"Drop Trooper Smith."

Trooper Smith stood. At eight feet tall and weighing more than half a ton, the Auto Trooper was designed for only one thing: killing.

Stell saw it, backlit by the burning truck, waiting with limitless mechanical patience for the order to kill. Zonies were swarming around it, screaming their frustration as their slugs and beams bounced harmlessly off its armor and defensive screens. Then, somewhere deep inside its metal body relays closed, current surged, weapons were activated, and the mini-computer controlling it began picking targets of opportunity. With deceptive slowness, it lumbered forward into the Zonie horde. Then, without warning the robot began to spew slugs, grenades, flechettes and coherent energy in every direction.

Ace Science Fiction books by William C. Dietz

WAR WORLD
FREEHOLD

FREEHOLD

William C. Dietz

ACE SCIENCE FICTION BOOKS
NEW YORK

This book is an Ace Science Fiction original edition,
and has never been previously published.

FREEHOLD

An Ace Science Fiction Book/published by arrangement with
the author

PRINTING HISTORY
Ace Science Fiction edition/March 1987

ISBN: 0-441-25186-2

Ace Science Fiction Books are published by The Berkley Publishing Group,
200 Madison Avenue, New York, New York 10016.
PRINTED IN THE UNITED STATES OF AMERICA

For my wife Marjorie,
who liked this one from
the start, and put up
with me while I wrote it.

PROLOGUE

The incredible heat of Freehold's sun beat down on the little pre-fab hut, turning its interior into an oven. In spite of the air conditioning, sweat poured off Bram's face as he bent over the open connector box. His blunt, capable fingers made the last connection and he straightened with a groan. His short, stocky body ached from hours of bending over.

The problem was sand. The problem was always sand. Sand in the windings, sand in the gears and, this time, in the connector box. Somehow the damned stuff managed to penetrate the triple-sealed box and pile up till it shorted out half the weather hut's instrumentation. And on Freehold, weather reports were very important indeed.

Bram picked up the tool pak, slipped his arms through the straps, and pulled it up onto his back. He snapped on his polarized goggles, sealed his sand suit, checked the action on his autorifle, and hit the release switch by the door. It opened, and he stepped out into the blowing sand, allowing the door to hiss shut behind him. Cursing steadily, Bram fought his way up the side of the first dune. Halfway up his legs were already tired. He knew it could be far worse, however. In fact, it was a nice day by local standards. Wind a steady fifteen miles an hour, with gusts up to thirty, temperature a cool hundred and five in the shade, if you could find any shade.

He felt the air conditioning in his sand suit shift up a notch as he struggled the last few steps to the crest of the dune. He paused there for a moment to catch his breath and wonder why he'd been stupid enough to come on foot. "Gotta stay in shape," he'd told his wife. Screw that. Next time he'd ride. He turned, eyes automatically sweeping the horizon. Sand storms, the huge tuskers called Sandies, lots of things could catch the unwary on Freehold. At first he thought it might be a mirage, a common enough phenomenon on Freehold, but deep down he knew it wasn't. The smoke boiling up to be whipped away by the wind was all too real, and the characteristic shimmer of the settlement's force field had disappeared. Something was very wrong.

Bram began to run, leaping and jumping down the side of one dune and then struggling up the next. His feet sank into the soft sand, his breath came in short gasps, and cold lead filled his stomach. With heart pounding, he started up the final slope toward the distant point where sand met sky.

Like all the working settlements on Freehold, Sweet Hole occupied a large circular depression below the planet's average surface. About ten miles across, the depression—or "hole"—was almost split in two by a huge subterranean river that surfaced at the south end of the crater and disappeared underground again at the north end. Surrounding the depression on all sides was a steep embankment of wind-driven sand. Bram got down and crawled the last few feet of the embankment, careful not to break the skyline. Sergeant Sanderson, the regimental drill instructor back on his native New Britain, would have been proud of him. Somewhere in the back of his mind he could hear Sanderson screaming, "Keep it down, Bram, or somebody'll blow it off!"

He kept it down as he neared the edge of the embankment and the wind brought him the stench of burning plastic and rubber. Smoke rolled up to be caught by the wind and jerked away. The muffled sound of gunfire confirmed his worst fears. Wriggling closer to the edge of the crater, he unclipped the binocam from its place on his chest and pressed the viewfinder to his eyes. Careful to shield the powerful lenses from any possibility of reflection, he pressed the zoom control—and flinched as a terrible scene of death and carnage leaped up to meet him. While part of his mind screamed, another part, carefully trained many years before, remembered to flick on the binocam's memory. It would tape everything he saw.

Sweeping the binocam from right to left, he saw that the battle was almost over. The battered black shape of the pirate shuttle dominated the scene, crouched in the middle of the settlement's main plaza like some sort of evil god, dispatching armor-clad demons to do its bidding. A veil of vapor and smoke swirled around it. Pirates darted in and out of the smoke on nameless errands, while others carted loot into the shuttle, and a handful continued to fire at the few remaining defenders.

Bram's heart pounded in his chest as the binocam found and held a view of the last of his friends and neighbors. They were fighting from behind a hastily erected barricade. He gagged, and almost turned away, when he saw that the barricade was made of bodies—bodies who had once been friends. But he forced himself to look, to bear witness to the horror below, knowing the binocam would preserve what he saw, hoping that with this record others could avoid the same fate.

So he watched. He watched as seventy-two-year-old Slim Hana took two slugs in the chest, and still managed to bury his knife in a pirate throat, slipping the blade in just above the man's armor. He watched the ten-year-old Barry twins aim and fire a gun twice their size, before an energy beam cut them down. Tears ran down his cheeks as he watched the pirates jump the barricade and prepare to rape his wife and daughter.

The beep from the binocam signalled maximum storage. Quickly removing his emergency locator beacon from a pocket, he turned it on, shoved it and the binocam into a weatherproof bag, and pushed it deep into the sand. When they came, they'd find it. Then he stood, careless of the skyline, and shrugged off the tool pak. Assuming the stance of a trained marksman, he brought the auto rifle up to his shoulder, blinked his eyes clear of tears, and carefully sighted in. With infinite care, he shot his daughter and then his wife. Then, sweeping his weapon in a careful arc, he methodically picked off the half-naked pirates who'd surrounded them. Bram paused for a moment to make sure he'd killed them all, uttered a long primeval scream of rage, and ran down the embankment, his weapon chattering in his hands, waiting for the inevitable impact.

CHAPTER ONE

Stell stood by the window, hands clasped behind his back, a long, lean silhouette against the soft light of Arno's distant sun. His green eyes prowled restlessly over the makeshift drill ground below. It wasn't regulation by any means. In fact, until recently it had served as a parking lot for hover trucks. Of course, the troops marching back and forth across it couldn't care less. They hated marching no matter where they did it. The few veterans were bored and slightly insulted, and the raw recruits surrounding them were scared and all left feet. But they must learn to work together, to function as a team, to follow orders without question. Marching had been used to teach those things for thousands of years.

Stell ran a hand over his smooth scalp, still shaved clean in the manner of the elite Star Guard. As he watched the orderly ebb and flow of troops below, it occurred to him that the basics of war were eternal. The passage of time might change the tools of war, but not the principles by which it was fought, or the reasons behind it. Greed, hate, a lust for power; together, they had always guaranteed soldiers something to fight and die for.

"To serve with honor among the stars." That was the motto of the Marine Corps, the reason he'd gone to the Academy, and his father before him. For years he'd believed it and lived it. Until the day they decided that "honor" had grown too expensive. Let the frontier defend itself. Let the Il Ronn and pirates keep each other in check. And let us have

1

lower taxes. That's what those toward the center of the empire had decided. Stell's brigade was among those chosen for deactivation.

He and the two thousand other members of the brigade were offered a choice: Honorable discharge and free passage to their home planet, or continued service in an authorized mercenary army. "Authorized" meant agreement in advance to fight only those wars approved by the Imperial government. So if they agreed to become mercenaries, the Emperor would continue to benefit from, if not directly control, their activities. And all for free.

In any case, the brigade had put it to a vote. Almost everybody considered going home, but they'd been gone a long time, they didn't have civilian skills, and besides, for most of them the brigade *was* home. So most stayed, and Stell was no exception. Now they continued to fight and die, not for freedom or honor, but for money. And Stell didn't like it. Three months had passed since the final battle of New Covenant. It was a dirty little religious war between two rival factions of what had been a single church. The brigade was brought in by the weaker side. They managed to win the war, but at a terrible price. In the end, after the disastrous and unnecessary final battle caused by the incompetence of their clients, they'd used hand lasers to carve more than five hundred graves into the rocky ground, including one for Colonel "Bull" Strom, their commanding officer.

As a result, Mark Stell rose from Major to Colonel, from Executive Officer to Commanding Officer, and from enforcer of policy to architect of it. And the worst part was that he liked it. He liked the freedom, the responsibility, and the challenge of command. And yes, he liked the power, too. All of which made him feel guilty as hell sometimes. Bull Strom had been like his father, brother and best friend all rolled into one. But Bull had been wrong, damn it! Dead wrong. He couldn't see the future the way it must inevitably be. Couldn't understand things had changed. Couldn't see that over time his beloved brigade was dying what the ancient Chinese had called "The Death Of A Thousand Cuts." As each body was lowered into blood-soaked soil, a part of the brigade died too. And when the dying was done, they'd be asked to move along, to do it all over again, until finally none of them survived. And as they were replaced, one person at a time, the brigade was gradually changing and would eventually become something Strom wouldn't have recognized, much less loved. As Stell watched the raw recruits wheel, turn, and crash into each other, he knew that time was growing closer with each passing day. It had to be stopped . . . but how?

"It's time, sir." The voice was a familiar basso, and Stell turned with a smile.

"Good to see you, Zack. What's the body armor for? We're going to dinner, not war." Although, where clients are concerned, one often precedes the other, he thought to himself. Sergeant Major Zachariah Como made an impressive sight. Standing a full seven feet tall, his black skin was only a shade lighter than the dull matte finish on his body armor. Broad at the shoulder and narrow at the hip, he looked like a recruiting poster and he knew it. Although his brown eyes were filled with intelligence and humor, there was also a natural wariness there, a detachment, past which few were ever allowed. Stell was one of those few. The Sergeant Major wore two hand guns at his waist and cradled a grenade launcher in his arms. Como replied with a familiarity reserved for times when they were alone. "You're a fine one to talk about appearances, Colonel; when's the last time you changed uniforms, anyway?" He indicated Stell's rumpled clothes with a grin.

Stell looked down at his uniform sheepishly. "You're right, Zack. It wouldn't do to let clients see what a slob I really am. But isn't body armor a bit much?" He began to strip off his dirty clothes.

Como snorted in reply. "Have you been outside since we landed? Hell, no. That might involve taking some time off— something you fear like death itself, probably because you don't know how to have a good time. But if you'd been out there you'd know why I'm wearing armor."

Stell knew Como was right. He disliked free time because he didn't know what to do with it. "Trouble?" he asked, stepping into a pair of gray dress trousers.

"More like total insanity," the other man replied shaking his head in wonderment. "They call it the Free Zone. I call it a free-for-all. We've been in some pretty wild places over the years, but this takes the cake. I've got a full section waiting outside to escort us to dinner, and I'm not sure it's enough. But I'm afraid to weaken the perimeter by taking more, especially with so many greenies in the ranks. So take my advice and suit up. Otherwise some Zonie may have you for dinner!'' With a grin and a wave he was gone, leaving Stell to finish dressing.

As he buttoned the last gold button on the bright red coat, Stell wondered about medals, and then decided against them. They belonged to the past. He shrugged on the harness and tucked the slug gun into the holster under his left arm. If Zack was worried, there was good reason. And although he hadn't been outside, he knew what the Sergeant Major was talking about. As usual, their last clients had been eager to get rid of them once victory was assured. No one wants a mercenary army sitting around while they go through the delicate process of forming a new government. After all, the power the brigade granted, it could also take away.

So they lifted off-planet, taking their pay and leaving their dead. And they came here, to Arno, to rest, regroup, and wait for the next war. Arno was an agricultural planet, settled by and organized around a single church. Kind of ironic in a way, considering they were on Arno to recover from a religious war on New Covenant. Anyway, the church Elders controlled all aspects of life on Arno, especially the economy. Early on, the Elders had realized it was the very same kinds of activity forbidden by their religion that earned the most foreign exchange. Which is to say that the sale of illicit drugs, sex, and weapons brought in more money from off-planet than did the sale of vegetables. So, eager to reap this much needed foreign exchange, yet afraid of a punitive god, they invented the Free Enterprise Zone, a wonderful device that would enable them to have their virtue and money too. And by confining all those from off-planet within the Zone, they could protect their flock from corrupting influences and still enjoy the benefits of interstellar commerce. And their invention served them very well indeed.

The Elders demanded and received what they called a ten-percent tithe on the value of all goods sold within the

Zone. In return, those within the Zone were free to do as they pleased. Free of restrictive law and regulation, the Zone soon attracted all sorts of enterprise, most of which were quite illegal on other planets. This fact didn't trouble the Elders in the least. Following the ancient religious dictum that the end justifies the means, they reasoned that, since the revenues thus generated would be used to import agricultural equipment, which would evenutally transform the planet into the Eden prophesied by the church's founder, Brother Esten Arno, then the Zone was, in the final analysis, moral. And from what Stell had seen coming down from orbit, they were well on the way toward their goal. Arno was a beautiful planet, much of it still wild, with large tracts of beautiful farm land that were broken here and there by the gentle flow of wide, slow-moving rivers. Arno was a nice place to live—if you weren't in the Zone.

The Free Zone was about twenty-five square miles in size. Because its boundaries were entirely artificial, it formed a perfect circle, a shape that the Elders' military advisors assured them would be vulnerable to attack, should those living within the Zone ever get out of hand. A shaped force field surrounded it, preventing entry or exit except through the one, closely guarded gate. Of course, that was rarely used, since citizens were not allowed into the Zone and Zonies were not allowed out. Most commerce arrived and departed via the spaceport located at the Zone's center. There was a second, smaller spaceport located on the other side of the planet, but it was dedicated to church-approved traffic and Arno's small navy.

Radiating out from the Free Zone's spaceport were concentric rings of activity. First came the dives and nightclubs catering to every imaginable taste in drugs and sex. Their clientele were mostly drawn from the ships touching down to load or unload cargo, but rumor had it that church Elders paid secret visits to places like the "Super Nova" and "Bloody Mary's"—two of the Zone's more celebrated dives. Beyond those were the illegal factories, illicit research laboratories, and warehouses. And, finally, the outermost ring was a warren of dilapidated domes, tenements, and shanties. Here the majority of the Zone's population returned each night. Most eked out a marginal life working in some factory, selling themselves for illegal research, or being used by those who frequented the bars and nightclubs. Others were not so lucky. They had no jobs and existed by victimizing those who did, until they themselves fell prey to the endless cycle of poverty and misery. For within the Zone there was no law, except that imposed on the weak by the strong.

This, then, was the area into which the brigade had been forced to go. Oh, they could have stayed in space for a while, or sought out another planet, but Arno was close and therefore less expensive to reach; plus, Stell knew that in the end they'd be forced to accept something similar, or worse. No one rolled out the red carpet for a mercenary army between engagements.

So the brigade paid the Elders an exhorbitant tithe, entered the Zone, and rented space in what had recently been a Yirl drug refinery, and an illegal weapons factory before that. The complex of buildings, plus the parking lot outside, now comprised brigade HQ. It wasn't as secure as he'd like, but so far the brigade's obvious firepower, aggressive patrols, and violent reputation had prevented raids by the criminal element—although Stell wasn't sure the word "criminal" served any useful function in the Zone. But such attacks weren't unheard of. When it seemed worthwhile, someone would recruit a temporary army and use it to attack a drug factory or some other profitable target. And, because of its weapons and equipment, the brigade would certainly qualify as "profitable."

So Stell slipped into the *A*-suit and sealed it. He checked the load on the short, ugly assault rifle he favored for street fighting, and opened the door. As he left his office, the two sentries outside snapped to attention. He nodded and they fell in behind as he marched down the hall toward the lift tube. Moments later he was outside, and almost gagging on the heavy odor of rotting garbage and backed up sewers. He swallowed and made a note to get the area cleaned up. Without any form of central control, utilities in the Zone were a haphazard affair.

As he walked to the street he noticed that the light had grown dim as Arno's sun neared the horizon, retaining barely enough strength to throw long shadows across the duracrete beneath his boots. Sergeant Major Como's convoy sat idling at the curb. It consisted of four vehicles: three open hover trucks of various makes and lineage, plus an ancient limo. There was something vaguely familiar about the rounded shape sitting in the rear of the open vehicle. For a moment Stell couldn't place it, but when he realized what it was he laughed, and turned to find that Sergeant Major Como had materialized at his side. "Sorry about the vehicles, sir, but as you know, the bastards wouldn't let us bring any of our own stuff down."

Stell knew Como was referring to the Elders' refusal to allow them any armor. While they rode around in whatever they could dredge up, there were a couple of hundred prefectly good vehicles aboard the brigade's three transports, presently in orbit around Arno. If the thought of mercenaries made the Elders nervous, the thought of mercenaries riding around in tanks probably drove them crazy.

"But I see you found a way around that," Stell said, indicating the rounded shape in the back of the limo.

Como's face registered elaborate innocence. "You mean trooper Smith, sir? I agree he's tough, but certainly no match for armor."

Nodding in mock agreement, Stell said, "Now that I look again I see you're absolutely right, Sergeant Major. That is trooper Smith. Ugly bastard I must say. By the way, Sergeant Major, my compliments on our transportation," Stell said, eyeing the aging vehicles that made up the convoy. "I see that in addition to your other accomplishments you're able to raise the dead."

The joke got the predictable laugh from those near enough to hear it. Stell knew it would make the rounds of the barracks later, making him seem less remote and more human to the troops. As he climbed into the truck he felt guilty about how easily he could manipulate them. But leadership hadn't come as naturally to him as it did to some. Bull Strom had been a good example. He had that mysterious ability that allows some to walk into a room full of perfect strangers and effortlessly make each into a friend and admirer. Lacking that kind of charisma, Stell developed a more calculated style of leadership which, though quite effective, seemed somehow artificial and therefore less genuine.

Stell chinned his radio switch on. "Where's Major Malik?" he asked, looking around for his XO.

Fifty feet away, in his own vehicle, Como shrugged his shoulders. "He told Sergeant Wilkens he was planning a surprise inspection of the perimeter, sir."

Stell was annoyed that Malik hadn't seen fit to show up for final orders, but the surprise inspection was a good idea. It would keep the greenies on their toes. As the convoy jerked into motion, Stell's eyes began a systematic search of their surroundings. He was looking for the little things, clues which had often made the difference between life and death: the hint of motion in an upstairs window, the glint of reflected light off a weapon, the stalled vehicle that shouldn't be there. But finding nothing, he turned his attention to the convoy. The natural tendency to bunch up could be suicidal. A tightly grouped convoy could be destroyed with a single shoulder-launched missile, or a well-placed bomb. But the vehicles stayed well separated under Como's watchful eye.

Cautiously, the convoy wound its way through darkening streets, twisting and turning like some nocturnal snake gradually moving further away from the safety of its lair. And, as the sun dipped below the horizon, Stell felt a prickling in his scalp and knew they were not alone. The wash of their headlights was quickly lost in the darkness that had descended around them. People weren't seen, only sensed, as their dark, uncertain forms scurried to avoid the light and were tracked out of sight by infrared scanners.

Stell shivered in his armor, doing his best to ignore the ancient instincts pumping adrenaline through his system, urging him to run, to hide from the unknown things that stalked the night. Then darkness turned to day, as powerful flares went off. The intense light drove the filters in Stell's visor to the edge of burnout. Swearing, he switched to infrared just in time to see the attackers come swarming up out of the sewers like maggots fleeing a disturbed corpse. There were hundreds of them, all dressed in disposable white camouflage suits, which were gradually turning black as the flares burned down. They moved quickly to surround and isolate each vehicle in the convoy. Then they opened up with slug throwers and energy weapons that cut the night into a thousand streamers of light and dark.

Stell chinned his mic switch. "Automatic weapons, left and right flank, fire. Grenade launchers, left and right, fire. Snipers, pick targets ahead and fire. Clear a path for your vehicle but watch out for those in front of you, there's enough people shooting at us already." If the joke got a laugh, it was lost in the roar of sound as the troopers opened up. Thanks to Como, they were all hand-picked veterans. A quick glance told him casualties were light so far. Only one of the troopers in his truck was down. The others were cutting down Zonies in swaths like wheat at harvest. But as quickly as they died, more boiled up out of the sewers, dropped from rooftops, and surged out of dark passageways to join the fray. There was a burst of static, followed by Sergeant Como's calm voice. "Green four to green one."

"Go ahead, green four," Stell replied, squeezing the trigger on his assault rifle and stitching a line of white holes through one of the infrared blobs surging toward him.

"We have a prisoner, green one, and he's been egoed."

"Understood, green four," Stell replied, churning over the new information. Some, if not all, of the Zonies had been ego suppressed, probably through use of illegal drugs, and then memprinted with a hatred of the brigade, or all people wearing A-suits, or whatever. It really didn't matter. What mattered was that the Zonies wouldn't react the way they should. Instead of realizing they were being decimated and running or surrendering, they would just keep coming until they won, or until they were all dead. Ego-suppression techniques were illegal everywhere—except, of course, in the Zone.

Sweeping his gaze over the convoy, Stell saw the greatest danger lay in being swarmed under. His troopers were better armed and trained, but the Zonies outnumbered them at least ten to one. Given that advantage, plus their suicidal frenzy, they couldn't lose. Unless . . . Suddenly a Zonie landed right in front of him. With a shock he realized she was just a teenager, her camouflage suit hanging in folds on her skinny frame, eyes enormously dilated, lips drawn back in a snarl. He watched, fascinated, as she brought up her cheap, disposable power gun, aware that some remote part of himself had reacted, wondering vaguely who would win. Then he felt himself pull the trigger and watched the side of her head disappear in a spray of blood and brains. Stell forced his eyes away from her crumpled form as he spoke. "Green one to green four."

"Go ahead, green one," Como replied.

"Stand by to drop trooper Smith on my command. Initiate program *D* with a ten-minute hold."

"That's affirmative, green one; trooper Smith on your command."

Peering over the truck's cab, Stell was cursing the darkness when a sudden flood of white light washed over him. Startled, he thought another flare had gone off. Then he realized the last truck in the convoy, the one just behind the limo, was on fire. The surviving troops bailed out and ran forward, trying desperately to catch up with the moving limo. As he watched, one stumbled and fell, then another, both quickly disappearing under a wave of advancing Zonies. Pounding the side of the truck in frustration, he issued new orders. "Green one to green four. Stop the limo, drop trooper Smith, and pick up survivors."

"Affirmative, green one," Como replied.

Raising his glasses, Stell saw the limo silhouetted against the burning truck. Trooper Smith stood, unfolding himself into vaguely human form, and stepped down onto the pavement. Meanwhile, the rearmost troops laid down covering fire as survivors from the burning truck caught up and piled into the limo.

As trooper Smith disappeared in the direction of the advancing Zonies, Stell wondered if their drugged minds would recognize what they faced. Probably not. But they would soon experience what it could do. Standing eight feet tall, and weighing more than half a ton, the Auto Trooper was a machine designed for only one thing: killing. It did its job very well. A military derivative of the famous Autoguard, the robots had the destructive capability of an entire section of Imperial Marines. But since Auto Troopers were incredibly expensive, they would never replace the cheaper flesh-and-blood humans who created them. At least we have job secur-

ity, Stell thought wryly. Como had violated the spirit, if not
the letter of their agreement with the Elders by bringing the
robot down from orbit, but Stell didn't plan to point that out.
They would probably lose the valuable machine, but they
would save most of the section, a trade he'd happily make
any day of the week.

With the survivors aboard, the limo's driver wasted no time
catching up with the rest of the convoy. Turning his glasses
slightly, Stell saw the Auto Trooper, backlit by the burning
truck, waiting with limitless mechanical patience for the order
to kill. Zonies swarmed around it, screaming their frustration
as their slugs and beams bounced harmlessly off its armor and
defensive screens. Then, somewhere deep inside its metal
body relays closed, current surged, weapons were activated,
and the mini-computer controlling it began picking targets of
opportunity. With deceptive slowness, it lumbered forward
into the Zonie horde. Then, without warning the robot began
to spew slugs, grenades, flechettes and coherent energy in
every direction. It was a sight Stell would never forget. In a
lifetime of battles, he'd never seen such slaughter. The robot
never missed. Each projectile hit its mark. Every beam of
lethal energy found a target. Row after row of Zonies were
cut to bloody shreds. Those to the rear pushed their way
forward, slipping and sliding in the slush of flesh and blood
under their feet, eager to take their turns in the hail of lead,
steel, and deadly energy. Men, women and children all hur-
ried forward to die. The worst part was the mindless, empty
expression they wore. Somehow, they seemed more machine-
like than the metal monster that destroyed them. They were,
or had been, people. Loving, hating, happy, sad . . . people.
Mercenaries in their own way, they were lured by promises of
god knows what, betrayed, and chemically altered into cheap,
disposable troops. There was no honor in killing them, only
survival. Stell turned away. Sick at what someone had done
to them, sick at what he was doing to them, yet allowing it to
go on. To do otherwise would be a betrayal of those who
trusted him. But he swore a silent oath to find those responsible and make them pay.

Glancing around, he saw most of the Zonies had turned
away from the convoy to attack the robot. They were like

moths drawn to a flame. Whether acting on their own or responding to some external direction, he couldn't tell. Whatever the reason, he was grateful. Calling for more speed, Stell held on tight as the convoy drew quickly away. Ahead he saw only darkness. Lowering the useless binoculars, he bit his lip in frustration. The Zonies had been used like a hammer to drive the convoy forward. Logically, therefore, an anvil waited somewhere up ahead. If they continued, they'd be smashed against it. His mind searched desperately for an answer, a way out, and finding none, he felt the first stirrings of panic.

Forcing himself to breathe slowly, to relax, he made his mind a receptive blank. He could almost hear Bull Strom saying, "When things get toughest son, that's the time to let go. Otherwise your emotions will get you all jammed up. The answer's there . . . but you gotta be quiet to hear it. So let your mind go blank. That's when the answer will come." And when it did, Stell couldn't help but laugh out loud, causing the troopers nearest him to look at each other in surprise, shrug their shoulders, and laugh too. Another story for the barracks.

Moments later Sergeant Major Como laughed as well, a deep basso belly laugh, as the small tactical computer by his side confirmed the feasibility of Stell's plan. He admired the pure simplicity of it, and knew that because it was so simple, so obvious, most officers would have missed it. Bull would've loved it, Como thought as he chinned his mic open and delivered the good news. Minutes later the convoy came to a full stop. The troops jumped out, placed demolition charges, and formed a column of twos with the wounded to the rear. Fortunately, only two of the wounded had to be carried on improvised stretchers. They departed in double-time, with Stell in the lead and Como bringing up the rear. Even if the unit was cut in two during an ambush, both halves would have leadership.

As they jogged along, Stell occasionally referred to the map that Como's computer had printed out. Far behind, a series of muffled explosions signalled the convoy's destruction as the demolition charges went off. "Never leave 'em anything useful," that's what Bull had always said.

Numerous twistings and turnings brought them to a shabby

duracrete building. It wore an equally grimy sign that read,
"TRANSCAR TERM NAL." It was part of a Zone-wide
system originally installed by the Elders to attract industry.
Since then, the Zone's business tenants had maintained the
system to move raw materials and finished products to and
from the spaceport. And, since the Elders prohibited air travel
within the Zone, most people had to use it too. In front of
the terminal, fifteen or twenty Zonies had gathered around
two trash fires, warming their hands and talking in low tones.
For the most part they were dressed in rags and castoffs,
though a few more recent recruits wore slightly better attire.
A trickle of equally grubby passengers entered and left the
terminal, each dropping something into a large bucket as they
passed between the two fires, but otherwise giving the two
groups a wide berth. Sighting the mercenaries, both groups
quickly drifted together, a variety of weapons materializing in
grimy hands, avarice gleaming from deeply shadowed eyes.

For a moment, Stell thought the ambushers had found
them. But he quickly dismissed that idea, certain they
faced a band of common thugs. The ambushers would've
been all over them by now. Motioning the troops to stay put,
Stell carefully slung his assault rifle across his back, and
stood with empty palms out. As he waited, his hard green
eyes swept the mob, taking inventory one man at a time.
Most eyes turned aside refusing to meet his, but here and
there a few challenged him with open defiance. One of those,
a big burly man standing toward the center of the crowd,
drew Stell's attention. Here was their leader. Tiny, arrogant
eyes peered out of a full, meaty face topped by a mass of
greasy black hair. His voice whistled through a small, lipless
mouth.

"Well, gentlemen, what have we here? Some customers
what haven't paid their toll, that's what." As the man stepped
toward the front of the crowd, the others quickly moved out
of his way. "Now you wouldn't want to ride without payin',
would you soldier boy?"

"How much?" Stell asked evenly. If possible, he'd rather
pay than fight over some petty extortion.

The other man eyed Stell and his troops with a calculating
stare, ran a filthy rag over his forehead and grinned a slow,

insulting grin. "Every fourth weapon should do it, soldier boy. Normally it'd be more, but I'll give you a group rate. Just stack 'em next to me as you go by."

Stell nodded. Obviously the other man had no intention of being reasonable. Either that, or he'd severely underestimated the opposition. Stell sighed. Either way it didn't make much difference. He took two steps to the right. "Pay 'em, Corporal."

Stepping up from behind him, Corporal Flynn flamed the first rank of men with one long-practiced motion. Five of the would-be extortionists, plus their leader, died instantly. Only a few blackened chunks of flesh and a dusting of ashes marked where they had stood. At Stell's signal, Corporal Flynn released the trigger and her flamer returned to standby.

Without a word, the surviving members of the mob backed carefully away into the shadows and disappeared. Stell posted a rear guard, and led the rest of the section down a frozen escalator and out onto a filthy loading platform.

He placed Corporal Flynn in charge of twenty troops, with orders to escort the wounded back to base. They would catch a transcar headed in the other direction and be there in a few minutes. As Flynn turned to leave, Stell stopped her. "That was good work back there, Corporal. Thanks."

Flynn looked away self-consciously, her light skin flushing dark, accentuating the freckles sprinkled across her pug nose. "They were sure stupid sir, thinkin' we'd just cave in like that. I reckon they won't make that mistake again."

Stell smiled. "At least not with you around, Corporal." His smile turned to a frown as he said, "Keep an eye out for Zonies on the way back, Corporal. And when you reach base, report to Major Malik. Tell him about the Zonie ambush, and for god's sake, tell him to check the sewers under HQ. There might be more down there than a bad smell!"

Flynn laughed and replied formally, "I understand, sir, and will comply."

Stell nodded, returning her salute, and watched as she led her troops onto the overpass leading to the other tracks. He noted with satisfaction that she sent scouts across first, and had the wounded to the rear. She'd do just fine. Hopefully, Malik would get his message in the next half hour and do something about it. Once again he felt the distrust and disapproval his executive officer always elicited from him and pushed it aside. Even Malik couldn't screw this up. But he wished he knew why someone was jamming all the brigade's frequencies up and down the bands. Was it connected with the brigade, or just coincidence? Either way, he didn't like it.

Moments later a transcar arrived and they all piled on, weapons at the ready, rear guard jumping on at the very last second. Tense troopers scanned nervous passengers for any sign of hostility. There was none. Just the usual looks of fear and resentment familiar to any mercenary soldier. The transcar gently accelerated and the walls of the tunnel became a blur. Stell slumped down into a seat and stared out through a grimy, scratched window. He felt sure they'd escaped the anvil. But someone had gone to a lot of trouble and expense to set that trap. Who? Why? Those questions occupied him for the rest of the journey.

CHAPTER TWO

Their destination wasn't much to look at. A seedy hotel, once fashionable but long since outstripped by newer establishments located further from the noisy spaceport. "Shall I secure it, sir?" Sergeant Major Como's expression made it clear he thought he should.

"Yes, thank you, Sergeant Major," Stell replied. "In spite of our obvious charms it seems we're not overly popular in some quarters; better to be safe than sorry."

"Yes, sir," Como replied with a grin as he turned to give orders to the troops. With the wounded, plus their escort gone, they could establish only the lightest perimeter, but anything was better than nothing. Ten minutes later Stell entered the hotel's rundown lobby with Como at his side and two handpicked men close behind. A shriveled up old man sat at the reception counter, looking every bit as worn as the establishment he served. He wore ancient electroptic goggles replacing eyes lost years before after overdosing on Yirl drug. The goggles gave him a frog-like appearance, and the long, narrow tongue constantly flicking in and out of his wide mouth enhanced the similarity. His voice emerged as a servile whine. "Welcome to Arno's finest, noble sirs. How can this humble old man be of service?"

"We're here to see President Kasten," Stell answered evenly. "Where could we find him?"

The old man's tongue snaked in and out thoughtfully. "Kasten . . . Kasten, hmmm, the name does have a familiar

16

ring, noble sir," he said doubtfully, his left hand scratching a bald head, the right palm up, waiting for a tip.

"Maybe this will improve your memory, old man," Como said impatiently and placed the barrel of his slug gun in the clerk's waiting palm.

The old man jerked his hand back as though burned. "Third floor, Suite *B*," he snapped resentfully, turning back to the porno holo still playing below the counter. As soon as Stell and Como were out of sight, he picked up the com-set and punched in a series of numbers.

On the sixth ring, in a plush hotel room on the other side of the Zone, a beautiful woman with long black hair flicked on the com-set next to her bed and listened without answering. "They're here," the old man said, and he hung up.

The woman smiled a cold smile, and turned to the naked man in bed beside her. "Your first attempt was a failure, Major. I hope you'll do better the second time around." As her cool fingers slid toward his groin, Major Peter Malik wondered which she meant, the ambush of Stell's convoy, or their recent coupling. He hoped like hell it was the ambush.

The lift tube was out of service, so Stell and his men walked up three flights of stairs, and then down a drab hall to the door marked Suite *B*. Standing on either side of the door were two hard-looking men dressed in stained leathers. One had a dark beard, quick bright eyes, and a large hooked nose. The other was too young to shave, had acne, and a thatch of yellow hair. Long exposure to sun and wind had tanned their skins a dark brown. Both wore sidearms and cradled assault rifles. They regarded the approaching soldiers with interest but without alarm. They think they can take all four of us if necessary, Stell noted with interest. Looking at them, he decided it was a distinct possibility. His respect for their prospective employers were up a notch. Freehold evidently produced some tough customers. They were still fifteen feet away when the man with a beard said, "That's far enough gentlemen. Can I help you?"

Stopping as ordered, Stell was careful to keep both hands in sight. "We're here to see President Kasten," he replied. "My name's Stell, and this is my aide, Sergeant Major Como."

The bearded man nodded in acknowledgement, and whispered into a wrist mic, his eyes never leaving Stell. Receiving clearance via the implant in his right ear, the guard smiled. "They're expecting you, Colonel. Go right in." In spite of the bearded man's friendly demeanor, the younger guard only grudgingly opened the door. A very serious young man, Stell decided. Stell smiled his thanks and entered with Como close behind. The two troopers remained outside.

After passing through an antechamber, they emerged into an open, airy room that had seen better days but still managed a feeling of used elegance. Comfortable furniture surrounded a worn rug, while indirect lighting cast a muted glow against once-red walls. Two men and a woman rose to greet them. "Welcome, Colonel Stell," the larger of the two men said. He extended his hand, a smile of greeting on his round, tanned face. "I'm Oliver Kasten." Kasten was a big man, once athletic, now starting to put on a little weight. Stell liked his firm grip and open gaze.

"This is my daughter, Olivia," Kasten continued with a gesture, "and over here we have Senator Austin Roop." Stell smiled at Olivia Kasten and shook her offered hand. It was cool and firm. Her touch sent a tingle of excitement through him and the subtle widening of her eyes told him she felt it too. They were brown eyes, deep and calm; the flecks of gold floating in them matched her sun-streaked auburn hair. She was beautiful, and well aware of it, smiling at his frank appraisal. "It's a pleasure to meet you, Colonel Stell."

"The pleasure is mine," Stell replied, holding her hand just a little longer than necessary. "My apologies for our appearance and late arrival."

"And rightly so," Senator Roop remarked, looking Stell up and down in a critical manner. "Punctuality is usually considered a military virtue." Roop's face was handsome, in a hard, rigid sort of way, marred only by large pores, which gave his features the texture of weathered stone. Brittle blue eyes glared at Stell in open challenge.

Oliver Kasten cleared his throat, preempting Stell's reply. "Really, Austin. The Colonel is our guest. Please accept our apologies, Colonel Stell. I'm afraid Senator Roop's political party doesn't favor the idea of hiring you. He's here to make

sure I don't do anything rash." Roop scowled, making it
clear he desired no forgiveness. But before he could say so,
Olivia said, "You'll admit, Colonel, that for a politician
Austin is refreshingly direct. I can't imagine why they keep
electing someone so honest!"

Roop forced a smile, evidently thinking better of what he'd
been about to say. "Olivia's correct, as usual, Colonel," the
Senator said extending his hand, "I was out of line. I hope
you'll forgive me."

But as they shook hands Stell saw no apology in the other
man's hard blue eyes, and knew he faced an enemy. "Of
course, Senator," Stell said easily. "A thick skin is another
well-known military virtue."

"And while we talk, this man stands here bleeding,"
Olivia said, her voice tense and concerned. Turning, Stell
saw she was right. Blood was seeping from a rip in Como's
A-suit. While body armor would take a lot of punishment, it
wasn't indestructible. Como had evidently been nicked by a
high velocity slug and, in typical fashion, had ignored it.

The next few minutes were filled with a bustle of activity
as Olivia retrieved a professional looking med kit from her
luggage, and proceeded to apply self-absorbing staples and a
dressing to the gash in Como's right shoulder. As she worked,
Stell told Kasten and Roop about the Zonie ambush, and their
subsequent escape. When he'd finished, there was a moment
of silence as the other two men absorbed what they'd heard.
Stell took note of the meaningful look they exchanged just
before Kasten spoke.

"I'm terribly sorry, Colonel. I can imagine what the loss of
those men and women means to you. As you've probably
guessed, there's a good chance the attack was directed at us
as much as you. It seems there are those who don't want
Freehold to obtain your help." Kasten shot Roop an openly
critical glance, which the Senator chose to ignore.

"I'm afraid Oliver and I disagree as to the cause of the
attack, Colonel Stell," Roop said smoothly. "Personally, I
doubt there's a connection. There's no shortage of criminal
types around here, as I'm sure you're aware. However, I
certainly join him in extending sympathy regarding the loss of
your people."

Spoken like a true politician, Stell thought as he said, "Thank you, Senator. I appreciate that. Whatever the reason, there's nothing any of us can do now." Except find the bastard who planned it, and kill him, Stell thought to himself.

Kasten nodded soberly and Roop said, "Quite right, Colonel. What's done is done. Accept it and move on. I've always admired that in military people. I wish my fellow politicians could understand it." Roop aimed a meaningful look in Kasten's direction.

"That's enough business for now gentlemen," Olivia said firmly as she sprayed the final dressing onto Como's shoulder. "I suggest we give the Colonel and his aide a chance to freshen up."

Two hours later they had finished a wonderful meal of authentic Freehold cooking. The Kastens had brought all the necessary ingredients with them. Heavily spiced vegetable dishes played a major part, with only small portions of meat. Due to its climate, most of Freehold's food was grown in large hydroponics centers. Stell learned that eventually the settlers hoped to irrigate their deserts using water from the huge underground rivers that crisscrossed the planet. Then they would be able to grow a wider variety of crops, and import herd animals. Until then, however, lesser fare would have to do. Stell found the dinner quite satisfying and, when it was over, he settled back, cigar in hand, to enjoy some excellent Terran coffee.

Dinner conversation had centered around the merits of big-game hunting on various planets, something Roop was an expert on; 18th-century literature, a passion of Kasten's second only to politics; and an extremely funny commentary by Olivia on the internal politics of the Emperor's court, which she had observed firsthand while visiting there with her father. Stell and Como had taken their turns as well. Stell told short, humorous anecdotes suggested by the conversation, and Como shared a long, absolutely hilarious tale about a leave fraught with misadventure, all culminating in an intoxicated performance as first zirth player in the Alberian World Symphony, and the difficulty he'd faced when called upon for a solo—and how one coaxes music from a ten-foot-long reptile that closely resembles a boa constrictor.

Since no one could top Como's story, they agreed to retire to the sitting room and discuss business. Once everyone was seated, with drinks in hand, Kasten pressed a button on a remote control unit and a section of faded red wall slid aside to reveal an old but serviceable holo tank. Turning to Stell, Kasten said, "Colonel, in order to understand why we're interested in your services, a little history might come in handy. With your permission I'd like to narrate a holo prepared by my staff. I think it'll make our situation clear."

Stell nodded his assent as the room darkened and the holo tank swirled into life. The first thing he saw was the blackness of space. Then a pinprick of light appeared at the center of the blackness, gradually growing larger and larger as the camera approached it, until finally a large, moonless planet hung before him.

"That's home," Kasten said simply. "Freehold. It was discovered and claimed about forty years ago by Intersystems Incorporated."

Kasten didn't need to tell Stell about Intersystems Inc. Everyone was familiar with one of the biggest companies in the human empire. Intersystems, and two other equally large companies, were known as the Three Sisters. The name stemmed from the fact that they often seemed to function as a family, usually to their mutual benefit and someone else's loss. While Intersystems was huge, and involved all sorts of manufacturing and banking enterprises, it was well known that a large part of their income came from the incredibly expensive and risky business of finding, claiming, and selling planets.

"Here's some info on climate and so forth that you'll find interesting," Kasten remarked as words and numbers appeared to overlay the planet. He laughed, and then added, "Believe me, Colonel, it's even worse than it looks!"

Stell scanned the data and found that Kasten wasn't kidding. It probably was worse than it looked . . . and that was bad enough. Seventy percent of Freehold's surface was classified as "arid," or "semi-arid," which always sounds better than "desert." Ten percent was devoted to polar ice caps. That left two narrow temperate zones to divide the polar regions from the broad section of arid land banding the middle of the planet. As if that weren't bad enough, the hot air rising from the huge deserts inevitably came into contact with the cold air generated at the poles, producing incredible winds. Propelled by the wind, the desert's almost limitless supply of sand quickly became billions of tiny projectiles, making travel on much of the planet's surface extremely difficult, and habitation close to impossible. Then, just to make sure no one got bored, the place had been blessed with an interesting array of animals and plant life, all of which was just as mean as the planet itself.

"I take it tourism doesn't play a major part in your economy," Stell commented dryly.

Kasten laughed and Roop looked elaborately bored. Olivia smiled as she picked up the narration. "No, Colonel, there's no danger of that. However, there is a lengthy part of the year during which the temperate zones are actually quite pleasant. In fact, those who can afford to, have villas there." The holo changed, showing a series of shots featuring lush vegetation, pleasant looking villas, and small, fresh-water lakes. "Unfortunately," Olivia continued, "our natural resources are located elsewhere."

The pleasant scenery disappeared. It was replaced by a shot from some sort of atmospheric craft skimming just above the planet's surface at a high rate of speed. Below, a seemingly endless expanse of dry, wrinkled land sped by, broken only by occasional networks of canyons and ravines. These had obviously been cut by flowing water, so Stell assumed there was a rainy season. Then Kasten picked up the narration with an amused chuckle.

"As luck would have it, the Creator chose to put all our natural resources out here. It's mostly desert, occasionally interrupted by broken terrain, and never what you'd call 'pleasant.' Dry as hell most of the time, and then damned near underwater during the brief rainy season. That's when we get the flash floods and mudslides. We'd almost welcome those, if we could use that water for agriculture, but no such luck. Within hours, all the water seeps down through the topsoil or sand, dribbles down through the porous rock that underlies most of the surface, and joins one of the large underground rivers that crisscross the planet."

The picture changed to show a wide shot of a huge crater.

A large river surfaced on one side of the crater, flowed across, then dived underground again on the far side. "As you can see, the action of the underground rivers, combined with the wind, forms large craters. Most of our working settlements have been built at the bottom of such craters to take advantage of the water and get out of the wind." As the camera slowly zoomed in, Stell saw the bottom of the crater was thickly covered with structures of various kinds, though domes seemed the most popular—probably because of their low wind resistance. The broad, uncluttered streets frequently met in square or circular plazas paved with colorful tiles, testifying to the settlers' foresight and their determination to make what they had attractive.

Of course the river dominated the town. For the most part, both its banks had been left clear, allowing for high water during the rainy season, and an unimpeded view of the river from most of the settlement. Green grass and trees grew down to the edges of the river banks, interrupted by only a few functional looking buildings with rounded corners and a squat, boxy look. People were everywhere—eating picnic lunches, or simply strolling along the many foot paths. Around them, children ran and played while the sun sparkled on the river. Stell was struck by what they had done with their hostile environment, and impressed by the planet's potential.

"That's the settlement of Sweet Hole," Kasten said, his voice low and bitter. His huge fists opened and closed as if methodically crushing all life from an unseen enemy. "At least, that *was* the settlement of Sweet Hole." The holo shifted to a different view, and in spite of the fires and the battle being fought in the streets, Stell immediately recognized it as the same settlement. There was total silence in the room as the holo played. Stell noticed the footage was jerky and random, having none of the flow and polish of the earlier pictures. But he quickly forgot that as his attention was drawn to the squat shape of the shuttle, the men running in and out of it, and the people who were fighting and dying all around. He felt sick as he watched an old man take two hits and still manage to stick his knife in a pirate throat. He saw children cut down by energy weapons, and men in armor jumping a barricade of bodies to surround a woman and her child. Then the holo went dark and it was over.

For a long moment, no one spoke. Finally, Kasten cleared his throat, his voice cracking slightly as he spoke, "And that, Colonel, is why we need you."

CHAPTER THREE

Corporal Flynn listened to the rattle of automatic-weapons fire, and the heavier crump of grenades, and wondered what to do. Everything had gone smoothly up till now. While the ride on the transcar passed without incident, she'd decided to get off two stops early just in case, and her caution had paid off. The moment they'd left the transcar she'd heard the sounds of battle. From the sound of it, HQ was under attack. She immediately tried to make radio contact, first with HQ, and then with Colonel Stell, but all the freqs were still jammed. She was on her own.

As they moved cautiously through deserted streets, the sounds of fighting gradually grew louder. When she figured they were within half a mile of base, she called a halt and scouted around until she found a small, burned-out duracrete building. The walls were thick enough to take some punishment; and there were enough windows to permit defensive fire. The open ground surrounding the building was covered with rubble and garbage, not enough to provide attackers with cover, but maybe just enough to slow them down. It wasn't perfect, but it would have to do. She watched as the wounded were placed inside and made comfortable. They were her responsibility. The brigade never left its wounded.

She remembered the pain in her leg where the round had ripped through her flesh—like a bad muscle cramp, only worse. They'd been packed into the chopper like sardines.

The doors had been taken off to make it easier to load wounded. They were about to lift when Colonel Strom had staggered up to the chopper with a wounded soldier over his shoulder. She'd seen the pain etched in his features as he'd heaved the trooper into the crowded interior.

She'd heard the pilot as he leaned across his dead co-pilot's body and yelled over the urgent whine of the turbines: "Leave him, Colonel. He ain't gonna make it anyway, and I'm overloaded already."

The pilot had suddenly found himself staring down the barrel of a huge slug gun. "Either we all go . . . or we all stay . . . which is it gonna be, son?" The pilot had looked up from the gun into eyes just as black, and turned wordlessly back to his controls. Then Colonel Strom had climbed aboard and pulled the wounded trooper further away from the door.

The engines had been wound up tight, screaming under the strain, as the ship had wobbled into the sky. She had watched the trickle of blood dripping out the door quickly become a spray, making thousands of tiny red dots against the side of the aircraft as it limped toward base.

As Strom had sat down, wedging himself between two bodies, she had seen the pain in his eyes as he looked out at the endless carpet of broken men and machines which passed below. Hundreds of their people were dead or dying—all to settle doctrinal differences between two branches of New Covenant's single church.

Suddenly, the Colonel's eyes had met hers and he smiled. "Looks like you caught one, trooper. Doesn't look too bad though. A few days in an automedic and that leg'll be as good as new."

For the first time, she'd noticed the dark stain across the front of his uniform. "I'm fine, sir . . . but you've been hit bad. Can I help?"

Colonel Strom had shook his head and coughed, the brassy taste of blood filling his mouth. "No thanks, trooper. I'll be fine. Could use a little nap, though. But somebody's got to watch our friend up front." He indicated the native New Covenant pilot. "He doesn't understand that we've never left our wounded, and never will."

"Don't worry, sir," she'd replied, pulling a double-edged

commando knife out of her boot sheath. "Either we all go, or we all stay."

"That's the stuff," he'd answered. "Thank you." And with that, Colonel Bull Strom had died, just as he had lived, surrounded by his beloved brigade. A little bit of her had died with him.

"All right," she said, "you five: Rigg, Dudley, Alvarez, Su, and Mantu. Set up interlocking fields of fire and keep your eyes open. I'm counting on you. Dudley you're in charge."

"Gotcha, Corp . . . okay, you heard her . . . let's get organized."

Then, with her remaining fifteen troopers strung out in skirmish line behind her, Flynn headed for HQ. If it was under attack she knew it was her duty to help. But now they were a couple of blocks away and she couldn't figure out what to do. She'd watched wave after wave of Zonies fling themselves against the brigade's defenses, only to be cut down in bloody heaps. Gradually, the bodies had piled up until they became useful platforms from which the next wave of Zonies could launch their attack. Because the light-sensitive camo suits continued to function after their owners were dead, the piles of bodies seemed to come and go according to the light of battle, adding a gruesome, surreal quality to the scene.

As far as Flynn could tell, the brigade was easily holding its own without any help from her. In fact, from the occasional snatches of conversation that leaked through the jamming, it seemed like no contest. She was about to order her troops back, when suddenly the jamming dropped out for a moment and a frantic voice broke into the command channel. "Watch out! They're comin' outta the sewers! Oh god, there's hundreds of 'em!" The words were cut off by a long, drawn-out scream that made her blood run cold. There was a moment of shocked silence, before a voice Flynn recognized as Captain Wang's cut in, issuing crisp, clear orders in the same calm voice he used to deliver his dreaded lectures on sexual hygiene. What happened to Major Malik? she wondered.

Maybe the Zonies got him. If so, the attack wasn't a total loss.

Flynn ducked back behind the corner she'd been peeking around and tried to think. Damn! It was all her fault. The Colonel had told her to warn them about the sewers. . . . and she'd failed. Damn, damn, damn.

"What now, Corp?" The voice belonged to Trooper Stickley, better known as Sticks. He had a round, moon-like face, trusting brown eyes, and a gentle personality. As a result, people tended to underestimate him. A serious mistake, if they tried to push him around. Sticks was rated "Instructor" in unarmed combat. Looking at him, Flynn was immediately struck by the fact that he wasn't worried at all. Sticks just knelt there waiting for her to tell him what to do. His faith in her was like a transfusion of strength and determination. With it came an idea just weird enough to work.

"We're gonna do what we always do, Sticks," Flynn said, getting up with a grin. "We're gonna kick some ass!" Moving quickly from one trooper to the next, she provided each with enough information to do their part, plus someone else's should they be hit. Once everyone had been briefed, she watched them take off, and timed them to their assigned stations. Then, with Sticks at her side, she ran full out for the large sewer grating that marked the middle of the nearest intersection. As she ran, she ignored the Zonies who continued to attack the perimeter a few hundred yards ahead. If they saw her, she would know soon enough.

Reaching the square grating, they dropped to their knees, bare hands frantically scraping at the accumulated garbage covering it. The putrid smell coming out of the sewer made her gag, forcing her to gulp the contents of her stomach back down, but making her happy nonetheless. It was the smell of success. Once the grating was clear, they grabbed the open latticework and heaved. Nothing happened. Flynn looked up to find Sticks grinning at her, rivulets of sweat cutting white tracks through the dirt on his face. "One more time, Corp!"

She grinned in return and, bracing themselves, they heaved once more. Hard muscles bunched and writhed along Stick's shoulders and arms. A vein stood out on Flynn's forehead. Suddenly, she felt the grating pop loose and almost fell over

backward. Laying it aside, she felt dizzy from the effort and
from the fumes that engulfed her. Strangely enough, Sticks
seemed unaffected. Seeing her discomfort he shrugged. "Hell,
Corp, it ain't no worse than Doc's socks after a week of
manuevers."

Flynn laughed, a small part of her brain noting that such
behavior wasn't rational when any second the Zonies could
notice and kill them, while the rest of her mind worked on the
problem at hand. Picking up a light piece of plastic wrap, she
tore it into tiny pieces and released them over the sewer
opening. To her satisfaction, they floated up for only a
second before being sucked down into the blackness below.
That meant the Zonies had broken through enough gratings
inside the brigade's perimeter to create a positive air flow in
that direction. Praying she wouldn't kill half the brigade
along with the Zonies, Flynn chinned her mic, waited for a
short break in the jamming, and gave the order. Triggering
her flamethrower, she aimed it down into the sewer. It gushed
orange-yellow flame. She knew the rest of her troops were
doing likewise with improvised torches.

At first the flames blew straight back, burning all the hair
off her face and arms. But then the gases trapped by countless
blockages caught fire, creating a blue inferno. Suddenly she
felt lead fingers plucking at her suit and heard the screams of
enraged Zonies. She and Sticks ran for the cover of the
nearest building, where they turned and cut down the handful
of pathetic creatures headed their way.

Meanwhile, the fires started by Flynn and her troopers
followed the supply of gas, howled down the pipes to the
nearest intersections, split four ways, and then took off to do it
all over again, in a chain reaction that wouldn't end until all
available fuel was consumed. Flames followed pipes into
other sections of the Zone, starting countless fires and causing
tremendous damage. But the blue inferno also headed straight
for the brigade's compound, just as Flynn had intended. In
seconds, it reached sewers still packed with Zonies. Some
burned to death, their screams echoing through the miles of
pipe underlying the Zone. Those who didn't burn were suffo-
cated as the raging flames consumed all the available oxygen
and filled the sewers with carbon dioxide. Inside the com-

pound, huge gouts of blue flame shot twenty feet into the air. Hundreds of Zonies, pinned down around the sewer openings, died instantly. The rest were cut off from any possibility of retreat. They fought to the death.

Because the attacking Zonies had forced the brigade's personnel back and away from the sewer opening, none of the troopers were hurt or killed by the flames. While the brigade got off lightly, thousands of Zonies had been killed or wounded. The screaming went on and on as the brigade's medical personnel struggled to deal with the massive casualties. They could expect no help from the Elders or the other residents of the Zone, so they did the best they could, often being forced to use stunners on the wounded, who otherwise continued to attack with teeth and fingernails.

Meanwhile, Flynn gathered her people together and, with wounded in tow, made her way back to the compound. They had to climb over piles of dead Zonies to reach the gate. Inside, it wasn't much better. It smelled like burned pork.

Once she had delivered the wounded to the overflowing infirmary, and released her troops to other details, Flynn climbed one of the three remaining observation towers that marked the corners of the compound. She told the weary troopers manning it to take a break. After they had left, she gazed out across the endless drifts of bodies, the countless fires burning in the distance, and then down into the tiny compound she'd killed so many to protect. Why do we do it? she wondered. Because it's us or them, the soldier in her answered. But looking down she knew there was another reason. Because for the moment the killing ground below was home, the tiny figures moving from one wounded Zonie to the next were family, and because there was nothing else. And she knew they'd soon leave to do it all over again somewhere else. The tears rolled down her cheeks for a long time before she went down to help with the wounded.

CHAPTER FOUR

As the room lights came back up, they turned to Stell, waiting for his reaction. He didn't have one ready. Stalling for time, he made an elaborate ritual out of lighting a new cigar. Whoever shot those pictures had guts. He wished he could meet them. But he knew he wouldn't and why. The thought made him sad. At the same time, another part of him stood aside observing and analyzing. It said he couldn't afford such emotions, that too many people depended on his objectivity, that if he failed, they too would die. Had died. How many lost today? With a sudden pang of guilt, he realized he didn't know.

"Colonel Stell?" Kasten's voice jerked him back into an embarrassing silence.

"Excuse me," Stell replied with a twisted smile. "I'm terribly sorry about the settlement. Your people were very brave. Pirates?" Stell knew pirate raids on frontier planets like Freehold weren't all that uncommon. Out along the edge of the empire Imperial Navy patrols were few and far between. Some even said that the Emperor allowed the pirates to exist because they helped keep the Il Ronnian empire in check, and did so at no cost to him. As a member of the Star Guard, Stell had always resisted those arguments, partly because they seemed disloyal, but mostly because he didn't want to believe the Emperor would put money before lives. But then they had demobilized his brigade, citing budget cuts, and had reduced the size of the Navy for the same reason. As a result, pirate raids had increased, and so had clashes between the pirates and the Il Ronn. So now he wasn't so sure anymore.

Kasten regarded him for a moment through steepled fingers before speaking. "Yes, Colonel, they were pirates. However, please don't think the raid you saw was a random event. Rather, we believe it's part of a larger pattern of activity."

"Speak for yourself, Oliver," Roop interjected. "We don't all believe in your wild allegations." Satisfied that he'd said his piece, Roop slumped back into studied boredom, his aging chair desperately seeking to accommodate his new position with a hiss of cranky pneumatics.

Kasten smiled tolerantly. "As you can see, the Senator and I disagree about why the pirates keep attacking, but more on that in a moment. First, a little more history. Are you familiar with Standard Planetary Agreements, Colonel?"

Stell frowned as he dredged up what little he knew on the subject. "I know it's an agreement of sale between a planet's owner, usually the Imperial government or a large company, and a would-be buyer, most often a group of settlers. Beyond that, I draw a blank."

"That's plenty," Kasten said with a smile. "Briefly, here's how it worked in the case of Freehold. Having found and claimed Freehold, and having assured themselves there were no massive mineral deposits, or other resources they cared to exploit, Intersystems advertised for buyers throughout the empire. Among the roughly 250,000 qualified respondents were my mother and father." Here Kasten looked affectionately at his daughter and winked. "I'm afraid you'll have to hear the story one more time, honey."

Olivia laughed, and reached out to squeeze his hand.

"So a consortium was formed," Kasten continued, "and each of its quarter-million members contributed equal shares of the five-million-credit down payment. The agreement called for another five million credits per Earth year for fifty years. At the end of that time, Freehold would become the sole property of the consortium and their descendants." Kasten paused to gather his thoughts. "If, however, the payments were missed for two years running, Freehold would revert to Intersystems Inc., and all payments made thus far would be forfeit.'' Kasten sighed and shook his head. ''It wasn't fair, but that's the best deal they could get. Thirty years have passed since then. As you saw earlier, Freehold is no garden planet. The early years were very hard. My mother died first, then my father, and thousands more with them. But we managed in spite of that. For the first few years we barely made the payments on time. Gradually, things started to improve. We found ways to deal with Freehold's hostile environment, even ways to profit from it.''

Now Kasten's eyes glowed with the fervor of a man on his favorite subject. ''Eventually we managed to produce a small surplus. We used that to buy the technology we didn't have, but needed. We put the technology to work and our surplus grew larger.'' The glow faded from Kasten's eyes and his shoulders slumped as if under a great weight.

''Then our good fortune stopped. As you might expect with a planet like Freehold, the weather is cyclical. We're still learning what makes it tick, but the geological evidence, plus our own experience, tells us that years of reasonably moderate weather can be followed by equal periods of bad. Two years ago we entered such a time and are only now coming out of it. Consequently, all sectors of our economy have suffered. Our surplus was quickly eroded, and then gone.''

Now the pain in Kasten's eyes turned to anger, huge fists opened and closed in frustration, and he fought to keep his voice level. ''Even so, we would have made it except for the pirates. Oh, we always had a few raids from both the pirates and Il Ronn, since the budget cutbacks most of the frontier worlds do, but nothing like this. Day after day, week after week, raid after raid the pirates pound away at us. And they've exacted a terrible toll, not just in material terms, but in human lives and suffering as well.'' Kasten's voice broke, and he turned away for a moment as he fought to regain his composure.

''They killed my mother two months ago,'' Olivia said softly. ''She was visiting one of the outlying settlements when it was hit. We miss her very much.'' Stell saw sorrow in her eyes overlayed with concern for her father. He started to speak, to suggest a break, but Kasten held up a restraining hand.

"It's all right, Colonel. I apologize for imposing my personal troubles on you and Sergeant Major Como, but my wife and I were very close, and I'm afraid I haven't adjusted well. I was going to say that, while we've done our best, we're no match for the pirates. We have no military as such; it's not practical for a population as small as ours, and there has never been a need. In the past, our Civil Defense Force has dealt with the occasional pirate or Il Ronnian raid."

"And quite well, too," Roop added, gazing at the ceiling.

"Maybe at first," Kasten acknowledged, "but not lately. Their weapons and training beat anything we've got. Plus, they have the element of surprise on their side." He shrugged and smiled wanly. "We've missed one yearly payment and we're about to miss another. And that's why we're talking to you, Colonel."

Stell knew Kasten was right. From what he'd heard, the pirates were well organized, well equipped and well trained. They had to be in order to survive. The ironic part was that originally the pirates had been soldiers, too—soldiers on the losing side of a long, bloody civil war. The war wound up destroying the confederation it sought to perserve; from its ashes had risen the present empire, the creation of one man, the first Emperor. Most had accepted his rule, tired of the endless civil war and eager for peace. But some had refused, and were sent to a lifeless prison planet known as the Rock.

The Rock had once been a mighty fortress built by the old confederation against an Il Ronnian attack that never came. It was converted to a prison simply by turning the orbiting weapons that guarded it away from the emptiness of space and toward the planet below. So when the scattered remnants of the rebel fleet gathered one last time in a glorious but hopeless attempt to free their imprisoned comrades, the attack met with unexpected success. The Rock's weapons were pointed in the wrong direction. The Imperial Marines guarding the planet paid dearly for their mistake, and were quickly slaughtered. The prisoners were free. But were they? Where could they go? The Rock was right between the human and Il Ronn empires. To flee in either direction meant death. Besides, there weren't enough ships to lift them all off. So once again the planet's weapons were turned toward space and the possibility of attack. Their prison had become their home.

However, as homes go, the Rock was far from hospitable. The confederation's military engineers had used hell bombs to turn the planet's surface into an endless plain of black glass. They'd known that without factories, homes, and a civilian population to worry about, a well-defended planet could stand off any fleet ever assembled. So they scrubbed the planet clean of all life and created the perfect fortress. Unable therefore to grow their own food, and without an industrial base, the newly freed prisoners were soon forced to raid other planets for their necessities. At first, they justified such raids as a fitting revenge on those who'd caved in to the Emperor. But as time passed, the high ideals of freedom and justice that originally guided them gave way to naked greed and hate. In this fashion, soldiers in a once-noble cause became nothing more than organized thieves and killers.

Stell wondered, "What's to prevent us from ending up the same way? We already kill for money." Turning aside from the obvious answer, Stell chose to think about the military problem instead. "What about the Il Ronn?" he inquired. "What have they been doing during all this?"

Kasten looked thoughtful for a moment, and then replied, "Come to think of it, the Il Ronnian attacks have fallen off recently."

Roop groaned. "Thanks a lot, Colonel, now he'll find something ominous in *that*. Just what we needed."

Stell laughed with the others, but made a mental note to obtain more information on Il Ronnian activities in that sector. He would have expected an increase in Il Ronnian attacks on Freehold, not a reduction. First, because of the pirate activity in the area, but also because of the generally increased contact between two growing empires. What had once been a thick cushion of frontier worlds serving to separate them had been gradually reduced as more and more planets were absorbed by both sides. Now that cushion was very thin and conflict was inevitable.

While man had encountered hundreds of intelligent races among the stars, only the Il Ronn posed a real threat. Not because they were more intelligent or advanced than other alien cultures, but because they alone shared man's relentless ambition, and were ruthless enough to pursue it.

The Il Ronn were an ancient race, having preceded man into space by thousands of years. Fortunately, theirs was a cautious and methodical culture in which important decisions were reached by consensus. As a result, their empire expanded in a slow, deliberate manner—each new acquisition first being carefully considered, and each gain being consolidated before another was attempted.

Meanwhile, the human empire grew in great, uncontrolled leaps. Periods of tremendous expansion resulted in advances that would take the Il Ronn hundreds, even thousands of years to accomplish. Unfortunately, many of the human gains were soon lost, either through internal bickering, competition, or just plain laziness. The result was two empires of roughly equal power. The Il Ronn continued a planned and inexorable expansion, while the human domain grew in fits and starts, driven more by the engines of greed and profit than by any unified plan . . . or so it seemed to Stell and many others.

Kasten took a sip from his drink and addressed Stell, while pointedly ignoring Roop. "As I was saying, lately the pirates have come in force. And they haven't limited their efforts to the looting of produced wealth, either." The politician searched the soldier's face for signs that he understood the significance of those words. "They're destroying the means of producing it, too. Power plants, factories, laboratories—you name it. If they can find it, they destroy it." Kasten smiled wryly. "Or, as Olivia puts it, they're killing the goose that lays the golden eggs. Something they've never done before, and something that makes no sense. Unless, of course, there's a greater profit in destroying rather than raiding us. And that, Colonel Stell, is why I'm so certain the pirates are cooperating with Intersystems. Nothing else explains the facts."

"So you think that Intersystems is paying the pirates to step up their attacks, thereby destroying your means of production and forcing you to miss your next payment," Stell mused out loud.

"Exactly," Kasten replied, leaning back in his chair with the satisfied expression of someone who has made his point. "If we miss the next payment, Intersystems gets Freehold back, they keep the payments we've made so far, and they can sell a developed planet for a higher price."

It made sense, up to a point. While Stell suspected that Intersystems was quite capable of it, he couldn't escape the feeling that Kasten wasn't telling the whole truth. For one thing, Olivia looked distinctly uncomfortable, plus, Kasten's voice lacked conviction, and his eyes slid toward Roop as though seeking support. Stell was glad he'd requested an intelligence report on Freehold. Maybe that would give him some answers.

"Really, Oliver," Roop said, shaking his head in pretended amazement. "I think that's pretty thin. It's possible, I suppose, but you know as well as I do that there's not one shred of evidence to prove it. The whole thing's preposterous." Roop seemed to enjoy Kasten's obvious discomfort. Kasten frowned angrily, opened and closed his mouth as though tempted to speak, and then restrained himself through a major effort of will.

They were hiding something. Roop was lying, and for some reason Kasten was going along with it, albeit reluctantly. Why? Stell decided to keep his suspicions to himself and see where the conversation led.

His brow furrowed in apparent concern, Roop said, "The problem is that while we waste time and energy looking for nonexistent plots, the destruction goes on. I admit that what the pirates are doing seems stupid, but who says they're smart? I agree we should deal with the problem, but I think there's an alternative to importing a mercenary army." Roop nodded apologetically in Stell's direction. "No offense, Colonel, but outfits like yours cost a lot of credits. Not only that, but even if you're successful, your presence on Freehold is almost certain to lead to more destruction and bloodshed. Instead, why not spend the money on a negotiated settlement with the pirates? Wait, Oliver, give me a chance; distasteful as it may be, it would probably be cheaper in the long run, and would certainly save lives." Roop looked eagerly from one person to the next, seeking support.

Kasten snorted in disgust. "Negotiated settlement my ass! Protection money is more like it. And even if you're right, once we pay, where will it stop? How much will be enough? Damn it, man! Can't you see that we'll be slaves?''

Roop's lips formed a thin smile. "An interesting point, Oliver. But I'd say the greater danger lies in what you propose. Once Colonel Stell lands his personal army on Freehold, we'll live at his pleasure. If he desires slaves . . . then that's what we'll be. Or maybe that's the idea, maybe you're tired of elections and want to be King instead of President—is that the problem, Oliver?''

"Father—'' Olivia's voice was concerned as her father leaped to his feet, face flushed with blood, big hands shaking.

Then a huge chunk of wall disappeared as the hotel took a direct hit from a shoulder-launched missile. As the noise of the explosion died away, the first of the Zonies swung in through the gaping hole, mouths twisted by incoherent battle cries, weapons spewing death.

Stell was out of his chair, moving toward Olivia and firing his handgun without conscious thought. One, two, three Zonies fell, gaping holes through their chests, cheap weapons rolling from nerveless fingers. He grabbed Olivia's wrist and jerked her out of the way as an energy beam cut her chair in half. To his left, Sergeant Major Como brained a Zonie with a chair and took his weapon. He used it to good effect, cutting a bloody swath through the oncoming mob. Meanwhile, Kasten brained a Zonie with a heavy ashtray and dropped another with a well-aimed punch. Stell shot two more, their bodies almost touching the muzzle of his weapon as it went off, the impact of the heavy slugs knocking them backward. Peripherally, Stell saw Roop go down, a slash of scarlet across the side of his head, a giant Zonie poised to strike another blow. Before he could move, Olivia scooped up a fallen energy pistol and fired. The beam cut off one leg at the knee. Unbalanced, the Zonie crashed to the floor like a fallen tree. He was crawling toward Roop when Stell finished him off.

Whirling back to face the Zonie attack, Stell saw them jerk and fall in a macabre death dance as Kasten's guards and his own troopers entered from the hall and opened up. Moments later, it was over. The room was silent except for the muffled sounds of fighting from outside, the groans of wounded Zonies, and the pinging of cooling weapons.

CHAPTER FIVE

Staring out of his office window, Stell couldn't believe the destruction in the compound below; it stretched as far as the eye could see. In the far distance, fires started by the sewer gas still burned, columns of black smoke marking the locations of buildings that hadn't paid their premiums to the Zone's privately owned fire companies. Below, his medical personnel loaded truck after truck with wounded Zonies being transported to the Zone's two privately run hospitals. They would be cared for at brigade expense. It didn't make sense . . . but they couldn't just leave them there, either. The experts said that, given time, most of them would recover. He sighed. Counting those killed in the ambush, the attack on headquarters, and the attack on the hotel, they'd lost twenty-three people. It was happening all over again. Twenty-three more cuts. Twenty-three more deaths for nothing. Arno had turned into a very expensive and unpleasant vacation.

Upon his return to HQ, he received a full report from Captain Wang. The young officer had done an outstanding job. He and Corporal—no, make that *Sergeant* Flynn. He would have her promotion entered in the muster today. But Wang hadn't been able to answer the question that bothered Stell most: Where the hell was Major Malik when the fecal matter hit the fan? As executive officer, Malik had been in command. Yet, when the Zonies attacked he was nowhere to be found, so Wang had assumed command. Stell didn't like Malik and never had. He'd joined the brigade a year before,

39

hired by Strom because they were short of experienced officers. On paper, Malik had all the right credentials. He had graduated from the Academy in the top third of his class, chose the Marines over the Navy, distinguished himself in a number of actions, and rose to the rank of Captain in record time. His promotion to Major had come as a result of Strom's death, just like Stell's promotion to Colonel. But Stell had always wondered why a man with Malik's record, and probable future in the service, had resigned his commission to join a mercenary outfit. Unlike the rest of the brigade, he had chosen this life . . . something Stell couldn't understand. In any case, he didn't like Malik and never had . . . a feeling that was mutual. The man was arrogant, egotistical, lazy, stubborn, and sadistic to boot. In fact, it was partly these qualities in Malik that made Stell worry about what the brigade would eventually become. After all, the man was second in command—if Stell were killed he'd take command, and no doubt shape the brigade in his own image. The thought made Stell shudder. Now Malik was either AWOL or missing in action. Because Stell didn't like him, he forced himself to keep an open mind. But if he was AWOL, god help him.

Meanwhile, Sergeant Major Como had a section out looking for him. Like every officer above the rank of lieutenant, Malik had a tiny mini-beacon surgically implanted below his right shoulder blade. Powered by his body heat, the device would last forever. More than once, such beacons had guided medics to wounded officers, and on one occasion, had led a rescue team to Stell's position behind enemy lines. Now Malik's beacon would allow them to track him down. Initial readings put him ten miles away, in one of the worst parts of the Zone. There was no logical reason for Malik to be there, but Stell forced himself to reserve judgment.

In the compound below, figures scurried around preparing for lift-off. Shortly after Stell's return, the Elders had sent word that the brigade was no longer welcome on Arno . . . and had forty-eight hours to get off. Of course, they would have lifted anyway. The Zone was no place for rest and relaxation. Plus, they had a new client—the planet called Freehold. The agreement had been hammered out on the fly.

Stell had arranged for Kasten and his party to be evacuated to
brigade HQ in a heavily armed convoy, since they obviously
weren't safe in the hotel. As they wound their way through
the flames and chaos touched off by Corporal Flynn, Stell and
Kasten began the delicate process of feeling each other out.
Kasten began by requesting the brigade's standard rates. Stell
replied there was no such thing as a standard war, and
therefore no such things as standard rates. The brigade charged
according to services actually rendered, with a standard minimum, and escalation clauses covering the unexpected. Nonetheless, he agreed to supply some examples of past engagements
and approximate cost. As he did, the politician turned white.

"Roop was right, you certainly aren't cheap," Kasten said,
forcing a crooked smile.

"True," Stell answered with a shrug, "but like the ancient
saying goes, you get what you pay for, and we're the best."

Kasten nodded. "I don't doubt it, Colonel, but I honestly
can't say if we have enough credits left to pay you. I guess I
was somewhat optimistic about your fees. Maybe Austin's
right after all . . . it's a choice between giving the planet to
you or the pirates!"

Stell laughed, saying, "If so, I assure you we are the more
pleasant choice." However, Kasten's joke stimulated a line
of reasoning that both surprised and intrigued him, and he
made a mental note to pursue it later. Meanwhile, the two
men worked out a compromise. Kasten couldn't hire the
brigade without the consent of Roop's opposition party. Even
if the necessary amount of money was available, he lacked
sufficient authority to spend it. But, since Roop was still
unconscious, Kasten had the leeway to hire the brigade on a
provisional basis, pending a final decision by Freehold's Senate. If the Senate vetoed the idea, the brigade would be paid
for time spent; if Kasten's proposal was approved, the mercenaries would already be in transit. Since they had to leave
Arno anyway, the agreement wouldn't impose a hardship on
the brigade. Stell smiled, remembering the twinkle in Kasten's
eyes as he said, "Frankly, Colonel Stell, Austin would do our
planet a great service if he'd just stay unconscious a little
longer. Without him mucking around I wouldn't have any
trouble getting the Senate's approval!"

Stell's thoughts were interrupted by the buzz of his comset. Without turning, he said, "Yes?"

"There's a man here to see you, sir," Sergeant Wilkins, the headquarters clerk, said disapprovingly. "Says his name is Sam. Won't give any other name, sir."

Stell grinned. "Send him up, Sergeant."

"Yes, sir," Wilkins replied reluctantly.

A few minutes later the door to Stell's office flew open, and a disheveled young man strode in and flopped onto the couch that Wilkens had dredged up from somewhere. "You call this an office?" he said, looking around critically at the dingy walls and shabby furniture. "I've seen Finthian bordellos with more class than this."

"Hello to you too, Sam," Stell said, dropping into a chair and swinging his boots up onto the scarred metal surface of the old campaign desk. "It disturbs me to learn that one of my officers is so familiar with Finthian bordellos . . . and a lady officer at that."

Captain Samantha Anne Mosley stuck out her tongue at her commanding officer, peeled off the wig she wore, and shook out her medium length blonde hair. She wasn't especially pretty, but that was an asset in her line of business. The last thing an intelligence officer needs is a memorable face. On the other hand, she wasn't ugly either, kind of cute in fact, something which hadn't escaped Stell's notice. Intelligent brown eyes twinkled under bushy unplucked brows. A nose a shade too large was softened by full, sensuous lips. And Stell knew from personal experience that the male clothing hid a very nice female body.

"Hello, Mark," she said. "It's good to see you. Excuse the charade, but this dump isn't a nice place for a defenseless girl to wander around in." She looked him up and down with the proprietary air of an older sister.

Stell snorted in disbelief. "Defenseless my ass. You're about as defenseless as a Linthian Rath snake . . . but I'm glad you're back, you had me worried."

"Why?" she asked with a smile. "You know I'm indestructible."

"Yeah," he said. "I know you think you are, anyway." For a moment they sat, sharing the comfortable silence of two

people who know each other very well. For nearly two years
they'd enjoyed a close relationship. Although the love affair
had eventually run its course, it ended in an amicable parting
of the ways, and they had remained good friends. The relationship made Stell feel guilty sometimes, but he couldn't
bear the thought of ending it. He wondered what he'd do if
faced with the necessity of sending her on a mission with
little chance of survival. He wasn't sure, but he knew she'd
hate him for the slightest hint of favoritism, which made him
admire her even more, and in turn made the problem worse.

She pulled out a dopestick and puffed it alight. Stell frowned
in disapproval as always and, as always, she ignored him.
"You've been busy," she said waving vaguely toward the
outside. "Any connection with my mission?"

Stell nodded. "Lots. I'm hoping you'll be able to shed
some light on the whole thing. But first, I'd better bring you
up to date." Quickly, he reviewed the Zonie attacks, his
meeting with Kasten and Roop, and the subsequent attack on
brigade HQ. When he finished, Sam stubbed out her dopestick
and lit another. As she spoke, her eyes narrowed in concen-
tration.

"There's a connection all right, although for a while it
looked like a standard client recon, and a boring one at that. I
landed on Freehold using a deep cover as a sales rep for a
small shipping line called Tri-Star. Supposedly, I was looking
to set up regular runs to Freehold. First I talked to the
government types at the planet's capital, a place called First
Hole. I told 'em I represented a small shipping line interested
in serving Freehold, but was concerned about the unusual
number of pirate raids, and asked if they could shed any light
on the situation. All I got was the runaround. They didn't
have the foggiest idea why the pirates had increased their
raids, but the government was working on it, and I shouldn't
worry my pretty little head. So I headed for the boonies. At
first, I couldn't find a damn thing there, either. Those who
knew weren't talking, and those who didn't wouldn't shut up.
From all indications, the economy centered around limited
mining operations, light industry, and the production of some
sophisticated ceramic products. It seems a long period of bad
weather had hit the first two pretty hard, so I figured their

surplus must be coming from the last, and it made sense. Given all that sand, and the almost limitless hydroelectric power available from those huge underground rivers, specialty ceramic products were a natural. Then, too, I learned the finished products were often small, light, easily transportable items, just the sort of things pirates love."

"With that in mind, I traveled around telling anyone who'd listen that my company was offering top prices for exotic ceramic products." Sam laughed. "You wouldn't believe the bribes I was offered—including a variety of sexual services that would make you blush. Anyway, it seems that the settlements operate as cooperatives, each in competition with all the others. So everyone I talked to did their best to promote their products and knock the competition's. And in their eagerness to win my business, they also dropped odd bits of information."

"With lots of help from you, I'm sure," Stell added dryly. "Were you dressed as a man or a woman?"

"Whichever it took," she teased. "Now pay attention, because I'm getting to the interesting part. After a particularly alcoholic dinner with the chairman of the local co-op, I received a drunken tour of the settlement's power plant—a big, sealed building right down at the river's edge. I had tried to get inside similar buildings and had failed. Once inside, there was all the stuff you'd expect in a hydroelectric plant: giant turbines, power grids, all the rest. But there was also a section that my host seemed determined to avoid. So when he left for a moment to relieve himself, I took a peek."

Stell wasn't fooled by her light conversational tone. He knew the risks she had taken.

"After getting past a variety of locks, sensors and other stuff, I knew I didn't have much time in there. So I didn't try to figure anything out, I just taped as much as I could." With that she pulled a micro-viewer out of a hidden pocket in her rumpled clothing and handed it to Stell. Holding it up, Stell gave the viewer a gentle squeeze, and it dutifully played back. Although the two-dimensional picture lacked the depth of a holo, it still produced good detail and color. The shots were fast and jerky, reflecting Sam's haste as she had raced against the clock and her host's full bladder. Occasionally he touched the screen to freeze a shot for a longer look. First he saw a complicated maze of pipes and tubing that seemed to snake in and out of large, sealed metal boxes. Then the camera ran along a laboratory bench covered with printouts, specimen bottles, tools, and other less-identifiable junk.

Handing the viewer back, Stell said, "Very impressive. What is it?"

Sam smiled. "That's what I asked the big brains on Techno before I came here."

Stell knew Techno was an artificial satellite that had started hundreds of years before as a small research station. Over time it had grown, one module at a time, until it matched the size of Earth's moon. It was a small, independent and self-sufficient universe, inhabited by a variety of top-flight scientists and technicians, all working for the highest bidder. It was rumored that they had developed secret weapons of incredible power with which to defend their artificial world. So far, no one had tried them on for size.

"And what did our high-priced friends have to say?" Stell asked.

"They say the folks on Freehold have come up with an interesting source of revenue. One which will make them very rich, if they can produce it in quantity . . . if they can get it to market, that is. The eggheads told me they'd been puzzling over the stuff coming out of Freehold for some time. So, using their existing research, plus the information I provided, they were able to do a pretty good analysis. Evidently, that maze of pipes and stuff is all part of a sophisticated water-filtration system. So sophisticated that the brains estimate it's capable of filtering out a piece of matter only a couple of microns across. The stuff on the work bench confirms that, and also suggests that the system is set up to recover a single mineral, one that is evidently present in large quantities in those underground rivers."

"Any idea what mineral that might be?" Stell asked.

Sam grinned and lit a new dopestick from the butt of the last. "I thought you'd never ask! The brains call it *thermium*. They say it's the secret ingredient that makes Freehold's ceramics so special. Nobody's been able to duplicate them, and I guess plenty have tried. Evidently, they are unbelievably heat resistant. There's nothing on the market like them, and there's thousands of possible applications, in everything from weapons to mom's toaster. Techno made me a generous standing offer for any thermium I could bring them.''

Stell frowned thoughtfully. ''That explains a lot. If this mineral is something new, and extremely diluted in those underground rivers, that would account for how Intersystems missed it during their original survey. And, if it's as valuable as you say, it explains why they want the planet back—so much so that they're willing to strike some sort of deal with the pirates.''

''Exactly,'' Sam agreed. ''And it also suggests how Freehold has managed to make those payments up till now. They're not living in the lap of luxury or anything . . . but those specialty ceramics have kept them from going under. But why make the ceramics themselves? Why not market the thermium and let others manufacture the products?''

''I don't know,'' Stell admitted. ''But maybe they think it's important to build their own industrial base. They seem like an independent bunch.''

''An independent bunch who're lying like hell,'' Samantha said, jabbing a dopestick in his direction. ''Why haven't Kasten and, what's his name, Roop, told you about thermium, instead of pretending it doesn't exist?''

''Because,'' Stell said soberly, ''they're convinced that potentially we're just as bad as the pirates, and in a way you can't blame them. Once dirtside, we could easily take everything they've got. I think Kasten wants to tell us . . . but Roop's stopping him.''

Both were silent for a moment as Sam blew out a long stream of scented lavender smoke. ''No,'' she said finally, ''I guess you can't blame 'em. If I had a home, maybe I'd do the same.''

Just then, Stell's com-set buzzed. ''Yes, Sergeant?''

''The Sergeant Major's on his way up, sir.''

''Thanks, Wilkens,'' Stell replied, as a tremendous commotion began out in the hall.

Seconds later a small, ragged figure was shoved into the room, kicking and screaming abuse, with Sergeant Major

Como close behind. "Sit down," Como ordered sternly, pointing at a straight-backed chair.

The skinny little girl jerked her arm away and spat defiantly at Como's feet. "Screw you, mister," she said. "Who died and made you an Elder, anyway?"

The Sergeant Major looked down at the spittle on his highly polished boots and then back up with an expression that had terrified full-grown men. The girl promptly sat down.

"And what have we here, Sergeant Major?" Stell asked with an amused expression.

"Face the other way, child," Como ordered, his voice gruff but kind.

The girl made a face, but stood obediently, turned, and sat down straddling the chair. Stell saw the back of her pathetic little dress had been ripped. Working carefully, Como gently pulled the edges of the garment apart to reveal her bare back. Stell winced at the sight. Someone had made a deep slash in her back and then stitched it up with sloppy sutures. Bloody drainage oozed down between protruding shoulder blades to disappear under her filthy dress. Turning to Como, Stell said, "Malik?"

The other man nodded wordlessly. Stell swore under his breath. The bastard. He'd had his mini-beacon removed and inserted in the girl. That way the beacon had continued to function and had misled his pursuers. He'd done it this way knowing that the needless cruelty of it would make Stell furious.

"That isn't all, Colonel," the Sergeant Major said with disgust. "Come take a look at this." Stell stood and walked over to the girl. He saw she was shaking with fear. He touched her shoulder gently, as Como used a clean dressing from his own med kit to wipe the bloody drainage away. And there, carved into her flesh, was a message: "Dear Stell, I've decided to resign my commission in order to pursue other interests. Too bad the ambush didn't work, but I'm sure we'll meet again. Peter Malik."

CHAPTER SIX

The Senate chambers were spacious and cool, a relief after the searing heat of Freehold's noonday sun. Built deep underground, they could withstand anything up to a direct hit from a hell bomb, and Stell's military eye approved. However, the decor was anything but Spartan. Freehold might not be a wealthy planet, but the pride of its citizens was visible in the colorful murals covering the walls, and their hopes for the future could be seen in the holo that covered the ceiling. Clever artwork had been combined with electronic wizardry to show Freehold as it might be, hundreds of years in the future. The planet depicted in the holo was crisscrossed by a network of irrigation canals fed by the underground rivers. Green forests covered hundreds of square miles, giving way to carefully tended farms, and grassy plains dotted with thousands of grazing animals. Hovering as it did over the Senate, this vision of what Freehold could become was more than art—it was an affirmation, a unifying purpose.

Physical comfort had not been neglected, either. Tiers of comfortable chairs rose in orderly progression toward the rear of the room. The front seats formed a gentle curve facing a low stage and a transparent wall. Beyond the armored plastic flowed a huge underground river. Its power and purpose dominated the room. Cleverly placed lights made it seem as though sunlight was filtering down through its mighty currents, creating an endless dance of light and dark. Against such a backdrop, man's affairs would always seem puny and

insignificant, Stell mused. For while men might argue and
debate, the rivers ruled Freehold. From them came life-giving
water, power to run man's machines, and the tiny bits of
mineral matter over which they were willing to fight and die.

"And that's where I come in," Stell thought, settling back
in his seat. He watched curiously as Freehold's Senators filed
in singly and in small groups. Most were still dressed in the
pressurized sand suits that were a necessity outside. Stell
noted that most were armed. This was no gathering of a
privileged elite. These people were used to danger and hard
work, things that Stell understood. Many glanced his way as
they entered, talking softly with those around them. The
debate was already underway.

Kasten had met him at First Hole's small spaceport, and
from his comments, Stell knew the chances weren't very
good. Roop was fully recovered and working hard to organize
opinion against hiring the brigade. Kasten had been equally
active since they'd parted company a week earlier, but feared
Roop's party was making inroads with the independents.
And, since the two political parties were roughly equal in
size, the independents would very likely settle the issue.

Once again Stell went over his plan, searching for flaws or
acceptable alternatives. But no matter how many times he did
so, and regardless of logic, it felt good in his gut. He remembered the orderly rows of alert faces. The backdrop of scorched
duracrete. And the sickly sweet smell of death that surrounded the brigade as they listened to him speak. They stood
at ease, listening attentively, smiling and nodding their encouragement, as though listening to a favorite child recite his
lessons. They admired and respected him, but, with the natural cynicism of the lower ranks, they also thought him a bit
naive, and maybe a little crazy. He, in turn, admired and
respected them, but couldn't understand how they could accept his idea so passively, so unemotionally. They didn't
scream objections or cheer with enthusiasm; they simply accepted his suggestion like they had accepted a thousand orders, with cheerful acquiescence. So when he was finished,
they voted their approval, and climbed aboard the transports
that would take them to the spaceport. But among their ranks
there were some with whom his words and ideas hit home,

expressing feelings they'd had but couldn't find words for.
One was Sergeant Flynn, who stood watching as he stepped
down off the ammo case, looking at him almost the way the
devout would regard a saint. But she was toward the rear of
the milling crowd, so he didn't see her.

Stell's thoughts were interrupted as a tall, thin man with
thick black hair mounted the stage and called the session to
order. Glancing around, Stell thought there were a surprising
number of empty seats, until he realized they weren't actually
empty. Each was filled with a faint, almost transparent, holo
of the Senator to whom it was assigned. As the lights were
dimmed, the holo took on more substance, until it was difficult to tell them from their flesh-and-blood neighbors. Evidently, some of the more distant Senators chose to remain at
home rather than travel to the capitol.

As the man with the black hair droned through the minutes of
the last meeting, Stell's eyes were drawn again to the powerful
flow of the river. He allowed his mind to merge with the
peaceful blueness, releasing all tension and gathering strength
for the coming battle. Although it would be fought with
words rather than weapons, it would be a battle nonetheless,
and maybe the most important in the brigade's history. The
opposition would bring superior numbers to the conflict, and
they would be armed with fear and greed. Stell felt sure that
Roop's actions were somehow linked to thermium. But Roop
had been present during the Zonie attack. And he'd been
wounded to boot. So it seemed unlikely that he'd arranged for
the attack. Anyway, Stell's strategy depended on surprise,
compassion, courage, and the desperation of the planet's citizens. "Remember son, timing is everything," Strom had
counseled him many times. "The power of a secret weapon
lies in the timing with which you use or reveal it. So don't let
'em know what you've got till the last second, and then use it
to the limit." With that in mind, Stell forced himself to wait
patiently.

With routine matters finally out of the way, the black-
haired man introduced Kasten, and as the President mounted
the dais, Stell admired his poise and presence. Kasten appeared relaxed and seemed to be enjoying himself. There was
a spring in his step and a gleam in his eye. As the polite

applause died down, Kasten's eyes swept the audience, gauging the Senate's mood. He chose his words carefully.

"Ladies and gentlemen of the Senate, fellow citizens of Freehold, thank you. The matter before us today is serious indeed. How we deal with it will determine our future, and that of our children's children. We are deciding nothing less than our collective destinies. There are few among you who haven't already shed tears for friends or loved ones lost to the violence of the past few months—violence that threatens our lives, our homes, and our freedom. Some here believe the violence can be ended by peaceful means . . . that we can buy off the pirates. Nothing could be further from the truth. The price for cooperation with the pirates is slavery. Not just for us, but for all future generations as well. A poor legacy for our children. What's more, such payments would ignore the real source of our problems, the true reason why the pirates continue to attack, and that ladies and gentlemen is the avarice of Intersystems Incorporated.''

There was much more. Kasten did a skillful job of arguing his case, laying out each point in logical sequence, wrapping it up with the inescapable conclusion that, lacking sufficient strength to defend themselves, they should hire a force that could. There was, however, no mention of Intersystem's real motive—thermium. Kasten didn't bring it up, even though he could have used it to strengthen his arguments. Did the assembled Senators know about the precious mineral being filtered out of the underground rivers? Surely they must. But did the general population? Given a system of competitive co-ops it seemed likely, though not certain. In any case, there was apparently some kind of unwritten agreement between the parties not to mention thermium publicly. They evidently feared that publicity would bring even more trouble their way; and they might be right, but the secrecy was distorting the decision-making process while benefiting the pirates and Intersystems. So how would they react when Stell brought it all out into the open? He couldn't tell, but it had to be done.

Kasten sat down and Roop took the stage. He had an oversized white bandage wrapped dramatically around his head, serving to remind all present of the wound he'd suffered in their service. His eyes burned brightly as he accepted his applause and nodded indulgently to his supporters. When the applause died down and he spoke, it was with the patient conviction of a parent lecturing an errant child.

"Ladies and gentlemen of the Senate. The President has stated his case most eloquently. In fact, I agree with most of what he said. Everything, in fact, except his conclusion. Stated simply, President Kasten suggests that the pirates, or Intersystems Incorporated, want our planet. He goes on to say they are determined to take it by force. Never mind the lack of proof of such a conspiracy, he suggests that since we're not able to effectively defend ourselves, we should hire others to do so. He even goes so far as to suggest that any other solution will result in de facto slavery. Well my friends, I suggest our money is better spent on peace than war, and that the only person likely to enslave us sits right here in these chambers!" With that, Roop pointed a quivering finger at Stell. His supporters applauded loudly, and all turned to look curiously in Stell's direction.

Roop snorted in derision to bring their attention back to him. "But let's ignore all that for a moment and just look at practicalities. Even if Colonel Stell and his brigade were a band of angels, we couldn't afford them. Not at the usurous rates they're accustomed to receiving. I remind you that we are in danger of missing our next payment to Intersystems Incorporated. Clearly a plan to spend more money than we have on mercenaries isn't going to help us make that payment." Roop paused, a smirk touching his lips as he allowed the silence to grow, enjoying the power it gave him. "With that in mind, and considering that President Kasten has seen fit to break precedent and introduce an outsider into the affairs of the Senate," Roop again glanced meaningfully in Stell's direction, "I think it only fair that my party be allowed the same freedom. So it's with great pleasure that I introduce gentlebeing Lady Almanda Kance-Jones. She currently serves Intersystems Incorporated as the Planetary Account Executive for Freehold. Since her company has been the subject of no small amount of suspicion in these matters, it seems only right to allow Intersystems the right to reply through Executive Kance-Jones."

There were more than a few gasps of amazement and

muttered objections from members of Kasten's party. Those were quickly drowned out by the applause generated by Roop and his cronies. Stell's mind raced, trying to calculate the impact of Roop's move. But his attention quickly shifted as Almanda Kance-Jones ascended the dais. To say she was beautiful would be an understatement. She was without a doubt the single most beautiful woman he'd ever seen. Her beauty burned like a flame, but to his eyes it was a cold flame, for as she faced the audience her eyes were like ice. He knew such flawless beauty could not possibly be natural and testified to the work of the empire's most skilled biosculpters. Long, jet-black hair fell in gentle cascades to frame a perfectly proportioned oval face. She wore a unisuit, which molded to her perfect figure and shimmered softly in the light. She was fascinating, but in the same way a snake about to strike is fascinating, and, like every other man in the room, Stell couldn't take his eyes off her.

Her voice was smooth and modulated, touched with just a hint of huskiness, yet very feminine nonetheless. She spoke with a disarming directness. "Ladies and gentlemen of the Senate, thank you for allowing me to speak. I fully realize how unusual this opportunity is and promise not to abuse it. With that in mind, I'll keep my comments brief. First, let me assure you Intersystems is not behind any plot to steal what's rightfully yours. Nothing could be further from the truth. I cannot explain why the pirates have chosen this time to increase their raids on your planet, except to say you're not alone. Since the empire's well-known military cutbacks, all the frontier planets have come under more pressure from both the pirates and the Il Ronn. But to suggest that Intersystems is in league with the pirates is . . . well . . . misguided." At this point, her expression made it clear that she would have preferred to use stronger language than "misguided." "While I admit that if the attacks prevent you from fulfilling your contractual obligations, Intersystems might benefit, I assure you we would rather have you succeed under the original terms of our agreement, and thereby have you as customers in the future. As an outsider, it would be presumptuous of me to advise you on how to run your government, but I must say that Senator Roop has impressed me with his good judgment and concern for your affairs. Thank you.''

As she stepped down and disappeared toward the rear of the room, there was only a flutter of applause. No matter whose side they were on, representatives of Intersystems Incorporated would have only limited appeal to the majority of Freehold's Senate. Nevertheless, there was no denying the impact of her words. For those already inclined toward Roop her comments could be decisive.

Then Roop took the floor again, clutching a sheaf of printouts in his hand and holding them aloft like some sort of trophy. ''Ladies and gentlemen of the Senate, I'd like to thank Executive Kance-Jones for her comments, and bring your attention to the petition I hold in my hand. It is addressed to the Emperor, and has been signed by all the members of my party; it asks him to prohibit the brigade in question from meddling in our affairs. It may interest you to know that since these mercenaries were 'authorized' by the Emperor, he has the power to redirect their activities! I urge each of you to sign. The petition will be sent to Earth by message torp immediately after this session is adjourned.'' With a smile of triumph, he marched off the stage to loud applause.

As the black-haired man rose and took the dais, Stell's heart sank. If a sufficient number of Senators signed the petition, there was little doubt the Emperor would carry out their wishes. Then the brigade would have to withdraw, or challenge the might of the entire empire. ''Ladies and gentlemen of the Senate, on behalf of President Kasten, I would ask that you hear one more speaker. While he has no official status on our planet, Colonel Stell commands the army in question, and his comments will no doubt be relevant. I might add that Colonel Stell has agreed to answer any and all question you may have at the conclusion of his remarks. Are there any objections?''

All heads turned towards Roop. He smiled and shook his head. ''I have no objection . . . and I look forward to asking the Colonel some questions about the cost of his services.''

The black-haired man said, ''That being the case, it is my pleasure to introduce Colonel Mark Stell. Colonel?''

Stell made his way up to the dais. As he looked out at the blur of strange faces, it seemed hopeless. All he saw was suspicion and hostility. Then there was movement in the back of the room as a massive door opened and closed. For the briefest moment, his eyes met Olivia Kasten's, and her smile of encouragement sent a wave of confidence through him. Looking out again, he forced a smile and said, "Ladies and gentlemen of the Senate, on behalf of myself and my brigade, I greet you. I wish the occasion of my visit to your planet were more pleasant. Unfortunately, these are difficult times. As you know, life isn't easy on a frontier planet. If it were, the Emperor would live out here, instead of on Earth!" Stell's joke served to break the ice a little, reaping scattered chuckles and at least one "You can say that again!"

"But even though frontier life is hard, you've suffered more than most. Again and again the pirates have attacked. Again and again you have fought back, but to no avail. Ladies and gentlemen, the time has come for honesty." Stell paused, allowing his eyes to roam the audience. Did he see glimmers of sympathy here and there? "You and I both know why they continue to attack. It can be summed up in one word: thermium. And if you're not familiar with its recently coined name, I suspect you still know what I'm referring to."

There was a moment of shocked silence, followed by consternation, confused babble, and then cries for quiet mixed with demands for Stell's arrest. Holding up his hands to still the noise, Stell said, "Hear me out."

Again all eyes turned to Roop, who shrugged and smiled a crooked smile. "Let him speak, he's making my case better than I could." There was nervous laughter as many nodded in agreement. The black-haired man, who had risen to point out that Stell still had the floor in any case, took his seat.

As the noise died down, Stell did his best to smile and appear relaxed, while inside every nerve was stretched wire tight. "Yes, I know about the mineral you filter out of your great rivers," he said gesturing to the living mural behind him. "I know it's heat resistant beyond any similar material known to man. I know it's the crucial ingredient in the exotic ceramic products for which you are justly famous. And, ladies and gentlemen, if I know, then you can be sure the pirates and Intersystems Incorporated know, too!''

This time the room was completely silent as Stell's words struck home, each Senator privately admitting what he or she had known all along. ''I don't blame you for keeping thermium a secret for as long as you could,'' Stell said quietly. ''In your place, I would have done the same. Why ask for trouble? But the time for secrecy is long past. I learned of thermium through the routine intelligence appraisal we always do before accepting a client. Somehow, the pirates learned about thermium too, and so did Intersystems. You've got it and they want it; it's as simple as that.''

''And what about you, Colonel?'' a Senator yelled, looking to Roop for approval. ''Don't you want it, too?''

The black-haired man rose to object, but Stell held up a restraining hand. ''A fair question Senator, and one which I'll happily answer. Not with a simple 'no' that you wouldn't believe anyway, but with a proposal—one which should not only put your fears to rest, but will also enable you to fight off the pirates . . . and make your next payment on time.'' Stell saw that he now had their full attention. ''We do want something from you,'' he said earnestly. ''But it isn't your wealth. When I landed this morning, I gave President Kasten a sealed container and asked him to hold it until now. Inside, he'll find applications for full Freeholdian citizenship from every member of my brigade.'' Suddenly, the entire room broke into excited conversation, forcing the black-haired man to call repeatedly for order. When all was quiet once again, Stell said, ''So you see, we don't want anything which isn't ours. All we want is a chance. A chance to earn a place among you, a chance to have a home. In return, we offer our services for *free*, just as members of your Civil Defense Force already do—just as any loyal citizen would do if their planet were attacked. I submit, by the way, that as citizens of Freehold, Senator Roop's petition would become a moot point.''

The room exploded into excited conversation. Looking out at the sea of faces, Stell saw everything from amusement to rage. Oliver Kasten beamed his approval, Olivia smiled her encouragement, and Roop was livid. Eventually, the black-haired man managed to restore order. Although Stell knew he still had the floor, he said calmly, "I believe Senator Roop has a question."

"How kind of Colonel Stell to allow me to speak," Roop said sarcastically as he stood and scanned the room. "Ladies and gentlemen, you heard it from his own lips. First he planted spies among us to learn our secrets, and now he's using the information thus gained to blackmail us into granting citizenship for his entire brigade! After all, why steal the planet if you can take it without firing a shot?" Roop's hard eyes moved from person to person, challenging each to object. "So, before Stell insults our intelligence further, I move his absurd request for mass citizenship be unanimously denied, that any consideration of using his services be tabled, and that he be escorted off the planet immediately." With a look of smug satisfaction, Roop took his seat to mixed applause and objections.

The black-haired man rose and said, "As Senator Roop knows, Colonel Stell still has the floor, and while he does, no vote can be taken. Colonel Stell?"

Stell looked out at the audience and wondered what to do. Roop had the advantage. He was used to dueling with words, and the battle was taking place on his home ground. Maybe it was stupid to try. After all, in spite of its potential wealth, Freehold wasn't much of a planet . . . and maybe they could do better. But he couldn't dismiss Kasten's hopeful look, Olivia's smile, or his own emotions. If there was a chance for the brigade to earn a home—a place where they could belong—and a future, then it was worth fighting for.

"May I speak?" The voice came from the darkness at the back of the room. Stalling for time, Stell nodded his consent.

"Senator Elwar Bram has the floor," the black-haired man said, as a short, stocky man stepped out into the light. He brought with him a sense of physical vitality and power. He was not handsome, yet women had always flocked to him because of the gentle strength of his eyes and hands. His rugged, sun-darkened features made a proper setting for bright-blue eyes that shone with anger. He spoke with an intensity born of deep feeling. "What the hell's going on here? Have you all gone crazy?" Senator Bram's eyes swept the chambers. "We're fighting for our lives and losing. My brother and his family are dead. Each of you have lost someone or something. Yet some of you are ready to give them more. Well I'm not. For me it's gone beyond politics. Today I speak to you not as an independent, but as a man. A man who is pissed off and tired of losing. And what's this crap about not accepting any help?" He pointed to Stell. "This man has offered to fight beside us for the right to live here, to make Freehold his home. I say we accept his offer, and damned quick. And if he and his people profit from living here, then so much the better; there's enough sand, hard work, and pain here for everyone. As for Intersystems . . . hell, they'd piss on your boots and tell you it was raining." He paused grimly, "I vote for Colonel Stell's proposal, for fighting back, and for self-respect!"

Two-thirds of those in the room stood, their applause reverberating off the durasteel-reinforced walls, filling the chamber with a thunder of sound. Bram's speech had swung the Independents to Kasten's side, and the first battle was won. Stell felt himself grinning like an idiot. The brigade had a home.

CHAPTER SEVEN

As Freehold's sun sank toward the distant horizon, Stell sat perfectly still, afraid his slightest movement might destroy the magic of the moment. The sky was painted orange and gold. A warm, gentle breeze wafted in from the distant desert and skipped gently over the lake, rippling its surface, and pushing tiny wavelets toward shore to slosh softly at his feet. Across the lake, the fading light washed the villa with orange and gold, making it look like a castle from some ancient painting. Around him insects hummed, and nocturnal predators emerged to eat them, their luminescent wings glowing as they flitted from perch to perch. It seemed like a fairyland, an enchanted place where the heat, grit, and hardship of the planet's bad-lands were kept out by some magic spell—a spell so fragile it would be broken if he so much as breathed. Knowing he could eventually come to a place like this would make months of hard work in the desert seem worthwhile. And suddenly the dream was gone, as he remembered all the work that remained undone, and all those who depended on him to do it. But he forced himself to shake it off for just these few hours. Surely he was entitled to that?

"Beautiful, isn't it?" Olivia asked, appearing by his side. "Are you glad you came?"

"Yes," he answered looking up into her eyes, "it is beautiful, and I am glad that I came." ·

She smiled at the compliment as she set the tray of fruit and cold meat on a low table between two chairs. Then she

59

paused for a moment to look out over the water, the scent of her perfume drifting around him. Right then he wanted her more than any woman he'd ever met. Then, as quickly as it came, the moment was gone and they sat down to eat. They ate in a companionable silence, savoring not only the food, but each other, and the natural beauty surrounding them.

Later they went for a walk through the villa's gardens. They had been designed and tended by Olivia's mother and, since her death, by Olivia. This was no garden of formal squares and circles, but a more subtle place, where flower and shrub were placed so artfully that everything seemed to flow together, yet did so within a larger purpose. Occasionally, Olivia would pause to point out some feature of particular interest, and would make a face and laugh when he refused to look, keeping his eyes on her instead. And as they walked it felt good to take her hand in his, to feel her shoulder brush his arm, to hear the soft murmur of her voice.

When they mounted the villa's wide, sweeping veranda to watch the sun's final moments, it seemed very natural to put an arm around her waist. And when she turned to look into his eyes, it seemed equally natural to meet her lips with his, and to lose himself in the soft warmth of her arms. As the sun dipped below the horizon, they turned and entered the villa, leaving the darkness behind. But far out in the gathering blackness a shooting star burned bright as it entered Freehold's atmosphere and fell toward the surface of the planet.

The meteor flared brightly on Com Tech Chu's screen. She frowned in annoyance, flicked shiny black hair back from her face, and watched the screen as her fingers tapped out a quick rhythm on the keyboard. The fragrant cup of blue New Indian tea by her side sat momentarily forgotten. High above the No-Hole tracking station where she worked, a ragged network of satellites responded to her commands—tracking, probing, and measuring the meteorite as it fell. Chu placed an ancient Chinese curse on the pirates who had routinely destroyed a good part of the network each time they staged a raid. Satellites were expensive . . . and Freehold just couldn't afford to replace them fast enough. But how was she supposed to do her job with only half a network? She'd complained bitterly more than once, but it didn't do any good. She relaxed as reassuring data flooded her screen. It was just another rock falling from the sky. For some reason there'd been a lot of them lately, but the rock showed no signs of propulsion, weapons, unusual radiation or life, so no sweat. A quick check revealed no danger of a hit on a settlement, so she turned her attention back to her tea, and swore when she found it was cold.

Inside the meteorite, Quarter Sept Commander Feeg watched his instruments carefully, grunting in satisfaction when the probing beams were withdrawn. He wasn't surprised. After all, his ship was very small, barely large enough to hold him, and carefully screened. That, and the pathetic condition of the planet's satellite network, plus the incompetence of the humans, had already allowed more than two hundred members of the elite Sand Sept to land using the same ruse. As the disguised assault boat continued its downward plunge, friction caused the rock sprayed on its surface to glow, and heat began to build inside the tiny craft. But even when the interior reached a hundred degrees, it was still a bit chilly by Il Ronnian standards, and Feeg wished he'd thought to wear a heat suit. Still, from what he'd heard during his briefing, the surface was quite warm, and that, combined with the substance called thermium, accounted for Il Ronnian interest in the planet.

As Freehold's surface rose to meet him, Feeg returned his attention to the controls. While the on-board computer handled most of it, planetary atmospheres could be tricky, often requiring the intervention of a skilled pilot, just one of Feeg's many qualifications. His sharp talons flicked in and out of the small indentations in the keyboard, firing his control jets, and smoothing out his glide path. With the added weight of the disguise, the little ship not only looked like a rock . . . it flew like one, too. Just seconds prior to touchdown, a double line of infrared landing lights popped into existence on his nav screen. He lined up the small ship between them and put it down with a gentle thump. As his landing gear touched the hard-packed sand, the lights disappeared. Even if there had been a satellite looking that way at that precise moment, the brief flare of infrared against the background of warm sand wouldn't have excited notice.

A few minutes later, Feeg was wrapped in the warmth of a borrowed heat-cape, watching as the ugly little assault boat disappeared into the underground hangar. Once the sand-covered lid was slid back into place, you could walk over it and never suspect the fortress hidden below. The location had been chosen with great care. Here the sand was shallow, allowing the underground construction for which Il Ronnians were justly famous, and a small tributary of a great sub-surface river could be tapped for power and water. Feeg touched a hand to rubbery lips at the thought of that holy substance.

An armed hover car made a few passes over the area, erasing all traces of the landing, and then stopped a respectful distance away, careful not to shower him with blown sand. As he walked to the car, Feeg inhaled deeply of the clean night air. Yes, he thought to himself, it is a planet worthy of our race. Beautiful expanses of clean sand, clinging like warm flesh to the planet's skeleton of rock, all of it fed by veins and arteries filled to overflowing with the holy fluid. It was, in fact, a nicer planet in some ways than the Il Ronnian home world. All things considered, Freehold's mineral wealth would be like an additional blessing, an omen of good things to come, a blessing on the race. But first he must cleanse it of all impurities, much as a priest must wash the sacred symbol of his Sept before offering it to those assembled before him. The analogy pleased Feeg as he imagined himself presenting a miniature Freehold to the Council of One Thousand. But first he must deal with the humans. Already they fought among themselves, making his task easier. How stupid they were! Still, they could be stubborn, these humans. They had been underestimated before. He scowled as he climbed into the car, nodding to the two bodyguards appropriate to his rank, and growled at the driver. "You have your orders, execute them." Without a word the driver put the car in gear, goosed the turbines, and skimmed off across the sand.

Senator Austin Roop swore continuously as he paced up and down in front of his hover car. He cursed the sand under his feet, the stars in the sky, and the goddamned pointy-tailed Il Ronnians who'd asked him to meet them in the middle of the night. No, damn it, the coded radio transmission had *ordered* him to come! How dare they? Who did they think he was, some errand boy? He'd done what they asked, hadn't he? Why treat him this way? The more he thought about it the madder he got. But deep down, below the anger, he was afraid. Not just a little bit afraid, like when he got up in front of the Senate, but gut sick afraid. It was an emotion he didn't feel often. Time after time he'd faced big game on a variety of planets, most of it quite lethal, and on many of those occasions he'd been scared. But never like this. He stopped pacing for a moment to listen. But all he heard was the pinging of his hover car as hot metal cooled in the night air. He could jump in it and go. There was nothing to stop him. But the thought of double-crossing them scared him just as much as did the thought of facing them. For all he knew, some of them were out there in the dark watching him that very moment. The mere thought sent a shudder through him. He resumed his pacing, but darted glances every now and then into the dark surrounding him. Damn them . . . why did it have to be clear out here, in the middle of the night? Looking at them in the daylight was bad enough . . . but at night. . . . Suddenly, he heard the tell-tale whine of distant turbines and whirled to face the sound. He composed himself slowly and carefully, just as he'd done a hundred times before speaking in the Senate. But try as he might, he couldn't lose the knot of fear that twisted his guts when the hover car appeared out of the night.

He flinched as the car swung insultingly close, spraying him with sand. The hover car's door whined open, releasing a blast of heated air and spilling light out onto the sand. Feeg was silhouetted for a moment as he stepped out. Roop felt his guts twist. He'd met Il Ronnians before, but he'd never get used to the way they looked. He remembered spooling through his father's Bible as a little boy, looking at the 3-D illustrations, and how the chill had run down his spine when he came to the one depicting the devil. Feeg was that illustration come to life. He was tall, standing on long, spindly legs, which ended in cloven hoofs that seemed to float on top of the sand. His skin was leathery and hairless. Eons before, its reddish hue had provided Feeg's ancestors with protective coloration on a world of red sand. His skull was bony, his deep-set eyes hidden by the deep shadows cast by a prominent supraorbital ridge. One long, pointed ear lay flat against his head. The other ended in a stump, sliced off by a pirate, accounting for both his passionate dislike of that breed, and his nickname among the troops, "Old One Ear." His long tail twitched back and forth like a cat's before wrapping itself around his waist.

As Roop had grown older, he had of course learned about the academic debate surrounding Il Ronnian physiognomy. Some experts believed the alien's devil-like appearance accounted for the almost instant dislike each race had for the other. They suggested that, after thousands of years of exposure to a negative image closely resembling the Il Ronn, most people couldn't view them objectively. Of course others disagreed, pointing out that from all evidence the Il Ronn had preceded man into space by thousands of years, and had perhaps visited Earth, treating primitive man with something less than kindness and thereby earning their reputation for evil. Still others said the resemblance was purely coincidental, and the enmity between the two races was the natural product of conflict between two aggressive, expanding empires, now separated by only a thinning band of unclaimed frontier worlds.

But regardless of who was right, for Roop, the Il Ronn were inextricably linked with that illustration in his father's Bible, and the fear and loathing that went with it. Nonetheless, he drew himself up straight, forced what he hoped was a confident smile and, using his best political manner said, "Hello, I'm Senator Roop. And you are?"

Feeg didn't reply. Instead, he looked Roop slowly up and down as though examining an interesting specimen at a zoo. Roop felt himself blush as the knot of fear in his gut grew even tighter. Having completed his inspection, Feeg said calmly, "You have accepted payment. You have failed. Explain."

Mustering what dignity and courage he could, Roop said, "And why should I explain anything to you? I don't even know who you are."

Feeg regarded him thoughtfully, and then said, "I am the one who will have you killed if you do not answer my question.'' His two bodyguards stepped forward, their assault rifles at port arms.

"You wouldn't dare!" Roop replied.

Feeg smiled—a terrifying sight, because as his thin lips pulled back they revealed rows of carnivorous teeth. He looked slowly around the horizon. "Oh, but I would dare. I am sure many people are lost in the desert each year and never found. Hover cars break down, radios fail, people become tired and confused and wander off into the sand, never to be seen again." Feeg looked toward the invisible horizon as though he could see Roop wandering hopelessly into the wastelands. "Now," he continued, his voice as hard as durasteel, "answer my question. Why have you failed?"

Roop began to shake. First his hands, then his knees, then his whole body until his teeth chattered. He knew that if he wasn't careful he'd lose control of his bowels, and the thought scared him even more. Oh god, why had he gotten into this? "I . . . I don't know what you mean," he said. "I've done everything I was asked to do. How . . . how have I failed?"

Feeg's tail unwrapped from his waist to twitch back and forth in astonishment. Hands clasped behind his back, Feeg slowly circled the human as he spoke. "How have you failed, pathetic one? Would you call recruitment of an entire brigade of mercenaries into the citizenry of your planet a success? You were ordered to weaken this planet's ability to defend itself, not strengthen it." Feeg stopped directly in front of Roop, his eyes glowing like red-hot coals in the darkness.

"And I did," Roop argued desperately. "All along I've encouraged them to argue, debate and generally waste time. And it would've worked, too, if the mercenaries hadn't offered their services for free. How . . . how was I supposed to counter that?"

"The absurd machinations of your ridiculous government are of no interest to me, or to my superiors," Feeg replied. "We are interested in one thing only . . . results."

For a moment, Roop's resentment got the better of him. "You think you're so damned smart; did it ever occur to you that Kasten and his people are probably right? Chances are that Intersystems *is* in league with the pirates. Maybe they'll show up with a fleet tomorrow . . . and then where will you be?'' The second the words were out of his mouth, Roop regretted them and would have given anything to bring them back. He shrank waiting for the blow or bullet. It didn't come.

Instead, Feeg wore an expression of amused condescension. ''So the mouse has teeth. What a marvelous surprise! In answer to the mouse's question: No, fool, we do not worry about the pirates. Why should we? They only want thermium, as does the company you call Intersystems. We want the entire planet. Do you seriously think the pirates would willingly live and work here?'' Feeg gestured toward the desert that surrounded them. ''Why bother, when it is easier to take what they want—either for themselves or Intersystems, it makes no difference. In the end, this planet will be ours. The only question is whether you will live to witness it.''

Roop wasn't so sure that the pirates and Intersystems should be dismissed so lightly, but he could see there was no point in arguing, so he stood, with his head hanging, waiting for whatever the next few moments would bring. He thought about the small blaster in the sleeve holster on his left arm. At least he'd take the alien to hell with him! Much to his own surprise he almost laughed, and the thought dissolved the knot of fear in his gut.

''However,'' Feeg said thoughtfully, as if sensing somehow the change in Roop's emotions, ''perhaps a second chance is in order. I believe you are, in your own way, sincere. And if you aid us, we will not fail to reward you. When the planet is ours, you shall rule your kind, and who knows—perhaps you will serve us elsewhere, as well. All things are possible for those who are loyal and accomplish the tasks given them. So I offer you one more chance. Success will bring you wealth and power beyond your wildest dreams. Failure will bring you death.''

Outwardly, Roop listened attentively, the very picture of subdued obedience, but inwardly he gloried in the power he would have, even daring to wonder if he could eventually rid himself of the Il Ronnians, keeping it all for himself. He was still scared, but not immobilized, and as he swore his loyalty, he silently promised the ugly alien payment, with interest, for the fear and humiliation he had suffered. The two of them talked for many hours, finally parting company just as the sun peeked above the eastern horizon, their plans for taking over Freehold complete.

CHAPTER EIGHT

High above Freehold, the brigade's three transports followed one another in orbit. They were spaced far enough apart so that they couldn't be destroyed with a single missile, but close enough to make transportation between them convenient. They were huge ships, each capable of carrying a thousand people plus weapons, ammunition, food, and other supplies. Their size, plus the complex maze of duct work, antennas, observation platforms, and weapons blisters, made it obvious that they had been constructed in space and would never be able to negotiate a planetary atmosphere. For hours crowded shuttles had flitted between the ships and the surface of Freehold. Now they were all aboard.

Stell's eyes roamed *Zulu*'s wardroom from his seat at the head of the massive table. He ignored the people pouring in who chatted with each other and searched for their seats. In spite of them, it was a private moment. In many ways it was like coming home, and he found himself wishing Olivia were there, so he could tell her all the stories it brought to mind. But she was still at the villa where he had left her two days before. He smiled as he thought about the precious hours they had spent together. Exploring slowly at first, then a little faster, then racing from subject to subject, finding agreement after agreement, eager to learn more. By the time he'd had to leave, they'd been talking about the future. Something he and his fellow officers had done a lot of here. His eye was caught by the bar that dominated the far end of the room. It was made of Terran oak, and its highly polished surfaces glowed like an altar in a chapel of steel. How many drinks, stories and laughs had been shared while standing around it? And there, just to the right of the bar, if you looked carefully, you could make out the patch in the ship's durasteel hull. They'd taken a torpedo there, just off Momar II. Old Willy, the wardroom steward, had been killed instantly—but his beloved bar had survived without a scratch. Over the years the *Zulu* had been hit many times, but she'd always come through, just like the brigade itself.

Like all the brigade's ships, the *Z* was old, older than those serving in her. And, like her sister ships, the *Masai* and the *Shona*, the *Zulu* wasn't really a fighting ship. Her true role was that of transport. Oh, she had energy cannons and a few missile batteries, but they were mainly defensive and wouldn't do too much harm to anything but another antique like herself. Her main defense lay in the powerful screens that she could generate. She wasn't fast or pretty, but her huge drives could put out lots of power, a fact that had saved their lives many times and was a source of tremendous pride to her Captain, Amanda Boyko.

Captain Boyko had a wiry body, small, dark features, fiery eyes, and a temper to match. She sat on Stell's left, with her two peers, Captains Nishita and Kost, ranked beside her. Beyond them were former Captain, now *Major* Wang; Samantha, looking very uncomfortable in her dress uniform and puffing the inevitable dopestick; and, beyond her, a number of lieutenants, senior noncoms, and specialists of various kinds. To his right were Sergeant Major Como, Oliver Kasten, Austin Roop, Elwar Bram, several key industrial leaders and various members of Freehold's Defense Force. It was a council of war.

Once everyone was seated and looking his way, Stell stood and said, "First, let me thank all of you for coming on such short notice, but I assure you it is necessary. You are key people, and frankly all of us have some adjustments to make and not much time to do it in. For example, those of us who have just accepted Freeholdian citizenship must readjust to civilian authority." His eyes swept over his subordinates as he remembered the scene an hour earlier. *Zulu*'s huge launching bay had been pressurized and packed with troops, as were those of the other two transports. Kasten's melodious voice had tied them together via com beam as he led them in the oath of allegiance—and then the cheers, as he said, "It is my honor to invest each of you with the privileges and responsibilities of citizenship."

Stell forced his thoughts back to the present. "And," he continued kindly, "there are the members of Freehold's valiant Defense Forces who have fought bravely for their, strike that, *our* planet, and now find themselves part of a larger force with different traditions and methods." The members of the Defense Force beamed at this praise, but a few still looked concerned. Stell knew what they were thinking. "I assure each and every one of you that we have no intention of absorbing your units or usurping your place. More on that later . . . but for the moment, please remember that we are now citizens like you, and will obey orders just as you do."

Then Stell smiled in Kasten's direction. "And last, but certainly not least, are those of you elected to represent the people. Suddenly you have a much larger army than before, and a good one, if I do say so myself. To you, and to those you represent, we have pledged our loyalty, and given our promise to do everything we can to earn our place among you. And now I believe President Kasten would like to say a few words. Mr. President?"

Kasten stood, his personal presence quickly dominating the room, his eyes moving to make contact with each person present. His words were serious and deliberate. "Everything we've worked for is in peril. The forces that would destroy us are gathering, and we must meet them with courage, determination, and above all else, a unified effort. To that end, the Senate has recognized Colonel Stell's present rank, and promoted him to General." There was light applause, in spite of Roop's smirk and raised eyebrow. Ignoring Roop, Kasten continued, "Colonel Ivan Krowsnowski of our Defense Forces will serve as General Stell's Executive Officer." There was more applause, and a stocky, middle-aged officer with bright, determined eyes rose and half-bowed to those present. Stell liked him, and knew he was damn lucky to get him. Of course, politics had dictated the selection—fortunately Krows-

nowski was a professional soldier and well qualified for the
position. By making him executive officer, Stell was sending
a message to both the brigade and the Defense Forces: there
must be no friction between them. He couldn't allow rivalries
or competition. Soon they would be fighting side by side and
each must trust the other.

"In a moment, General Stell will tell you more about our
plans to defend Freehold," Kasten continued. "But before he
does, I want to say one thing more—let's make damn sure we
win!" He took his seat to the sound of cheers, whistles and
yells of approval.

Stell stood and grinned as the applause died down. "Let's
start with an appraisal of our strategic situation. Both computer and common-sense analyses point up the same problems. Our first and overriding concern is our lack of tactical
air support. As you know, all the raids so far have been quick
hit-and-run affairs against isolated settlements. The local Defense Forces have been overwhelmed by superior numbers
and firepower, and the pirates have lifted before reinforcements could arrive." There was a growl of agreement from
the Defense Force personnel. One crusty old noncom said,
"Damn right . . . we never had a chance."

Stell nodded his agreement. "And on top of that," he
continued, "each time they come and go, the pirates knock
bigger holes in our satellite network, making it that much
harder to detect the next raid when it comes. If they decide to
send a full-scale invasion force, we might not hear about it
until they walk into our living rooms." There was an appre-
ciative chuckle all around.

"So what's the answer, General?" Roop asked, placing an
insulting emphasis on the word "General."

Stell smiled patiently. "I'm glad you asked, Senator . . .
because I know you'll love the answer. What we need is a
full wing of fighter-interceptors that are capable of space *and*
atmospheric combat."

"Why not just wish for the Imperial Marines, while you're
at it," Roop suggested sarcastically. "Or do you intend to
lure them here with an offer of citizenship?" Even Stell's
officers laughed at that.

As the laughter died away, Stell smiled and said, "If I

thought it would work, I would. Unfortunately it's going to take hard, cold cash. Or at least the prospect of it.''

"Brilliant," Roop responded caustically. "Aren't you forgetting that we're broke?''

"No, Senator, I'm not," Stell answered leaning back in his chair. "But like Bull Strom, an old friend of mine, used to say, sometimes you've got to spend money to make money.'' The brigade personnel all smiled, remembering Strom and his many sayings. "Now, in order for us to make money—enough money to make this year's payment and avoid default—we've got to move fast. We've got, what—two months left until the deadline?'' A murmur of assent ran around the table. "So let's be realistic,'' Stell continued. "We've got one thing, and one thing only that could generate the kind of money we need in that time, and that's thermium. So, simply put, I suggest a crash program to produce enough raw thermium to make the payment. I know you would prefer to manufacture the final products yourselves, and I can see the long-term wisdom in doing so, but we've only got two months. Meanwhile, we try to recruit the wing we need on credit. It won't be easy . . . but hopefully our ability to refine and market thermium will convince them we're a good credit risk. If it works, we'll have a wing here to fly air cover while we refine the stuff, and to defend our transports when we take it to Fabrica.'' Fabrica was a heavily industrialized Imperial planet lying just inside the empire. It was an open secret in government circles that representatives from Fabrica had indicated they would take all the thermium Freehold was willing to sell.

A buzz of conversation started to circle the table and Stell held up a hand to silence it. "If someone's got a better idea, now's the time to get it on the table.''

A few heads turned toward Roop, but the Senator only smiled and said, "Who am I to stand in the way of democracy? If you want to put everything we've got into one basket defended by an imaginary wing of interceptors, who am I to object?''

"Who indeed," Senator Bram growled. "Roop's just playin' with himself as usual, so let's get on with it.''

Kasten cleared his throat and said, "General Stell's right. Thermium is our hole card, so let's play it.''

Most of the others nodded in agreement with the exception of Roop, his staff, and a few of the Defense Force officers. But the officers at least changed their minds when Colonel Krowsnowski asked for, and received, permission to speak. His bright-blue eyes swept the room like a laser. "As many of you know, I'm not much for talking. So I'm gonna keep it short and sweet. The General's right. If we don't make the payment, we're dead. To do it, we need air cover. And, personally, I'd sell my left nut to get it."

He sat down to cries of "Hear! Hear!" and "I'd like to help but I can't spare any." To which a female officer replied, "Hell, you can't give away something you don't have, John!"

As the good-natured commotion died down, Stell said, "Good, that's settled then. Now let's discuss deployment of the forces we already have. Colonel Krowsnowski and I have spent some time on the brigade's computer, and believe that a mix of brigade and defense force personnel will serve us best." And help to homogenize the troops, he thought to himself. "I said earlier that we wouldn't try to absorb the Defense Forces into the brigade. And we won't. So it's with considerable pleasure that I announce formation of a battalion called the Free Scouts. Colonel Krowsnowski will command—in addition to serving as my executive officer." There was loud applause from the Defense Force officers.

"Now," Stell said, touching a button in the arm of his chair, "here's what we'll do on the ground." The room darkened and a holo tank occupying an entire bulkhead swirled to life. It was linked with the brigade's computer and displayed surface maps, personnel rosters, unit names and much more. The ensuing discussion lasted well through lunch, and then dinner, finally ending amid a pile of used meal paks, crumpled print-outs, and full ashtrays. All things considered, Stell was pleased with their efforts. Units of the brigade had been assigned to bolster the defenses of each settlement, especially those where the crash program to refine thermium would be centered. Each brigade unit would be accompanied by a contingent of Free Scouts. The Scouts would provide initial liaison with the civilian population, counsel brigade personnel on local customs, and teach classes on planetary ecology and geology. All of which would help if a massive attack ever came. But almost as important were the secondary effects of the plan. Through working and fighting together, troopers and scouts would come to know and trust each other. Friendships would be formed. Love affairs would blossom and follow their natural courses. Babies would be born, and eventually the Free Scouts would merge into the brigade, and the brigade would fade into the civilian population. And when that happened . . . the brigade as such would cease to exist. But it wouldn't die. It would evolve, to live on as part of a culture it had saved, and for once it would all mean something. Stell remembered lowering Bull Strom's coffin into the ground. It won't be like the old days, Bull, Stell thought, but things change, and like you used to say, "If you don't bend, you'll break." Well, we're bending, Bull, we're bending.

As the meeting broke up, Stell ran into Austin Roop near the hatch. "A very interesting briefing, General," the Senator said. "Very well thought out. No hard feelings, I hope?" Stell shook the outstretched hand and plastered an obligatory smile on his face.

"Of course not, Senator. The loyal opposition is a good test of any plan."

"We agree then, General. Good luck!" And with that, Roop disappeared into the swirl of bodies heading for the launching bay where the shuttles waited.

The next two days passed in a blur of activity. First there were meetings with Captains Boyko, Nishita, and Kost on the dispersal of the transports. If the pirates sent a full-scale invasion force, the lumbering old transports wouldn't last ten minutes, and they'd be needed later. It was decided that once the ground forces had been landed and supplied, the ships would take up positions a long way out from Freehold, where they could serve as early warning stations. That way, they'd help compensate for the damage to the satellite network. If attacked themselves, the transports could take a random hyperspace jump. There was some danger of coming out of hyperspace in the middle of an asteroid, or right on the surface of a sun, but the odds were on their side—especially when compared with certain destruction by the pirates.

There were also logistics meetings, communications meet-

ings, strategy meetings, and meetings on how to eliminate
meetings. But finally it was over. Krowsnowski had his final
orders, and with a sigh of relief, Stell climbed into a small
scout borrowed from Captain Boyko and slipped off into
space. Samantha was at the controls, her work as an intelligence agent having long ago required her to qualify as a pilot,
and Sergeant Major Como occupied the third seat of the
four-person craft. Like most of its kind, the scout was designed for speed, not comfort. Her huge drives left little room
for the crew. Only that, and Stell's vehement protests, had
prevented Krowsnowski from sending half the brigade along.
Krowsnowski didn't seem to understand that recruiting an
air-space wing was something you did quietly, not with a
small army. Of course, both the Colonel and President Kasten
had opposed his going at all, saying he was needed to organize the defense of Freehold—and what if there was an attack
while he was gone? Which was a major part of why he'd
decided to go. If Krowsnowski was to be effective, he had to
gain self-confidence and earn the respect of the brigade—
something he'd have a hard time doing with Stell looking
over his shoulder every second. And besides, convincing a
wing to enlist in their cause wasn't going to be easy. Based
on the reputation of the brigade, Stell would have a better
chance than anyone else. At least, that's what he told himself.
Deep down, he wondered if he just wanted a break from all
the logistics, meetings, and boring detail. It would feel good
to be doing something for a change.

Having set their course in the ship's computer, Sam made
her way back to the tiny lounge and dropped into the seat next
to Como. She lit a dopestick and said, "Endo, here we
come."

"Endo?" Stell frowned. "Seems to me I've heard the
name, but that's about it." Weeks before, he'd ordered her to
find out which wings were available and where they were
based. He'd been so busy, and so eager to get away from all
those meetings, that he hadn't asked her where they were
headed.

"It's not exactly a major tourist spot," Sam agreed. "In
fact I believe Endo was originally called 'Endo The Line.' It
was discovered by the empire but ceded to the Zords as

partial settlement of some minor territorial dispute. It's not far from their home world. Anyway, they haven't done much with it so it's mostly undeveloped rain forest. The planet's got potential, if they ever get off their tentacles and get to work." The Zords were bidpedal and had four tentacles, two to a side, instead of arms. Smaller tentacles surrounded their oral cavities and were used to communicate via a very complex sign language, as well as for eating. They were not an aggressive race, apparently satisfied with a small, two-system empire, and specialized in banking rather than industrial concerns. However, their reputation as loan sharks, plus their insistence on institutionalized slavery, had acted to limit their overall success.

"Okay," Stell said. "Endo it is. And I take it there's a wing based there."

"Yup," Samantha answered, blowing twin streams of scented smoke from her nostrils. "And a good one at that. Falco's Falcons."

Stell frowned thoughtfully. "Never heard of them."

"This wouldn't be Commander Jack Falco, would it?" Como growled, snapping together the receiver and barrel of the grenade launcher he was cleaning with a loud click.

"The same," Sam replied, blowing a stream of smoke toward the overhead. "Although the Navy takes a dim view of cashiered officers using their former rank. I understand his people just call him Jack."

"That's right," Como said, thinking out loud. "He's the one who got court-martialed for chasing some pirates all the way back to the Rock. Broke every standing order in the book."

"Then, do we want him?" Stell asked. "Casual is one thing . . . undisciplined is something else."

"True," Sam agreed soberly, "but you've got to understand the circumstances. Falco was out on a training patrol with a flight of greenies right out of the Academy. By chance, they stumble on a liner—the *Jupiter*, if I remember correctly—and she's just been hit by pirates. I mean there they are, right in his sights, hightailing it for home. And as usual they've got a bunch of passengers who'll end up as slaves somewhere.

Well, I guess he just couldn't stand it. He threw the general orders away and led his students after them.''

Stell could easily imagine the scene. The liner drifting, looted and empty, her drives disabled by the crew as the pirates boarded, a brief and hopeless battle at the main lock, then men, women, and children herded aboard the waiting pirate ships for a journey into slavery. To know about such horror was one thing, but to witness it, and do nothing because the empire wanted to preserve the pirates as a buffer against the Il Ronn, that was something else. "And?" Stell asked.

Como and Sam grinned in unison. "He caught 'em," Como said. "First they freed the *Jupiter's* passengers and crew by cutting off the transports. Falco sent them back with two fighters apiece for escort. Then they went after the rest and burned 'em one at a time. I heard only two or three out of a dozen made it back to the Rock.''

Sam nodded her agreement, and said, "His court-martial followed. Fortunately for Falco, some of the liner's wealthier passengers felt he got a raw deal, chipped in together, and gave him a very nice reward. He used it to form Falco's Falcons. End of story.''

"Okay, I'm sold," Stell said thoughtfully. "He sounds like our kind of folk. He also sounds like he's good, and I've got a feeling we're gonna need him.''

CHAPTER NINE

Com Tech Chu swore softly to herself as the dots appeared on her screen. Pirates. Two . . . three . . . five . . . six altogether. Just like the people on the *Zulu* said there'd be. Like everyone else on Freehold, she'd been waiting helplessly for the last twenty minutes. Now, at least the waiting was over. But one of them was huge. A real monster. Great Sol, were they really going to land a ship that big? It was the size of a light cruiser. Quickly, her fingers danced over the keyboard. Com-beams obediently leaped out from the No-Hole tracking station to key locations all over the world. One was Colonel Krowsnowski's command center, deep underground, near Freehold's north pole.

Seconds later, Krowsnowski's crisp, concise orders were crackling out to units all over the planet. Within minutes, all locations had acknowledged his orders and were standing by. Without air cover, that's all they could do. Thanks to the warning from Captain Boyko, Krowsnowski had enough time to scramble three wings of fighters. Except he didn't have the fighters to scramble. So there they sat, with no air cover and most of the brigade still digging in. Well, he reflected, searching for a bright side, six ships can't take the planet. True, he answered himself, but they can take any single target, plus raise an awful lot of hell. And what about that big sucker? What would they do with that? All he could do was wait to find out. As he watched the little dots move across the plotting projection, he wondered what Stell would do in the same situation.

Deep below Freehold's surface, Quarter Sept Commander Feeg's tail twitched back and forth in frustration. The monitor in front of him displayed the pirate ships as blue arrows, five small and one large. What were the pirate scum up to? Surely they didn't plan to land a major war ship. Even they weren't that stupid. Or were they? A ship that size is very vulnerable on the ground. Damn them! Their continued attacks only served to mobilize the settlers even more. And that could interfere with his plan. Turning to an aide, he issued terse orders. Moments later a powerful micro-burst of code punched its way up through the atmosphere and out into space.

A few hundred miles away, on the edge of the settlement known as Two Holes, Sergeant Flynn squinted up into the sun. Suddenly a dot appeared, quickly became a blob, which resolved into a ship, and grew to blot out the sun. "Oh, shit," she said softly to herself. The brass weren't on Yirl drug after all. The ship was so big that it must be at the upper limit of what could land and still blast off again.

Standing next to her, Corporal Stickley shook his head in amazement and yelled over the roar of the descending ship. "What now, Sarge?" He grinned broadly, knowing what she'd say.

"Why, we're gonna do what we always do, Sticks," Flynn yelled back. "We're gonna kick some ass!" She made an obscene gesture at the ship and then ran toward the half-completed weapons pit. Or lose our asses, she thought. One or the other.

A few hundred feet above, on the bridge of the Brotherhood's light cruiser *Avenger*, Major Peter Malik reclined on an acceleration couch and watched the monitors above him. Ant-like figures were running in every direction. Didn't they know it was useless? He shook back his long yellow hair, savoring the moment, anticipating the pain and death, his breath coming a little faster. He was tall and rangy, almost gawky, but well muscled. Under bushy yellow brows, pale-green eyes gleamed with energy and vitality. The nostrils of his blade-like nose flared with excitement, and between his legs there was a familiar stirring. It was always like this before a battle, and he welcomed it.

As though sensing his mood, Lady Almanda Kance-Jones turned, laying ice-cold fingers on his arm. "Remember, Major, Intersystems wants the extractor and nothing else this trip. After all, that's the point of grounding this barge, isn't it?"

"Don't worry your little head about it," Malik replied condescendingly, completely missing the glint of anger deep in her beautiful eyes. "We'll get the extractor, plus teach my old friend Stell a thing or two about soldiering. By now he's got elements of the brigade sitting in every one of these little hell holes. We're gonna cut them to pieces. God, how I wish I could see his face just now!"

"The Major forgets himself," a low-voice growled over Malik's head set. The voice was that of Brother Mustapha Infam Drago, commander of the ship, and a full-fledged member of the pirate council. "This is my ship, and I'm not putting it down to satisfy the Major's personal vendettas. Now I desire silence while we land."

The ship was hovering over the settlement at a height calculated to cause maximum damage. Everything her drives touched was turned to molten slag. The heat caused beads of sweat to pop out on Flynn's forehead. She winced as the pilot deliberately moved the pillar of fire across the settlement, carving a swath of death and destruction a hundred feet wide. Homes, businesses, public buildings—all disappeared into the roaring inferno. Fingers of blue light leaped up from a dozen half-completed weapons pits to touch the ship with death. At least half were right on target, but the ship's powerful defensive screens simply shrugged them off. Answering beams of coherent energy lanced down to destroy one cannon after another. Next to her, Sticks continued his efforts to raise their commanding officer, a Free Scout named Mullins. "Delta two to delta six, come in delta six. Delta two to delta six, come in delta six."

Finally, a laconic voice answered saying, "Delta two, you can forget delta six. He went hero, and was last seen running toward the ship with a demo pack. I think you are in command, or will be in a few seconds."

Above them, Drago watched the ground coming up in the stern monitor, and cursed in a dozen languages as a solitary figure appeared from the left, racing the huge ship to the point where it would touch down. Then the figure was gone in a blinding flash of light, as the heat from the retros incinerated the man and set off the demolition charge on his back. Drago was temporarily blinded by the flash. The upward rush of exploding gases hit the ship at a slight angle, pushing it sideways just as the pilot put it down.

Malik and Lady Kance-Jones were thrown hard against their restraints as the ship hit, and then held, tipped at a slight angle. Malik released the restraints and quickly headed downship to join the raiding party. Almanda left her acceleration couch more slowly, taking the time to check her makeup in a small hand mirror before carefully stepping down into the command center where Drago was still rubbing his eyes. He was a small, bony man with sallow, waxy skin, beady eyes, and a short temper, but just now he looked like a little boy with something in his eyes. Kance-Jones laughed at the thought and turned her attention to the action outside.

"Damn amateurs," Flynn said wearily as the brilliant flash marked Lieutenant Mullins' death. "Always in such a hurry to get killed. Well, I guess that's what a chain of command is for." As she slid her binoculars across the settlement, she began issuing orders.

Thousands of miles to the north, Krowsnowski bit his lip as he watched the computer projection. Five of the enemy ships had split up to hit widely separated settlements. They were obviously intended as diversions. Yes, it was the big sucker he should worry about. Why Two Holes? He no sooner asked the question than the answer hit him. The bastards were after a thermium extractor.

"Remember . . . get the thermium extractor!" Malik yelled into his throat mic as he climbed into the huge tank.

"Roger, Major," his tank commanders answered one after another. A rectangle of bright sunlight appeared as the huge cargo doors slid open to the loud whine of hydraulics. One after another, the big crawlers rumbled toward the hatch and down the ramp to Freehold's surface. Malik rode in the lead tank and had insisted on manning the top turret himself. As he worked the foot pedals, traversing the turret right and left, he squeezed the twin grips and sent out streams of lead death, tossing the running figures about like so many dolls. Many wore the A-suits of the brigade. Those he lingered over, taking extra seconds to carve already dead bodies into pieces. Below, he felt himself grow even harder. Later, he'd give Almanda "I'm such a big deal," Kance-Jones a real good time.

"Delta two to all delta units. Fall back. I repeat, fall back," Flynn ordered as the last of the crawlers rolled off the ramp and headed for the group of buildings by the river. There was no way her people could stop tanks with assault rifles. She noticed that some of the crawlers had dozer blades and others mounted cranes. The last two were pulling trailers, and she wondered why. "Units three, four and seven," she said calling up the energy cannon still able to fire, "retarget on the armored vehicles and fire when you come to bear." At least the ship's weapons had been forced to cease firing or risk hitting the tanks. Moments later, one, then another, then all three of the energy cannon lashed out at the crawlers, immediately destroying two. While they couldn't beat down the ship's screens, they were more than equal to the tanks. She felt Sticks pulling at her arm. He motioned toward her com-set and she chinned it off. "Yeah, Sticks?"

"Command just called on sealed beam, Sarge—they say to take out the extractor plant, and fast. They say that otherwise the pirates will get it."

Of course! Why was she so stupid? The bastards were going to steal an extractor . . . and it didn't take a genius to figure out why. After all, what good's a planet loaded with thermium if you don't know how to extract it from the rivers that carry it? The pirates were afraid that by the time they managed to take the planet, all the existing extractors would have been damaged or destroyed in the fighting. Swearing a blue streak, she spun back toward the buildings by the river, only to see that it was too late. The surviving tanks were next to the buildings and parts of the extractor were already being loaded onto trailers.

Malik was standing on the bow of the lead tank, screaming orders. Slugs and energy beams flashed around him, but he hardly noticed. Deep down he somehow knew that it wasn't his day to die. The carefully placed shaped charges had opened up the side of the building with surgical precision. Dozer units had quickly moved in to push most of the debris out of the way. A specially trained crew had entered and used laser torches to slice the extractor equipment into easily transportable chunks. Now the last of those chunks was being swung onto the surviving trailer for the short trip back to the ship. Once it was in place and magnetically locked down, he took a minute to look at the flames and destruction, enjoying the moment, knowing Stell would recognize him when the battle tapes were analyzed. The tank lurched into motion under his feet and reluctantly he resumed his place in the top turret.

"Take out the trailer!" Flynn yelled into her com-set. "Aim for the trailer!" There was only one trailer left. If they hit it, at least the bastards wouldn't get what they came for. The cannon crews worked like demons to find the new target and lock onto it. One even managed to score a direct hit before it and its crew winked out of existence. Drago had opened fire with the ship's weapons. He'd held back for fear of hitting his own people, but he couldn't let the settlers destroy that trailer. The ship's guns burped twice more and the last two energy cannon disappeared as their accumulators blew up. In frustration, Flynn pulled her sidearm and aimed it at the ship. She kept on firing even after the magazine was empty.

"Nicely done, Brother Drago," Kance-Jones said, smiling a perfect smile. "Things have gone so well that I'm inclined to indulge Major Malik's desire to visit a few more settlements before we leave."

Drago shrugged. "Why not? They have no air cover and it will save us work later."

"Exactly," Almanda agreed smugly as she sat down and crossed her perfect legs.

Com Tech Chu looked, and then looked again. It couldn't be, but it was. Twelve more dots had suddenly appeared on her screen. And no warning from any of the brigade ships, either. So these ships must have had the planet's exact coordinates and come out of hyperspace right on top of it. Her heart sank as her fingers flew over the keys. This was it. With twelve more ships, they could take the planet. But wait— there was something different about the data flooding her screen. They weren't pirate ships; there was something alien about them. "Great Sol! Those are Il Ronnian ships!"

Though not normally a religious man, Colonel Krowsnowski had been praying. And when more ships appeared, he felt completely forsaken. It took him a moment to realize they were Il Ronnian ships. Little by little, he began to smile, and then laugh, and finally dance, grabbing a surprised Captain and whirling him about the room. "Goddamnit, there is a god!" he shouted. "And he's on our side!"

Drago frowned as he read the printout. Il Ronnian ships? Here? Now? How could anyone have luck that bad? But with the surviving tanks aboard, along with ninety percent of the extraction plant, he wasted no more time pondering his fate. Instead, he ordered his pilot to take off on full emergency power. Due to the ship's slight list, it took skill, but the pilot did it, and moments later they were racing skyward.

Feeg watched his monitors with anticipation as the ships of the Il Ronnian Star Sept swooped down on the pirate scum. Two were quickly vaporized. The others proved more difficult, however, fighting on even when outnumbered two or three to one. "The cruiser, my noble brethren," Feeg whispered aloud. "You must take the cruiser." And, sure enough, three Il Ronnian ships locked onto the cruiser and threw everything they had at her. But it wasn't enough. One by one, the larger ship's superior weaponry took its toll until all three Il Ronnian arrows had disappeared from Feeg's screens. His tail swished back and forth in frustration. Seconds later the cruiser, along with a single surviving escort, was gone, outside the atmosphere and then into hyperspace. In keeping with their orders, the Il Ronnian craft were soon gone as well. It wasn't ideal . . . but still better than an all-out pirate victory. But next time he might not be so lucky.

It was time to put his own plan for Freehold into motion. Unlike the excessive and unnecessarily violent efforts of the human pirates, his plan was simple, conservative, and therefore elegant—an enactment of his race's virtues. Feeg allowed himself a grunt of satisfaction as he left the console and headed for his afternoon sand bath. He was not looking forward to dealing with the pathetic Roop creature . . . but it must be done.

As the pirate ship made the shift into hyperspace, Malik felt the characteristic queasiness in his gut. As soon as it passed, he rolled over and took her, using his hardness like a spear, stabbing and thrusting his way toward the moment of release he'd waited for all day. Beneath him, Lady Kance-Jones smiled, taking him, channeling his violence, absorbing and, ultimately, controlling it. When the explosion was over, she ran a single cold finger down his spine, and as he shivered, Malik wondered why he hadn't enjoyed it more.

Flynn stood in the smoking ruins of Two Holes, looking up into the sky. "You're gonna pay for that, you bastards," she said softly. Then, hearing a faint noise to her left, she called Sticks, and together they ripped and tore at the wreckage until the muffled cries became the full-fledged screaming of a three-year-old girl. Picking her up and shielding her from the sight of her dead mother, Flynn said, "There, there. Don't cry honey. Everything's gonna be all right. Come on . . . let's go put everything back together. Next time we'll make the bastards pay."

CHAPTER TEN

Samantha lowered the ship carefully through Endo's eternal downpour, the soft glow of the instrument panel gently lighting her face, her long, slender fingers playing over the controls. Its drives causing enormous clouds of steam, she put the ship down with a gentle bump. Moments later, Sam and the two men were huddled in the main lock, looking out across puddled duracrete toward the gleam of distant light that marked the spaceport dome. It was night, and for a moment the rain fell in sheets, driven by a sudden gust of wind that soon scuttled off toward the dome as though inviting them to follow. "What a slime ball," Sam said disgustedly. "It's worse every time I come here."

"It does leave something to be desired, weather-wise," Stell agreed. "Where's the ground shuttle?"

"You're standing on 'em," Samantha grinned.

"Well, there's no point in hanging around here," Stell said. "Last one to the dome, buys!" With that he was gone, sprinting across the duracrete at full speed. Como was right behind him with Sam bringing up the rear.

"You cheated!" Sam said, panting heavily as they entered the run-down dome.

"Of course," Stell answered cheerfully. "Otherwise you might have won. Besides, you'd be able to run faster if you gave up those dopesticks."

"I think I'll just give up racing with cheats, instead," she said loftily, lighting a dopestick as she headed for the counter.

A tired looking Zord lounged behind it, his brown, leathery skin hanging in folds, his single eye regarding them with the cynicism of someone who's seen it all. One of the tentacles surrounding his oral cavity took a toothpick and shifted it to the other side of his mouth. There was an elderly Zord despondently pushing a broom on the other side of the room, but apart from him, the clerk was the only one there. Stell could see why—there certainly wasn't any reason to linger in the shabby lobby.

Since Zords have no vocal apparatus, Sam used universal sign language rather than speech. Fingers and hands moved in jerky patterns, to which tentacles responded with a writhing flow of motion. It was so fast that Sam could barely read it. She signed her thanks and placed something on the counter, which was quickly whisked out of sight by a brown tentacle. Samantha led them outside and into a large, six-wheeled, all-terrain vehicle. It, too, had seen better days. She signed their destination to the driver, whose single eye blinked once in reply as all four tentacles flicked out to take the vehicle's controls. Moments later they were lurching down a deeply rutted, muddy road.

"It's just like I figured," Sam said. "The spaceport clerk didn't know where Falco's people are, but suggested we look in Human Town. It's the obvious place."

As the name suggested, Human Town was mostly occupied by humans, though not exclusively so. While not out and out discriminatory, the Zords didn't welcome humans into their society, though they favored them as slaves. So those humans unfortunate enough to find themselves on Endo naturally gravitated to Human Town, where they could find others of their race. Since humans were one of the smallest minorities on Endo, their area was in the most undesirable and run-down corner of the small Zordian city. To Stell's eye, the city appeared to be nothing more than a random series of earthen mounds sticking out of a sea of mud. A few mounds sported dimly lit signs, announcing their purpose to those familiar with Zordian script, but most were dark and anonymous. As the driver wound between lumpy structures, only dimly seen in the eerie glow of intermittent street lights, Stell was quickly lost—until they arrived in front of a dingy little place made of mud bricks, which cheerfully proclaimed itself to be Joe's Bar and Grill in nice, clear, standard script. They had arrived in Human Town.

Joe's didn't pan out, and they tried two more dives before arriving in front of the The Starman's Rest. It was an ugly little place, carved from a soggy hillside, and then covered with a sod roof. They had to wade through a large area of churned-up mud and animal droppings to reach the front door. Stell noticed that animals and vehicles seemed to play about equal parts in Endo's transportation system. As they entered, the low murmur of conversation stopped as all heads swiveled their way. More than a hundred tired, bored, hungry eyes inventoried, calculated and judged before returning to their own affairs. Stell wasn't impressed. The clientele were as run-down as the place itself. The wooden floors hadn't been swept in years, the tables were littered with empty tankards, half-eaten meals, and full ashtrays. The air stank of smoke, unwashed bodies, and urine. The latrine was a shallow ditch running the length of the establishment's rear wall.

They picked a table that allowed them to sit with their backs to a damp dirt wall, and looked around. "I'm not sure I'd want to hire anyone who'd come here for lunch," Stell said to no one in particular.

Samantha was about to reply when she was distracted by a loud, screeching noise. The noise was coming from the other side of the room and seemed to be headed their way. Its source turned out to be a large Finthian male. He wore a stained apron over his multicolored plummage, and was plowing through the crowd as if it wasn't even there. Como's right hand strayed to the grip of a slug gun when the noisy alien reached their table. His screeching turned to a series of squawks, and his saucer-like eyes bulged with emotion as he grabbed Sam, lifting and swinging her around his head. Como started to rise, a growl deep in his throat, but Stell grabbed his arm. "Hold it, Zack—I think they're acquainted."

Sure enough, when the bird-like alien had finished swinging Samantha about, he put her down unharmed. She reached up, and did something to the box he wore around his neck, and his squawks turned into standard. "Molly! It's good to see you! She was the best bar maid I ever had, back on

Weller's World," he said in an aside to Stell and Como, one claw-like digit touching his beak. "Always spent too much time talking to customers . . . but you can't have everything. So how 'bout it Molly, you lookin' for a job?"

Sam laughed. "Work for you again? The meanest, ugliest, most credit-pinching old bird in six systems? You gotta be kidding." Her laughter merged with the alien's squawks of merriment, as Stell looked at Como and shook his head in amazement. Maybe someday he'd get used to Sam's multitudinous personalities and bizarre friends, but he doubted it.

At Sam's urging, the Finthian pulled up a chair and joined them. He was, it turned out, the proud proprietor of The Starman's Rest. His true name was "The one who flies like an arrow," but finding this somewhat unwieldy for business use, he went by the unlikely nickname of "Pops."

"Pops, my friends and I are looking for a guy named Jack Falco," Sam said. "I thought he might be hanging out here. We'd like to do a little business with him. Any idea where he might be?"

Pops looked around secretively and turned back, his voice a conspiratorial whisper. "It's not that I don't trust you, Molly my friend, but many seek the Commander, and not all wish him well. Perhaps if I knew more. . . ."

"Of course, Pops," Samantha replied understandingly. "Maybe this would help." She slipped something into the Finthian's claw-like hand. Whatever it was quickly disappeared into the inner recesses of his filthy apron. "I promise you that we mean Commander Falco no harm," Sam added reassuringly. One large saucer-like eye winked knowingly as the alien stood, switched off his translator, and plowed back toward the bar, squawking greetings to his regular customers and orders to his largely Finthian staff.

"Somebody will take us to Falco in a few minutes," Sam predicted. "Pops is quite a character, isn't he?"

"He's nothing compared to some of my officers," Stell replied with a raised eyebrow. "I have a feeling you've been keeping bad company again." She made a rude noise in reply. Just then, a grubby little street urchin of indeterminable sex emerged from under a nearby table and tugged at Stell's A-suit.

"You come me," it squeaked, and promptly dived under another table, scurrying away through an obstacle course of chairs, legs, tails, and an occasional unconscious customer. Stell stood, the others doing likewise, and followed the child's progress by the grunts, squawks and squeals of annoyed customers. As far as Stell could tell, none of their kicks actually connected with the source of their discomfort. Emerging on the far side of the room, the little bundle of rags disappeared through an open door to the right of the bar. As they approached it, Como gave Stell a questioning look, which was answered with a nod.

Samantha went through the door first, with Stell right behind. They found themselves in a long corridor. Its walls were made of raw earth and everywhere water trickled down to run into the ditch dug in the floor for that purpose. The child reached the end of the hall and waved a grubby hand in their direction before disappearing down a side tunnel. For the next five minutes, they followed the grubby little urchin—who always seemed to dodge around another corner just before they could catch up. Stell was soon lost, which was, no doubt, the whole idea. He had an unsettling feeling that they were going in circles. Finally, their little guide scuttled through an open door and they followed right behind. It was pitch black inside and Stell couldn't see a thing. Then, strong hands grabbed him from behind, pinning his arms to his sides as a terse voice said, "Don't move."

"Good advice, friend," Como said softly. "I suggest you follow it—unless you'd like me to decorate the far wall with your brains." Stell's arms were released, and he heard a squishing noise as someone took a step back. Then the lights came on, accompanied by the hiss of pneumatics as a metal door slid closed. Not everything was as primitive as it looked, Stell noted, and so much for their way out. Now he found himself part of a frozen tableau. In front of him, Samantha was motionless in the grip of a burly man who was surprised to find himself looking down the barrel of her sleeve gun. Behind him, Como stood with one of his handguns pressed to a man's head, the other covering the room. Unlike the tavern proper, this room was clean and reasonably neat. It was evidently part of Pop's private quarters. Facing Stell were four men and a woman, all sitting in a variety of mismatched chairs and holding efficient looking blasters, all of which were aimed at him. He noticed that they wore shoulder patches depicting a falcon's head on their silver flight suits. And they didn't look the least bit scared.

"This will never do," one of them said with a grin. He had wavy black hair, even features, calm brown eyes, and a neatly trimmed mustache. "If we all shoot each other, Pops will make a fortune selling our clothes and weapons and we'll die broke." With that, he slid his blaster into a thigh holster and the others followed suit.

"It's okay, Zack," Stell said, and the Sergeant Major holstered both his handguns.

Samantha smiled sweetly. "Thanks, honey . . . but you're just not my type." The burly man flushed and released her. As he did, the wrist gun disappeared up her sleeve. Gesturing broadly, she said, "Commander Falco . . . meet General Stell."

The man with the wavy black hair chuckled and met Stell halfway across the room. "It's a pleasure, General . . . I'm Jack Falco. Sorry about the reception, but well, we've had some unwelcome visitors of late." Falco introduced the others, all pilots in his wing, and Stell reciprocated by introducing Sam and Como. With the introductions out of the way, Falco pulled up three more chairs, motioned toward them, and said, "Now, General . . . what brings you to this mudball?"

Stell accepted a chair, and then proceeded to lay it out from start to finish. The pirate attacks, the possible connection to Intersystems, the brigade's decision to settle on Freehold, the tactical situation—he held back nothing. "And that's about it, Jack," he concluded. "We're in pretty good shape on the ground, but wide open in the atmosphere and above. And I hope that's where you come in."

Falco nodded soberly. "I'd like to. Normally, we'd agree on money, load up the wing, and your troubles would be over. But not right now, I'm afraid."

Stell raised an eyebrow quizzically. "Problems?"

Falco forced a grin. "You could say that. Actually, I

suppose it's kind of funny in a way. You see, the wing has been repossessed.''

"Repossessed?" Stell asked. "You mean, like taken-over by creditors?"

"Just one creditor, in this case," the female pilot answered. She was probably attractive, but the dressing that covered one side of her face made it hard to tell. "A slimy Zord named Ithnar Goteb, to be exact. This," she indicated the bandage, "was courtesy of his thugs."

"Carla was duty officer when they took over the wing," Falco explained. Along with the others on duty, she put up a fight. They left her for dead."

"We killed five of the rotten bastards, though," Carla added with evident satisfaction.

"In any case, General, we'd like to help, and we sure could use the money, but until we raise half a million credits, he's got our interceptors—plus, he's holding about a third of our people hostage. So I'm afraid it's no-go."

"Unless the General could front us some cash?" Carla asked hopefully.

Falco frowned and started to say something to her, when Stell's laughter stopped him. "I'm not laughing at you," Stell said holding up a hand, "it's just that we were hoping you'd accept *delayed* payment!"

The whole room broke into laughter at that, and when he could talk again, Falco said, "We're obviously a team . . . let's drink on it!"

There were murmurs of agreement all around, and the street urchin materialized to take their orders, then scurried for the door with a squeaked, "Me go now."

Once Pops had come and gone, leaving a round of drinks behind, the two groups toasted each other and traded war stories for a while. Then Stell asked, "All right, Jack, just as a point of professional interest, how did this guy—Goteb? —how did he manage to repossess a whole wing? And why would he? How does he expect you to make the money to pay him if he sits on your fighters?"

Falco looked embarrassed. "It is, as they say, a long story. Business hadn't been too good for a while, and we needed money to overhaul and upgrade our interceptors. They take a lot of maintenance, you know. Anyway, we decided to borrow it from Goteb. It seemed like a reasonable thing to do, because we finally had a client signed, sealed and delivered. As soon as we showed up in his system, the client would pay, we would pay Goteb, and everything would come out just fine. So we used the contract as collateral and borrowed the money from Goteb. We did the work on the inteceptors at a small airstrip near here because it's easier to do dirtside than in orbit. When we were done, we flew 'em to the *Nest*. She's our carrier. Then, per our contract, we took off for New Hope. That's where the war was supposed to be. But as we came out of hyperspace and approached New Hope, we were intercepted by a speedster with our client aboard. He says the deal's off. Seems peace is breaking out all over. 'Keep the downpayment,' he says, and 'good luck.' ''

"To which Jack says, 'That wasn't the deal,' " Carla said, picking up the story. "The deal was full payment on arrival, war or no war. 'True,' the client says, 'but you haven't arrived yet.' 'Oh yes we have,' Jack says. 'Take a look at your screens,' our client says, 'maybe you'll change your minds.' Well, we look at the screens, and guess what, there's two cruisers sittin' a few lights out, just waitin' for our client to say the word. They were close enough to cook us good before we launched a single interceptor, and *Nest* ain't up to dukin' it out with no cruiser, much less two of them." Here she paused dramatically, and then said, "Needless to say, we changed our minds!" Carla and her fellow pilots laughed uproariously, as though it was the funniest joke they'd ever heard.

When the pilots had calmed down a bit, Sam asked, "So when you got back here you didn't have enough money to pay off the loan?"

Falco smiled. "That's about the size of it. We gave Goteb what we had, promising to pay the rest as soon as we could, and he agreed. So we brought the wing down to do maintenance and practice atmospheric combat, and that's when the bastard nailed us. He hired some humans to ambush one of our supply vehicles coming out from town. They killed the driver and his assistant, loaded a big force-field projector in the back, and tried to talk their way past the guard station.

But Carla spotted them right away, so they clubbed her, shot the sentries, broke through the gate, and turned on the projector. We tried to help . . . but there's no way to break through that force field. That projector must be a monster, because it throws a field big enough to cover all our fighters. Short of bringing in some energy cannon, nothing's going to break it down. Meanwhile, Goteb says we either give him the money or he'll sell the interceptors *and* our pilots. About a third of our people were sacked out in there when it happened. And slavery's legal here, you know. Anyway, I think he'd prefer to sell our fighters and crew. He thinks he'll make more that way, and he's probably right. Meanwhile, we sit here waiting for the axe to fall.'' He shrugged eloquently. "It's as simple as that."

"So this is everyone who wasn't taken prisoner?" Stell asked, gesturing toward the pilots.

Falco shook his head. "No . . . there's some more. We take turns standing guard duty around the field. If they let that field down for even a second, we'll be on 'em like a Tobarian Zerk Monkey jumping on a fava fruit."

"What about the local authorities," Stell asked. "Doesn't all this violate a law or two?"

"Evidently not," Falco replied. "But to be honest, we haven't pressed the point. It seems that Goteb's brother is the Governor, or the Mayor, or whatever. In any case, I doubt he's exactly impartial."

"Just out of curiosity," Stell said, taking a sip of his drink, "what's the power source for that portable field generator, anyway?"

"The fusion plant in town," Falco replied, "but I know what you're thinking and it won't work. We thought of it, too. Blow the plant and shut down the field, right? Only trouble is, we had our own fusion generator at the airstrip . . . and he's got that for back-up. It's all hooked up and ready to go. Carla learned that much by bribing one of Goteb's tame humans."

Stell nodded thoughtfully, and turned to Sergeant Major Como. Well, Zack, what do you think? It kind of reminds me of that supply dump on Envo."

Como thought for a moment and then smiled. "Damn right, sir . . . I think it'll work."

Falco looked back and forth between them, trying to follow the conversation. "What might work?"

"Well," Stell explained, "a couple of years back we accidentally learned something about portable field generators. We had one set up around a supply dump on Envo IV, mostly to keep the wildlife out. Then, for some reason the fusion generator began to run wild. While the techs went crazy trying to dampen it down, the added power hit the force-field generator like a ton of bricks. For a second there we thought it would blow and us with it, but it didn't; instead, the perimeter of the force field leaped out another hundred twenty feet beyond max. Later, we found out there's a built-in safety factor over what's supposed to be max, for just that kind of situation. Of course, if you continue to feed it too much juice, for too long, then it'll blow."

"So?" Falco asked.

"So," Stell answered, "the force field didn't *slide* out a hundred and twenty feet, it *leaped*. By chance, it enclosed a couple of grazing Envo Beasts. Ever heard of them? No? Well, they weigh about three tons apiece, have the worst tempers this side of a Rath snake, and when they bumped into the field it must have zapped them with a static discharge, because they went berserk. Ten minutes later, our supply dump looked like a garbage dump."

Falco frowned for a second, as though trying to understand the significance of the story, and then gave a loud whoop of joy. "Of course! We position our people just outside the edge of the force field, goose the fusion reactor in town, the field expands and we're inside! General, you're a genius. If it works, you've got yourself a wing."

"And that's the general idea," Stell thought to himself as he smiled, and raised his tankard with the rest.

"A toast, everyone," Falco proclaimed solemnly. "To the perfect plan!"

CHAPTER ELEVEN

One rotation later, crouched in the blackness just outside of Goteb's force field, with Endo's eternal rain dribbling down his neck, Stell wasn't so sure about the perfection of his plan. What if this field generator worked differently? What if it didn't leap over them, but went through them instead? Or blew up? A thousand possibilities passed through his mind, each worse than the one before. Bull Strom had always said that he worried too much. "Listen, son, more than half of winning wars is just pure luck. So make decisions as best you can and then forget 'em. Chances are it's the luck of the draw anyway, so instead of worrying, you could be doing something worthwhile, like drinking or chasing women."

Stell smiled in the darkness. What was he doing out here when he could be chasing women? Trying to stay alive is real high on the list, he thought wryly. He sampled the night air, searching for the whiff of smoke from dopestick, the tang of fresh lubricant, the click of equipment, the scrape of a boot on gravel—all little things—but things that could save your life. However, the only smell was the damp night air, and the only sound was the monotonous hum of the force field. When it disappeared, he'd know Como and Samantha had taken the town's fusion plant. He hoped Sam wouldn't do anything stupid. Although she drove him crazy, he'd always be a little bit in love with her. Which brought Olivia to mind. He'd already faced the fact that he loved her. Her hair, her eyes, the smell of her clean, smooth skin, the little noises she made when they came together—each was a precious memory to be taken out and enjoyed time after time. And suddenly he realized that he finally had something and somebody to fight for, outside of the brigade. Even during his affair with Sam, she'd been part of the brigade, an extension of his profession, an echo of himself. He smiled. For the first time in years, it all seemed worthwhile. Even the huddled misery of the present. Sticking his head up for a quick peek, he saw the shimmer of the field, the glow of buildings beyond, and the shadowy movements of Goteb's guards. Looking right and left, he could barely see the indistinct shapes of Falco and his pilots, as they, too, huddled in the rain. For space jockeys, they were doing very well. He dropped down again, forcing himself to wait patiently. Sam and Como made a good team, and were probably mopping up the fusion plant at that very moment.

"Lightly guarded . . . isn't that what you said?" Sergeant Major Como whispered to Captain Samantha Ann Mosley.

They were crouched in a dark alleyway opposite the power plant, which was lighted up like a pleasure dome on Saturday night. Numerous Zordian guards stood at key points, while others wandered around in seemingly random fashion.

"Well, it was lightly guarded three hours ago," she whispered back defensively. "How was I supposed to know they doubled the guard at night? Besides, more guards makes it more interesting."

"And you are completely out of your mind, lady," Como growled cheerfully.

"Oh yeah?" she whispered. "Well, I'm not the one who's about to lead a bunch of pilots on an infantry assault against a heavily defended power station. You are." Even though she outranked him, it never occurred to Samantha to assume command. This was his area of expertise, not hers.

"That remains to be seen," Como answered softly as he swept a night scope across their objective. "If I can't get better intelligence reports, I may quit."

Sam snorted in reply.

Como paused for a moment, having completed his inspection. "At least they aren't very well trained. That'll help."

"But neither are we," Sam replied mischievously, indicating the pilots hiding on either side of them in the dark.

Ignoring her comment, Como mused out loud, "If we were trying to destroy the place, this would be easy. But somehow we've got to take out the guards without harming the plant."

Samantha looked thoughtful for a moment, and then whispered, "Maybe a diversion would help."

"Sure," Como replied. "A troup of dancing girls would be nice."

"They're Zords, silly. They couldn't care less about dancing girls. No, I have something a little more violent in mind. Tell your troops to watch their night vision and be ready to move fast." She glanced at her wrist-term. "Give me ten minutes."

"Be careful," Como whispered, but he was talking to empty space. She'd already faded into the night.

Como counted off the minutes on his wrist-term, warning the pilots on eight, and pulling down his own visor on nine. At ten, nothing happened. At eleven nothing happened and Como began to worry. On twelve, there was a brilliant flash of light as a personnel carrier parked next to the fusion plant blew up. Como grinned slowly. She was all right. Forcing himself to wait, he watched as guards ran in every direction, some waving tentacles as they signed orders, others fighting the fire, and everyone bumping into each other. Their total silence made it seem eerie, like a strange pantomime of disaster, yet the flames were real enough, crackling and popping loudly. When the confusion was at its worst, he signaled the pilots and the attack began.

At first, the Zords didn't even realize they were being attacked. The figures running toward them through the flickering light didn't look all that different from their comrades fighting the flames. But when one of the pilots let loose with a bloody-curdling yell, they got the message. The Zords couldn't speak, but there was nothing wrong with their hearing. So Como and the pilots opened up with slug throwers and energy weapons. To his left and right, Como saw guards jerk and fall.

Then he was past them, the grenade launcher jumping in his hands as he watched a series of explosions across the courtyard. He swore when the last one hit the power plant itself, causing a section of mud bricks to crumble and fall. If he damaged the plant, there'd be hell to pay. He heard a scream to his right and turned to see one of the pilots dancing inside a cocoon of fire. He'd been flamed. Another pilot finished him off.

As the Zords grew more organized, they put up a stiff fight. Many used their four tentacles to good advantage by firing two weapons at once, doubling their firepower. The pilots, unaccustomed to this kind of warfare, began to falter. Slinging his empty grenade launcher across his back, Como pulled both handguns and yelled, "Come on . . . the last one in there buys the drinks!" With a rolling yell the pilots rushed forward, blasters punching black holes through alien flesh; Zords fell, mouths open in silent screams. Como felt the impact as his A-suit took two hits, and fired both his guns, dropping two Zords—one ahead and one to the left. Then they were inside. A few guards had holed up in there, but they were quickly killed, or knocked out with stun guns and taken prisoner. Como threw a quick defense perimeter around the plant to handle the possibility of a counterattack, and then turned his attention to the control room. As they entered, the first things he saw were two bodies, one sprawled on the floor, another slumped over the control board. Leaning on the board beside the body, a crooked smile touching her lips, a wisp of smoke still curling from the barrel of her wrist gun, was Sam. "Nice of you to drop in," she said with exaggerated nonchalance.

Como shook his head in amusement. "Quit showing off and take command of the perimeter," he growled.

"It's good to see you, too," she replied sweetly as she headed for the door.

Como turned to confront a large control board full of keys, buttons, and flashing lights. It was all a mystery to him, but fortunately one of the pilots, a roly-poly young man with eight combat kills and the face of a choir boy, was a qualified power engineer. He'd been ordered to stay back and out of harm's way until now. He dumped the body onto the floor and slipped into the vacated seat. Cracking his knuckles experimentally, he frowned at the controls for a moment, and then went to work.

His movements were deliberate and precise as he touched one control after another. "Watch this," he said, pointing to a long light tube mounted horizontally at the top of the board. As he spoke, the light in the tube began to move from right to left. Soon it was out of the green portion of the tube and into the yellow. "Okay," the pilot said tersely, "here goes!" With one smooth motion he slid a control all the way to its stop. The light tube suddenly registered in the red and a loud buzzer went off—presumably signaling an emergency overload. The pilot said, "That does it, Sergeant Major. They're either inside the field, or dead. Either way, it's time to dampen this baby down before she blows." Como nodded his permission and wondered how Stell was doing.

To Stell, it seemed like he'd been listening to the soft hum of the force field forever. So when the sound disappeared, it took him a moment to react. By god—they did it! He leaped to his feet and whispered softly, "The screen's down . . . let's go!" To either side, pilots separated themselves from the shadows and quietly rushed forward about fifty feet, before dropping again to cover.

The buildings were closer now; light spilled cheerfully from poorly shuttered windows, the faint sound of Zordian music and human conversation drifted through the night. For some reason, Goteb had placed quite a few human guards at the strip. But they seemed more interested in talking to each other than looking for possible intruders. The force field had evidently given them a false sense of security. Glancing around, Stell saw Falco give him a "thumbs-up" from a few yards away. He returned it and waited for some reaction from the guards. Nothing happened. Maybe they were very lax, or maybe it was a trap. It looked too damn easy. He waited a minute, two minutes.

He was just about to order the pilots forward, when a door opened, the squeal of its unlubricated hinges making his heart leap. Two men and a Zord came out and ambled toward another building. "It's those idiots in town," the first man said. "They could screw up a wet dream."

The Zord signed something, and the other human nodded

in agreement. "Yeah, one of 'em probably goosed the generator by mistake. We'll just call 'em up on the radio and make sure everything's okay."

"I don't know," the first man said doubtfully. "Why isn't the land line working?"

Stell grinned. Because we dug up the cable at the terminator box and cut it, he thought to himself as the trio disappeared into a building. Then he gave a low whistle, which brought the pilots up and running. The wet, moss-like growth underfoot muffled the sound of their steps. One by one, two by two, the inattentive guards were stunned and left to be dealt with later. Then they hit the building where Falco's people were being held prisoner.

But this time they ran into a couple of guards who were wide awake and ready for trouble. They saw the pilots coming and ducked inside a door, slammed it shut and locked it. Stell motioned to Falco, who was armed with a blaster. The pilot quickly slagged the lock and a good chunk of the door surrounding it. Stell kicked it in, and launched himself into a forward roll. As he came up out of the roll, a lance of blue light flashed by, punching a black hole through the wall behind him. Spinning around, he fired twice, slamming a Zordian guard backward into the wall. He slid down it, leaving behind a smear of purplish blood.

Falco had taken out the second guard by the simple expedient of cutting him in half. "Messy, but effective," Stell commented dryly as he looked at the bisected body.

"Results are what count," the other man replied airily.

Meanwhile, Falco's pilots had burned their way through a second door to free their imprisoned comrades. Stell and Falco were suddenly surrounded by happy pilots and ground crew, all slapping them on the back and trying to talk at the same time. Aware that Goteb would soon send reinforcements, Falco moved among the crowd, grabbing people one at a time, giving them orders, and then moving on to the next. A few minutes later, only he and Stell were left; the wing was preparing to lift. Falco walked over and extended his hand. "Thanks, General. We owe you one."

"And I'm about to collect," Stell answered with a smile.

"By the way, you folks aren't bad for a bunch of vacuum jockeys."

Falco laughed. "Thanks again, General, that's quite a compliment coming from a ground pounder." He looked around the room. "Well, so much for this dump . . . let's go." Together, they walked through the blackened doorway and into the night. The rain had stopped momentarily and there was a hole in the cloud cover. Stell smiled as he looked up at the scattering of stars. One of them was home.

CHAPTER TWELVE

With a growing sense of satisfaction, Roop watched the Senators file in. The planning, the hard work, the fear—in a few minutes, it would all pay off. A tremendous feeling of well-being settled over him as he considered the implication.

At the rear of the chambers, Oliver and Olivia Kasten filed in behind some Senators and took their seats. Olivia noticed how tired and worried her father looked, and asked, "Have you heard anything about the reason for this emergency session?"

Her father frowned. "No, I haven't, honey. Austin's playing it real close to the vest. Unfortunately, the Senate rules are a bit vague where emergency sessions are concerned, and that allowed him to call this one without spelling out the reasons why. All he needed was prior agreement by twenty-five percent of the membership, and as you know, he's got that many people in his pocket. So all we can do is wait and see."

"But what could he possibly hope to gain?" Olivia wondered. "Any proposal requires a vote, and you've got the Independents solidly behind you—he can't win."

"I know, honey," her father replied, his brow furrowed with concern, "but with Stell off-planet, it would be just like Austin to try some kind of legislative sleight of hand. I've racked my brain, and stayed up all night with the Senate rules, but I can't figure it out. But I know he's up to something." He shrugged, tried to give her a characteristic smile, but failed.

Olivia's thoughts turned to Mark Stell. She wished he were there. Somehow, she felt certain that Roop wouldn't try anything if he were. But she also had other, more personal reasons. Thinking about him gave her a hollow feeling, as though a part of her was missing, a part she hadn't even known existed until the evening they'd shared at the villa. That night she had discovered a surprising gentleness and sensitivity beneath his obvious strength. Lying in his arms, she had listened as he told her about his life, about the brigade and his fears of what it might become—a twisted thing, forever killing without reason or honor. And he had listened to her, as she told him about the kind of world that Freehold could become. Bit by bit, their dreams had merged, until they began to take shape as a common goal. She felt her eyes drawn to the ceiling and its glorious vision of the future. It *could* be like that, she thought to herself. Together, we could make it happen.

Then Senator Whitmore, a tall, thin man with black hair, called the session to order. "Ladies and gentlemen of the Senate, I now call this emergency session of the Senate to order. Senator Roop has requested this session, and in keeping with our rules has submitted the validated signatures of at least twenty-five percent of our membership, all of whom agree that such a meeting is appropriate. I now yield the floor to Senator Roop."

With that, Senator Whitmore took his seat, while Roop rose and mounted the stage. Behind him, the river pulsed and churned its eternal rhythms, framing him with its strength and power. "Ladies and gentlemen of the Senate, first allow me to apologize for the short notice and any resulting inconvenience caused by this meeting. I assure you, however, that it is necessary. As you all know, we find ourselves in strange times, caught up in unusual events. I submit that such times and events sometimes require equally strange and unusual solutions. Such solutions are not for the weak and shortsighted. They demand fresh, innovative leadership with the courage to act." Here he paused, his eyes focused above the audience, as though seeing something they could not. Then his eyes flicked down to the Senate floor and he continued. "Recently, I saw such a solution, and had the courage to act.'' A rumble of uncertain conversation swept through the chambers. Roop smiled patiently holding up a restraining hand. ''Please allow me to finish. I would like to announce that, due to the extraordinary circumstances we find ourselves in, and the Senate's demonstrated failure to deal adequately with those circumstances, it's now necessary to replace our existing form of government with one that is more capable of dealing with the crisis.''

''This is outrageous!'' Kasten bellowed jumping to his feet, his face red with rage. ''You've gone too far this time, Austin. Guards . . . arrest Senator Roop for treason!''

The room exploded into noisy confusion as each Senator tried to be heard above the rest. The aging Master at Arms and two of his men were halfway up the stairs and headed for Roop, when they started to jerk and stagger under the impact of the heavy slugs. When the roar of the auto slug thrower ended, there was perfect silence for a moment as the Senators looked first at the crumpled bodies, and then at the twenty Il Ronnian troopers who'd appeared, as if by magic, from the emergency exits. Now they stood completely still, twenty impassive demons, their weapons aimed at the Senators. Expressions of shock and amazement filled the room, but nobody moved; to do so would obviously be suicidal. Then they heard the muffled sounds of fighting from the outside corridors. The sounds died away as Il Ronnian soldiers quickly dealt with the complex's remaining security guards. An alarm had gone out, but many minutes would pass before anyone came, and by then the alien troopers would occupy strong defensive positions.

Roop looked out at them, reveling in his power and position. They should have listened to him, but they had insisted on ignoring his advice, and now they would pay. He smiled.

''By god, you'll pay for this, you filthy traitor,'' Kasten said, jerking his arm from Olivia's grasp. But before he could move further, an Il Ronnian trooper appeared behind him and dropped him with a single blow from his weapon. Kasten fell back into his seat and Olivia moved to help him.

Roop shook his head in apparent concern. ''Please, there's no need for anyone else to get hurt. I'm sorry about the violence . . . but sometimes we must look to the greater good. This is such a time. However, I assure you the presence of Il Ronnian troopers is not cause for alarm. Far from it. They're here to help us. In fact, with their assistance, we will be able to avoid a great deal of bloodshed. Do you think the pirates will dare attack us when it's known that we're under Il Ronnian protection? I think not. Who chased the pirates away when they attacked a few days ago? Was it the mercenaries? No—it was a squadron of valorous Il Ronnian craft, arriving just in the nick of time. Now I would like you to meet the Il Ronnian officer who ordered those ships to assist us. For some time now, he's been living here on Freehold, right under General Stell's nose, waiting for a chance to help us. So, without further ado, it's my honor to introduce Quarter Sept Commander Feeg. Listen to what he says, do as he asks, and everything will be fine."

Feeg heard Roop's words only dimly. He stood in the darkness toward the rear of the chamber, his mind and thoughts lost in the river. He'd been that way since entering moments before. The river was the most beautiful thing he'd ever seen. His hand touched his lips over and over in the traditional gesture of devotion and respect. On True Home, where his race had evolved, the saliva thus deposited on the hand would almost instantly evaporate in the searing heat, symbolizing the return of precious moisture to the air, from which it must eventually fall as rain. Many holy chants had been devoted to the rain cycle. But here before him was a sight that dazzled his mind and overloaded his senses. The incredible power and beauty of the river was almost too much to bear. To stand and watch the flow of the holy fluid was to know God. Surely the Council would invest this place with the status of a great temple, and his brethren would travel from many light years away to worship here.

Roop cleared his throat. "Quarter Commander Feeg?" He was anxious now, as all of his suppressed fears bubbled to the surface; he feared that Feeg was somehow backing out of their agreement, leaving him to face the consequences alone.

With a major effort, Feeg tore his eyes away from the river and forced himself to concentrate on the present. He strode down the aisle, stepped over the dead Master at Arms as if he weren't there, and climbed the steps to the dais. Roop moved nervously to one side and stood well away from the alien. Feeg took a moment to gauge his audience. He had spent many hours watching holos of humans, studying them, learning the nuances of their facial expressions, body language, and attire. Now that effort paid off, as he scanned the faces before him. What he saw was a sea of fear, confusion, anger, and frustration. Good, let it be so. "There will be rules," Feeg began. "The first is that he who moves without permission, dies." As he spoke, he saw a number of his troopers jerk their eyes away from the river to watch the humans. They, too, had been mesmerized by the holy flow. Again forcing his mind to the matter at hand, Feeg continued. "The second rule is that he who speaks without permission, dies. The third is that all personal weapons will now be passed to the aisle for collection." There was a rustle of activity as a small arsenal of weapons was passed to the aisle and collected by a trooper. Feeg didn't doubt there were some hold out weapons, but to search for them now might weaken his psychological grip on the humans.

As the weapons were taken away, he said, "There will be more rules as they become necessary. Now I want to address myself to those of you not actually present, but attending by electronic means." Here and there his eyes detected the slight shimmer and transparency of the senators attending via closed circuit holo. He knew that others had already dropped out and were no doubt trying to organize some sort of response. It was important that he convince those still hooked up that any sort of resistance was hopeless. "The continued well-being of your fellow humans depends on you. I am about to issue certain instructions. These must be followed to the letter. Failure to do so will result in immediate death." Suddenly he pointed to an elderly woman with carefully styled white hair who was seated in the second row. There was the crack of a single shot and her head exploded, spraying blood and brains over the dozen people sitting around her. It happened so fast that it was over before they could even flinch. "That," Feeg said calmly, "is a simple demonstration of how serious I am."

Roop averted his eyes from the woman's body. By chance, she'd been one of his strongest supporters. But in turning away, he found himself impaled by Kasten's hard, brown eyes. The hatred there spoke for itself. The President had come around rather quickly, and Olivia was fighting to keep him in his seat.

"Now," Feeg continued, "learn this about my race: Unlike you, we are *not* needlessly violent. The death you just witnessed was necessary. It taught you to take me seriously, and that will *save* lives. I have it in my power to eradicate your kind from this planet. Instead, I will allow those of you who wish to leave to do so, taking whatever you can carry on your persons. A limited number of volunteers may stay under Il Ronnian rule, to be trained for future administrative positions on those human worlds that we may eventually choose to include in our empire. Those will report to Senator Roop."

A burly Senator, about halfway back, spit in the aisle to show what he thought of living under Il Ronnian rule and reporting to Roop. His head exploded under the impact of Il Ronnian slugs, his torso toppling forward and sliding down between the seats. "We are quite aware that expectoration is a form of self-expression among members of your race, and therefore a form of speech," Feeg said calmly. He didn't add that spitting was considered a serious insult among Il Ronnians, so serious that his trooper had probably fired without thinking. He would be punished later. "Now, listen carefully," Feeg said, "because I intend to say this only once. . . ."

As Feeg proceeded to lay out his plan for the human evacuation of Freehold, Olivia was amazed by his audacity. His plan called for the humans to not only do all the work, but to bear the expenses involved as well. Those Senators not being held hostage in chambers would be responsible for implementing the plan. They would supervise a phased evacuation. The brigade and Free Scouts would be taken off first, followed by members of government and the civil service. That way, Olivia noted grimly, all of the planet's leadership would be removed as quickly as possible, lessening any chance of resistance and making Feeg's task that much easier. Everyone not in the first two groups would be in the third. And, in spite of Feeg's earlier statements, it became clear that a number of key scientists and technicians would be forced to stay behind. Supposedly, they would be released once they had trained their Il Ronnian counterparts in thermium extraction and use.

Meanwhile, shuttles would carry everyone else up to the brigade's three transports, and any other ships that happened to be around, for transport to the destination of their choice. Not that anyone would be willing to take them, she thought sourly. But since the available ships couldn't possibly begin to move the planetary population of about four hundred thousand, Feeg recommended hiring some liners or other large ships for that purpose, and gave his permission to use whatever refined thermium was on hand to pay for it. Olivia admired his cheek, since it was now apparent that this was not a full-scale invasion, and that Feeg commanded only enough troops to hold the Senate. Therefore, he could hardly stop them from using the refined thermium in whatever way they chose. But by giving his permission to do so, he maintained the illusion of control. It was, she thought, a clever combination of actual threat, bluff, and bravado. It was well planned and well thought out. She sighed. But in spite of that, it wouldn't work. She didn't know what the free Senators, plus Krowsnowski and Stell, would do—but she knew they would never consider actually evacuating the planet. Feeg had obviously studied humans carefully, and his plan depended on the conclusions of that study, but he'd made some serious mistakes. And being her father's daughter, Olivia had no trouble figuring out where the Il Ronnians had gone wrong.

First, the Il Ronn had never fully understood the rift between the empire and the frontier worlds. In spite of all the evidence to the contrary, the aliens persisted in seeing the humans as they viewed themselves, as a single cohesive unit. So, when the empire introduced military cutbacks that allowed the pirates to raid the frontier worlds, the Il Ronnians interpreted that as a weakness of will and purpose on the part of humanity in general. Plus, during the numerous violent clashes between the Il Ronn and the pirates, they had probably noticed how deeply the humans valued the lives of individuals, even when it was not practical to do so, and had concluded that they wouldn't knowingly allow others to be murdered if it could be prevented. A serious miscalculation indeed, she thought wryly. In addition, the Il Ronn were ruled by a Council that reached decisions by consensus. Feeg no doubt viewed the Senate as roughly analogous to that Council, and assumed that without it the humans would be unable to make effective decisions. She almost smiled. The one thing we're really good at is making decisions for each other, she thought.

So the Council of One Thousand had undertaken a risky operation by human standards, but one which made sense according to their own observations, experience, and bias. If it succeeded, they would acquire a choice planet, and do so in a way unlikely to excite the wrath of the human empire. After all, there was no fleet, no invasion; the Emperor would look at the small number of casualties and ask himself, why get into a costly war with the Il Ronn over some frontier planet? Intersystems would object, but not even they had sufficient power to move the Emperor to war over a single planet. No . . . and even if the plan failed, or the human empire did react, the Council of One Thousand could always shift the blame to Feeg, depicting him as overzealous and misguided. Apologies all around and end of incident. She knew from her visits to court that such things had happened before.

And she knew the plan *would* fail. Those outside wouldn't and couldn't allow it to succeed. They would let every single person in the chamber die rather than lose the planet. And she knew that, in their place, she would do the same. Suddenly she felt very sad. It seemed so unfair. There had been so much to live for. But if it must be, then she would not allow herself to sink into self-pity. She straightened her shoulders and forced herself to listen.

Feeg had paused for a moment, allowing them to absorb what he'd said, and now he continued. "Those of you outside these chambers have six days to implement my plan or we will kill everyone within these walls. Some of my troopers have remained outside to keep you under surveillance. In addition, Senator Roop has recruited human spies among you. I will know if you make plans against me." The first claim was true and the second wasn't, but Feeg knew it would have psychological value. He ventured an imitation of a smile. However, the sight did little to relax his audience. "So I suggest you waste no time trying to free those held here. Your engineers have done an excellent job of construction, and nothing less than a full-scale attack by your Imperial Fleet could breach these walls. That is all. You have your orders, execute them.''

One by one, the holos of the Senators not actually there snapped out of existence, until only one remained. A designated observer no doubt. The rest would go to work, trying to deal with this new and unexpected crisis. Those within the chamber were still under Feeg's order of silence, so no one spoke. Each was trapped alone with his or her thoughts and fears. And in front of them the huge river pulsed with strength and energy, light shimmering and dancing gaily through its currents, as though it was laughing at their weakness.

CHAPTER THIRTEEN

Their departure from Endo had gone without a hitch. Stell and Como were aboard the *Nest*, with Falco and his wing, and Samantha had taken the small scout in toward the empire on a recon mission. Now that the mercenaries were back in possession of their interceptors, the local authorities showed little desire to debate the matter, which was probably wise, since Falco and his crew could have taken out the local air force in a matter of minutes. However, Falco *had* sent a message to Goteb, promising the payment they owed—minus a fee for time spent in captivity and their expenses. The Zord had not replied.

As the *Nest* entered normal space, she began broadcasting the recognition code Stell had established prior to lifting from Freehold. Moments later they had sealed-beam confirmation from the *Shona*, and an urgent request for Stell to come aboard. An hour later, Stell was sitting in the optional rear seat of Falco's interceptor, watching in admiration as the pilot slipped expertly into *Shona*'s launch bay, and touched down. They waited while the robolock settled over the cockpit. When the air pressure had equalized, Falco popped the canopy and climbed up a short ladder. Stell was right behind him. When they emerged in the corridor above, they were greeted by a grim Captain Nashita.

"Welcome back, General. I wish I could tell you everything is fine, but it isn't. The folks dirtside will sure be glad to see you."

Stell smiled. "Hi, Mike. They'll be even happier when they hear we have air cover. Jack Falco, meet Captain Mike Nashita."

By now they were three abreast and striding down the corridor. "Not *Commander* Jack Falco?" Nashita asked.

"The same," Stell answered with a grin.

"Well, you certainly insist on the very best," Nashita replied. "Welcome aboard, Commander. For what it's worth . . . they were wrong."

"Thanks, Captain," Falco said, returning the other man's handshake, "but the brass are never wrong. Isn't that right, General?"

"No comment," Stell answered with a laugh. Moments later they were seated in the *Shona*'s wardroom. "Okay, Mike . . . what's the problem?"

"Well, for starters we were jumped by the pirates," Nashita answered, dimming the room lights. "And with them was a familiar face." The holo tank swirled into life, and Stell watched the battle for Two Holes. His jaw tightened and his fingernails grew white when the camera zoomed in on Malik. He was standing on the bow of a tank, shouting orders as bullets and energy beams shrieked around him. Nashita described the battle and how it had ended.

"No sooner were the pirates gone . . . than the Il Ronn showed up again . . . and not to help us, either." The scene changed, and Stell watched what had transpired in the Senate, from Roop's opening remarks, to Feeg's final ultimatum. One of the free Senators had taped the whole thing and beamed it up to the brigade ships, along with orders from Colonel Krowsnowski.

When it was over, the room was silent, and all eyes turned to Stell. He sat, lost in thought. Over and over he saw the Il Ronnian trooper hit Kasten, saw the politician fall, and Olivia's anxious face as she bent over helping him. Damn, damn, damn. If only he'd thought of that possibility. But the pirates had never even come close to the capitol, and where the hell did the Il Ronnians come from anyway? Turning to Nashita he asked, "Have they found an Il Ronnian ship?"

The other man shook his head. "Not so far, sir."

"Any idea how they got in?"

"Nobody knows for sure," Nashita answered, "but all the evidence suggests that guy Roop. Senator Roop—he apparently smuggled 'em in the night before, and then let 'em in through the emergency exits."

"Any chance of us getting in the same way?" Stell inquired.

"I don't think so, General," Nashita replied, "but you should ask Colonel Krowsnowski that. I believe he's got people working on it."

"I'll bet he does," Stell said turning to Falco. "How fast can you get me dirtside, Jack?"

Falco grinned. "Faster than a horny asteroid miner checking into a pleasure dome."

Stell laughed in spite of himself. "That's plenty fast enough." He rose to go, and then paused for a moment. "They aren't complying with any of that crap, are they?"

"Not a chance," Captain Nashita answered grimly. "Colonel Krowsnowski made that real clear by sealed beam. But just in case the Il Ronn do have spies all over the place, everybody's going through the motions. The truth is they're stalling, looking for a way in."

Stell nodded. "Thanks Mike . . . keep your eyes peeled— for all we know there's an Il Ronnian fleet on the way." But as they walked back down the corridor and climbed into the interceptor, Stell decided an all-out invasion was unlikely. Why mess around with hostages? No—they would have brought their fleet in right off the top. So they were running a bluff, trying to get something for nothing. They could kill the hostages, and be killed in turn, but beyond that they were powerless. How simple it sounded. He could almost hear himself, in some other place and time, saying, "Well, it's regrettable, but we can't give them the planet, and if we can't rescue them, then I guess we'll just have to take the losses." Easily said, unless you knew their names, or had talked with them, or worked with them, or made love to them. As they plunged down through Freehold's atmosphere, he thought about Olivia and what she must be going through. It was, he reflected, much easier to fight other people's wars.

A few hours later he was on Freehold's surface, entering Krowsnowski's temporary command post just outside the capitol near the occupied Senate. It wasn't much to look at. A dusty collection of tents, inflatable domes, and haphazardly parked vehicles baking in the hot sun. Without benefit of a sand suit, his uniform was soon soaked with sweat. Activity swirled around him. Brigade troopers tossed him crisp salutes, much to the amusement of the Free Scouts, who nodded cheerfully instead. Stell took a moment to look around. "It's important to know the ground, son," Bull Strom had often said. "That's one reason why the defender usually has the advantage."

Like all cities on Freehold, the capital had been built in a depression created by one of the planet's great rivers. First Hole was the very first settlement. Like older cities everywhere, First Hole had been built in random fashion, as need dictated. Where the planet's newer cities boasted planned streets and pleasant plazas, First Hole was a jumble of buildings, domes and crooked, narrow byways. So when it came time to build the Senate chambers, they built them clear on the other side of the depression, well away from the city. Some hoped to level First Hole someday and start over again. Keeping that in mind, they built their newest and most important building as far from the old city as possible.

Because most of the Senate chambers were underground, there wasn't much to see. Only the soft curve of a dome broke the surface of the sand. But what a dome! It was made of iridescent stone that shimmered and refracted the sunlight into all the colors of the rainbow. And somewhere under it Olivia and a lot of other people were waiting for him. He shook himself out of his reverie and headed for Krowsnowski's tent.

The older man was waiting inside for him. Five or six members of his staff were also present, two bent over a pile of printouts, one operating a com-set, and the rest staring at Stell with obvious curiosity. In keeping with the informality of the Free Scouts, no one even thought to come to attention. "Welcome home, General," Krowsnowski said with obvious relief. "It's sure good to have you back."

"It's good to be back, Ivan. I'm sorry the poop hit the fan the minute I lifted off . . . but from what everyone tells me, you did a hell of a job."

Colonel Krowsnowski managed to look both pleased and

concerned at the same time. "I wish I could take the credit, sir, but I'm afraid we were just damn lucky. But more on that later. Right now we've got these damned devils in the Senate. Did they brief you aboard the *Shona*?"

Stell nodded. "Yeah. Any idea where they came from?"

Krowsnowski looked unhappy. "Yes, and you aren't going to like it. The sonsabitches have an underground base right here on Freehold!"

Stell frowned as he sat down in a folding chair and leaned back on two legs. "You're right, I don't like it. How is that possible?" His voice was calm, but his expression hinted at suppressed anger. As always, he was conscious that others were present, and how much they could, and would, read into his slightest expression. After all, trying to guess what the brass thinks is a game as old as soldiering itself.

The other officer sat down beside him. "We're not completely sure yet. We found it by checking all our infrared satellite photos the night before they took over the Senate. As luck would have it, we got a sequence of exposures that showed a convoy of vehicles just popping into existence right in the middle of the desert. The satellite computer system isn't programmed to set off any alarms over dirtside vehicular activity, since presumably it's all ours." Krowsnowski shrugged. "Anyway, all of a sudden there it is, right out of nowhere and headed this way. Sections of the trip are missing . . . because there are so many holes in our satellite network, but there's enough to be sure it was them. So I put a team on the spot where the convoy first appeared, and sure enough, there's a well-camouflaged underground base there. How they managed it we don't yet know, but when we get inside, maybe we'll find some answers."

Stell stared thoughtfully at the roof of the tent. Every cell of his being screamed for action, to get up, move around, do something. But he refused to give in to it. The time for action would come, but first they must have a plan. Again, he was very much aware of the staff surreptitiously watching him. His voice was perfectly level when he said, "Good work, Colonel. Even though the base is a mystery, at least we know they don't have a ship lurking just over the horizon. Within a

few hours we'll have some air cover of our own in place."
The staff perked up at that, smiles replacing frowns all around.

"So," Stell added, "that frees us up to deal with the
Senate. Has there been any contact with our alien friends?"

"Not really, General," Krowsnowski answered, reaching
over to flick some buttons on a portable holo tank. It shimmered into life.

Stell found himself looking at the Senate chambers. Senators were slumped in a variety of positions. Many had removed various pieces of clothing in response to the hot, dry
atmosphere upon which Feeg insisted. Some wore vacant
stares, others had looks of determined resistance, and a few
had expressions of terrified dread. It was easy to see why.
Standing at regular intervals around the walls were Il Ronnian
Sand Sept troopers. "They do look like they're straight from
hell," Stell mused. A nice psychological edge for them, he
thought. His professional eye automatically inventoried and
classified their weapons, body armor, and other equipment. It
wasn't going to be easy. "This is live?" he asked.

"It is," the other man agreed. "They allow video, although they won't talk to us. To use their words, 'You have
your orders, obey them.' "

Stell got up and walked over to the holo tank. He activated
the zoom control and went in on the rear of the room where
Olivia usually sat. She was asleep, her head on her father's
shoulder. Her face looked quite peaceful, especially in con-
trast to her father's. He actively glowered at the nearest Il
Ronnian guard. The makeshift bandage around his head suggested he'd done more than just glower. Krowsnowski looked
from the holo to Stell, but if he was curious, he kept it to
himself. A moment later, Stell flicked it off and returned to
his seat.

"Okay, Ivan, how about running down the tactical situation for me?"

The Colonel took a moment to light a cigar, talking around
it as he puffed it into life. "We evacuated the entire complex
shortly after it happened . . . with the exception of three very
good Scouts. They're in there . . . and very close to the
chambers. They have orders to maintain strict radio silence,
unless they detect either an attempt to kill the hostages, or a

break out. We haven't tried a frontal assault because the chambers were built to withstand anything up to a direct hit from a hell bomb. Every passageway is sealed with durasteel doors, and the corridors were laid out to provide defenders with one strong point after another. I might add that we estimate there's more than two hundred Sand Sept troopers in there, and as you know they're mean as hell. So at each defensive point we'd be up against tough, experienced troops, armed with everything from handguns to crew-operated automatic weapons. Simply put, it would be suicide. On top of which, the hostages would be dead a hundred times over by the time we got to 'em.'' There were murmurs of agreement from Krowsnowski's staff. ''On the other hand, the clock's ticking down to when they say they'll kill 'em all anyway, so we're damned if we do, and damned if we don't.''

Stell nodded. ''How much time have we got left?''

''Three days, minus a few hours,'' Krowsnowski answered. ''But we're assuming that the Il Ronn, and or that bastard Roop, have spies all over the planet. So we're pretending to mobilize for evacuation, but unless we start loading people on ships in the next few hours, the whole charade's gonna fall apart. So we're just about out of time.''

''The place sounds impregnable,'' Stell mused out loud. ''Who the hell designed it, anyway? Maybe the miserable bastard can figure out how to break in.''

''I believe I'm the miserable bastard you're looking for, sir,'' a woman said, stepping over from the table covered with printouts. She was middle aged, had a plain, honest face, shiny black skin, and a tight cap of kinky black hair. Her shoulder flashes identified her as a Captain in the Free Scouts. She grinned openly at Stell's embarrassment.

''I'm sorry, Captain,'' Stell apologized, ''but you sure design a mean fortress. In fact, this one is a monumental pain in the ass.''

''Thank you . . . I think,'' she said good-naturedly. ''Captain Wells, at your service. And in answer to your question, I've racked my brain, but I can't think of a way in.'' She paused for a moment, and then snapped to attention. ''However,'' she said. ''I formally request permission to lead a frontal assault, sir.''

Stell regarded her gravely. "Thank you, Captain. But talent like yours is too valuable to waste on a suicide mission. When this is all over, we're going to need you." Turning back to Krowsnowski and the others, he said, "A frontal assault is out. Carry on with the fake mobilization. I need time to think. We'll reconvene here in one hour. Dismissed."

With that, he got up and left the confines of the tent. All the maps, computer projections and printouts were doing more to confuse than enlighten him. He walked aimlessly for the better part of an hour. During that time he invented and rejected countless plans. Each seemed to lead to certain disaster. Finally, he found himself at the place where First Hole's giant river plunged back underground, having completed its brief journey on the surface. Thoughts churning, he sat down beside it, determined to make his mind a receptive blank, recalling once more Strom's advice: "When the answers won't come, let go." His eyes wandered, and his mind followed, down into the rush and gurgle of the water at his feet, which gathered briefly before its long slide down into stygian darkness. He imagined he was moving with it, cool water flowing across his hot dry skin, tugging at first, then pulling him smoothly downward, carrying him away from the surface and all its troubles. Maybe she would see him through the armored plastic, gliding past, on a mysterious journey that would take him deep and far. Then, with a jerk of realization, he had it! Or, at least, what *might* be it.

A few minutes later, he entered Krowsnowski's tent still panting from his long run across the sand. The hour had been up some time ago, so everyone was assembled and waiting. Como had arrived, and was standing slightly apart from the rest, waiting for Stell. "Hello Sergeant Major—glad you could join us," Stell said cheerfully. "Well people, I think I've got an idea . . . though it may be just as suicidal as a frontal assault. Where's Captain Wells?"

"Right here, sir," she said, stepping out of the crowd.

"Excellent," Stell replied. "Captain, be so good as to tell us everything there is to know about that spectacular view of the river that's available from the Senate chambers. Perhaps we can give them something to look at besides water!"

For a moment there was complete silence as everyone

thought about what he'd said, and then they burst into excited conversation. Stell held up a hand for silence. "Please, everyone . . . Captain Wells, what do you think? Providing we could survive the trip through the river, could we break through that armored plastic?"

Wells looked thoughtful for a moment, and then embarrassed. "I hate to admit it, sir, but, yes—you could. The possibility of an attack from the river never even occurred to me. I used materials strong enough to contain the river, but not the effects of demolitions. Some carefully placed explosives should blow it easily."

"But what about all that water?" Krowsnowski wanted to know. "Wouldn't everyone in there drown?" He visualized an explosion, armored plastic flying in every direction, followed by a tidal wave of water flooding into the Senate.

Wells was busily tapping out a rhythm on the computer keyboard. Schematics and three-dimensional projections flashed across the screen one after another. "Not necessarily, Colonel. When we designed the chambers, we allowed for the possibility of an earth tremor cracking the plastic and allowing the river to flood in. But when the water reaches four feet in depth, durasteel doors will be activated and will slam shut, sealing the chambers off from the river. Just a second . . . here—watch this." They all looked at the screen where the words "FLOOD CONTROL GATE: TEST THREE," appeared, along with a date and some other numbers. The words were replaced by a shot of the Senate chambers, which were obviously still under construction. Seats had been installed, but the room was naked of other furnishings. And, at the front, the river flowed by—safely contained behind armored plastic. Suddenly, two huge metal doors slid together between the first row and the stage. The river disappeared.

"Excellent," Stell said as much to himself as the others. They wouldn't have much time after blowing the plastic, but it *could* be done. "Now, is there any possibility that they've already closed those doors? I couldn't see the river on that live shot you showed me, Colonel."

"Absolutely none, sir," Captain Wells replied with certainty. "Like I said, we never anticipated this kind of situation, so there's no manual controls. Even the annual tests are computer controlled, and there's no way the Il Ronn can access the computer. It was shut down right after they took over.''

"Good," Stell said. "Colonel Krowsnowski, if you'd be so good as to put Captain Wells together with your best explosives people . . . I assume you have some folks who are experienced in dealing with these rivers? Excellent—they can design us a can opener.''

"Yes, sir!'' Krowsnowski said, happy to have a plan at last. He turned to a young Lieutenant. Moments later, Wells and the Lieutenant were on their way out to round up a man called ''Boom Boom'' McCall. In spite of his nickname, citizen McCall was a mining engineer, and something of a deity among explosives experts. Just then, the Com Tech called to Colonel Krowsnowski. His expression was grim. ''We just had a message from the Il Ronnians, sir.''

"Well . . . what was it, Sergeant?'' Krowsnowski said impatiently.

The Sergeant hit a key on his console. ''Here's a playback, sir.'' The picture within the holo tank swam into focus. They saw a man on his knees. ''It's Senator Holbrook,'' Krowsnowski said, anticipating what would happen next. Holbrook's head disintegrated as a Sand Sept trooper fired from point blank range.

As his body toppled forward, a tall Il Ronnian officer with one ear missing stepped into the picture. ''We are not stupid, humans. You are delaying while you try to devise a plan to free those held here. There is no hope of that. All you will accomplish are more deaths like the one you just witnessed. From now on, I will kill one hostage every four hours until you begin actual evacuation of your population. You have your orders, obey them.''

For a long time they all stood staring at the dark holo tank. The horror of what they'd just seen went beyond anything that could be put into words. Finally, Stell said quietly, ''Well, time is of the essence, so let's get ready as fast as we can.'' One by one, they returned to their duties.

Stell turned to Como. ''Well, Zack, what's our status?''

"The special environments team is on its way, sir,'' Como replied.

"You requested my gear?''

"Yes, sir, and mine." Disapproval was clear in Como's eyes. In his opinion this wasn't the sort of mission a commanding officer should lead, and Stell knew conventional wisdom was on Como's side. But he didn't give a damn. Olivia was in there with those murdering bastards, and he was going to get her out. It was a personal thing, right or wrong. And then there was Roop. If he got a chance, he'd save the citizens of Freehold the expense of a trial. Anyway, he'd qualified for the special environments team, just as he had for the brigade's other special teams, and there were quite a few. If necessary, he could have called up anything from glider pilots to a null-gravity handball team. Stell was a believer in special teams and cross training, although he had to admit they had spent darn little time actually swimming through underground rivers. He turned to Krowsnowski.

"It would sure help if we had some info on what we're gonna be up against. How about it, Colonel . . . is there an expert on these rivers who we could talk to?"

Krowsnowski bit his lip for a moment and then said, "As a matter of fact, there is. Professor Hammel is our leading hydrologist. I'll send for him." Moments later, a Sergeant was on his way to the professor's lab in First Hole.

"Well, Ivan," Stell said dropping into a chair. "I understand there was some excitement after I took off."

"That kind of excitement I can live without, General," Krowsnowski replied despondently, as he sat down opposite Stell. "The bastards managed to capture a thermium extractor and lift with it." The Colonel proceeded to give Stell a complete report on the pirate raid, carefully sticking to the facts, and not sparing himself in any way. Once again, Stell remembered Malik standing on the tank shouting orders to the pirates. His day would come, and the sooner the better.

When Krowsnowski had finished, Stell nodded. "All things considered, Ivan, I think you did an outstanding job. Nobody could've done any better. It's too bad they got the extractor, but what the hell, it's not going to do them any good without the planet . . . and I'll be damned if they'll get that!"

Krowsnowski laughed and looked relieved at the same time. He'd felt much the same way, but in spite of his respect for Stell, he'd been unsure of how his commanding officer might respond. Some CO's would have blamed him for the whole thing.

The sergeant who'd gone for Professor Hammel stepped back into the tent and cleared his throat. "Professor Hammel was already here sir."

"Show him in, Sergeant," Krowsnowski replied.

The Sergeant stepped aside, and a vigorous looking man, with a shock of red hair and a beard to match, stepped through the door. He was lean and sunburned to a brick-red color. Energetic green eyes darted this way and that, quickly taking inventory of the tent and those in it. "Hello, Ivan," he said cheerfully. "Why has a humble academic been summoned to the tent of the mighty?"

"Humble my ass," Krowsnowski responded with a grin. "General Stell, this egotistical bastard is Professor Irving Hammel, our leading hydrologist. As you can see, he's not much to look at."

"It's a pleasure, Professor," Stell said, shaking Hammel's hand. "Please call me Mark."

"Mark it is," Hammel replied, perching on an ammo case. "And my friends just call me Irv. What's up? For some strange reason, I sense you're after more than my good company."

"You're aware of the situation in the Senate chambers?" Krowsnowski asked.

The professor nodded soberly. "Yes, I am. Damn near got caught in there myself. Right after the emergency session, I was supposed to testify in favor of a larger appropriation for hydrology research. I was just pulling in when all hell broke loose."

"Well, with your help, Irv, I think we can give the Senators a lesson in hydrology they won't soon forget," Stell grinned. He went on to explain their plan to enter the river, allow the current to carry them to the armored window, blow a hole in it, enter, and take the Il Ronnians by surprise. "Obviously, we can't meet their demands," he concluded, "and this plan seems like a way to free the Senators with a minimum of bloodshed. But, can it be done?"

Hammel frowned as he considered Stell's plan. Finally, he

smiled and said, "Yes, I think it can be done . . . if you've got some certifiable lunatics to do it."

"We've got plenty of those," Krowsnowski replied wryly. "No offense, General."

"And none taken, Colonel," Stell answered. "Okay, Irv— tell me what we're up against."

Hammel stepped over to Krowsnowski's computer terminal and asked, "May I?"

"Of course," Krowsnowski replied.

For a moment only the tapping of keys broke the silence. Then a schematic filled the screen. "The first thing to realize, General, is that we have very little firsthand knowledge of what those rivers are like once they go underground. Our best source of information has been unmanned submersible drones, which we attempt to send from one place to another. I say 'attempt,' because only about three percent actually make it. Then we have what knowledge we've gleaned through a limited diving program. I might add that we've never attempted anything as ambitious as your plan. So what you're looking at here is a computer-assisted guess, based on drone reconnaissance, and information provided by the divers who helped build the very window you plan to destroy." He looked from one to another, his brow furrowed with concern. "They, I might add, entered and exited the chambers by means of a temporary lock, and were secured at all times by lifelines. A far cry from the free dive you propose." He shrugged. "Still, I said it was possible . . . and I meant it."

Hammel turned back to the screen. "Fortunately, we do have some information on this river. It's received more attention than most by virtue of flowing through the capital. Now this is our best guess at what the river currents look like, in cross section." He used an electronic arrow to trace the river's course. "You'll notice this section, right *here*." The arrow paused, and Stell saw that the river suddenly reversed its downward plunge and went sharply up. "This will probably be the most dangerous point in the journey. At this point the river is forced to dive down to get under this rock formation, *here*," Hammel said, pointing to a dark mass that hung over the point where the river reversed its direction. "At the bottom of this *U*-shaped turn, the current suddenly becomes much faster; it then passes through this narrow opening in the rock, which is only a few yards across. As you would expect, there's a tremendous current at this point due to the narrowing flow of water. It would be easy to become trapped—pinned, for example, to a rock face by the strength of the current and unable to move, or bashed into the rock walls.'' Hammel looked from Stell to Krowsnowski and then back again. ''But that's not all,'' he continued. ''Once you pass safely through the rock aperture, you'll have only moments to slow down and, somehow, stop. Otherwise, you'll be swept past the chambers and down-river.'' Here, the professor paused soberly. ''If that happens, and you're not caught on some obstruction, you will eventually be ejected into the small ocean near our south pole. Since the journey would take weeks, you would, of course, be dead.'' Hammel smiled. ''Naturally, this is all conjecture, since no one has ever done anything similar and lived to tell about it.''

Just then, Sergeant Major Como ducked his head into the tent and said, ''The diving gear's here, sir . . . would anyone care to take a dip?''

CHAPTER FOURTEEN

They stood in a row along the river, twenty of the very best the brigade had to offer, looking more like sea monsters than men. Each wore a Liquid Environment Suit, commonly referred to as a LES. The suits were designed to function in any liquid environment, but were most effective in good old H_2O. They were armored, self-propelled, largely self-repairing, boasted built-in weaponry, and were capable of providing the wearer with air, food, water, and limited first-aid for up to three days. In addition, each volunteer wore personal weapons and carried a pack filled with specialized equipment. Looking down into the river's mighty current, Stell wondered if all their equipment would be enough. Well, he'd soon know. He chinned his mic and said, "Well, like Bull used to say, last one in's a Tobarian Zerk Monkey!"

With that, Stell jumped in. As he sank into the cool, green water, the river's current grabbed him and pulled him along feet first. He chinned a switch, and a pistol-grip-shaped control handle flipped down from under each forearm to fill his hands. By twisting, pulling, or pushing them, he could control his speed and direction. He pushed them forward, sending jets of water out of nozzles located on the inside of each leg near his heels. He felt the suit slow until it was barely moving with the current. "Form up on your team leader," he ordered. One by one, those not already traveling feet first flipped end for end, braked, and formed a long, single line.

"All right," he said, "report. This is our only chance to solve any problems."

"I want my Mommy," someone said.

Another voice answered, "Hell, you don't even know who she was."

Stell grinned to himself as Sergeant Major Como's voice cut in. "In a few minutes you clowns can share your humor with some Il Ronnian Sand Sept troopers. Since they're about as smart as you are, I'm sure they'll be amused. Until then, cut the chatter. Sorry, sir. Team *A* all present and operational."

"Team *B* all present and operational, sir," Corporal Stickley added calmly.

"Okay, people," Stell said, "remember our briefing. We go as slow as possible into Devil's Dip." Devil's Dip was the name they'd given to the *U*-shaped curve, where the river suddenly ended its downward plunge and angled sharply upward. "It's going to be tight and fast when you hit . . . so pay attention. Those currents are going to turn us every which way but loose. Your armor will take lots of punishment but there are limits. And remember, we won't have much time after Devil's Dip. Team *A* comes out first, sets the net, and stands by to assist Team *B*. As you come out, Team *B*, make damn sure that we've succeeded. If not, set the back-up net, place the explosives like Boom Boom McCall showed you, and take it from there. We'll send you a card from the other end of the river."

That got a nervous chuckle, since everyone knew that if they missed the net it was all over. "Any questions?" No one replied, so Stell said, "All right then . . . good luck." They were moving faster now as the channel grew smaller, and the current became stronger, carrying the puny humans with it. To the river they were bits of meaningless debris, like the uncountable billions that had gone before. Their desires and wishes were nothing against the power of the river's mighty flow. Gradually, the walls were moving in and the river bottom was edging down. Stell cranked his propulsion system wide open against the current, but the river was winning. He moved faster and faster. Now he could see jagged rocks on either side through the misty green water. Then, little by

little, the water began changing from green to brown, as the
current stirred up more and more sediment. It whirled around
his mask, a trillion tiny pieces reflecting the powerful cone of
light from his helmet. A distant part of his mind wondered
which of the little pieces were thermium. This whole mess
was their fault. Then he laughed out loud, only realizing
afterward that his mic was wide open. He chinned it off,
knowing the others must think he was crazy. Just another tale
for the barracks. General Stell laughs at danger! Only, General Stell's gut felt like he'd had a couple of lead diving
weights for lunch. "Most natural thing in the world son,"
Bull Strom had said once. "Healthy, too. Show me a man
whose not afraid going into battle, and I'll be lookin' at a
fool. Hell, son, a man could get his ass shot off out there!"

Now the light quickly dimmed as the river plunged underground and its course became steeper. Seconds later, the only
light was that produced by his helmet, and the walls moved in
even more, until the river's entire volume was being forced
through a channel only fifteen or twenty feet wide. Now Stell
was forced to turn all his attention to controlling his course
and speed, which was increasingly difficult to do. In some
places the river had carved away softer material, leaving
projections of hard rock. Up ahead he saw one—a big, black
spear of rock, so hard that a million years of water had only
served to sharpen it. He was heading straight for it. Desperately, he worked the hand grips as he opened his mic. "Obstruction chest high . . . go for the bottom!" Behind him, the
others did as ordered, dropping to slide along just above the
bottom. Stell felt his own suit respond, and begin to angle
down. but he wasn't going to make it.

He hit the rock spire with incredible force. His head bounced
off the inside of his helmet so hard it seemed like the padding
wasn't there. Searing pain exploded behind his eyes and
darkness tried to drag him down. He fought it, tried to move
but couldn't, as the current pinned him against the rock. His
legs dangled down into the passageway under the rock, and
his head stuck up into the flow passing over it. Meanwhile,
his suit doggedly tried to repair the numerous small leaks
through which cold river water was leaking in, all the while
giving him the bad news via the readout in his helmet.

Suddenly, something grabbed his ankles, and he felt himself jerked downward and off the rock. It took him a second to realize what had happened: Como had grabbed him as he passed under the obstruction, and now the current was carrying them both feet first into Devil's Dip. Stell felt his head clear as the suit injected him with a stimulant and pain killers. He noted that the suit's pumps were keeping up with the leaks . . . so far. "Thanks, Zack. I'm okay . . . watch yourself."

Como didn't reply. He didn't have time. They were moving almost straight down now, and he was worried about what would happen at the bottom. He could have saved himself the effort. Once they hit bottom, the river took control. As the river's volume hit Devil's Dip it bounced back up, swirling and pounding against rock walls, tossing Stell and Como around as if they were grains of sand. One by one, the rest of the team followed and became part of the insane malestrom. They were thrown against rock walls, bounced off the bottom, shot up into the ceiling, and knocked into each other like billiard balls. One trooper from Team *A* was knocked unconscious and swept away, his suit ripped and torn, water pouring in. Two troopers from Team *B* were literally torn apart. Sticks saw their arms, legs, and torsos all mixed together, jerking up, down, and sideways as though dancing a macabre performance at the river's request. Then, as though bored with its creation, the river tore its grisly toy apart and swallowed the pieces whole.

When the river decided to spit them out, it pushed them almost straight up; streams of bubbles poured from their leaking suits. Having been first in Stell and Como were first out. Adrenaline pumped through Stell's body and his thoughts churned. The hardest part was just ahead. In a few minutes they would pass the armored observation window. He struggled to pull the pack off his back and drag it around to the front. In it was the net. Its purpose was simple—to stop them from being carried past the window, and down-river to their deaths. He pulled the rip cord and let go. The river jerked it away as Stell did his best to brake. It would be five seconds before the pack exploded and threw the net across the channel. If he wasn't careful, he could be sucked past the net and down-river. Then *B* Team would have to give it a try with their net, though he hoped they wouldn't get the chance. The river pushed him forward. Up ahead, the glow of artificial lights marked the location of the observation window. Then he felt a dull thump as the pack exploded, releasing net in all directions. Everywhere it touched, a special mastic bonded instantly to the rock, forming an unbreakable anchor. Stell hit with such force that he bounded back against the current before coming to rest again on the net. "The corner!" Como yelled.

Instantly, Stell saw what he meant. One corner of the net had failed to make contact with the river wall and was flapping loose in the current. They had to close the gap before someone was swept through the hole. Desperately, they clawed their way hand over hand toward the loose corner, trying to reach it before the next man came, but knowing deep down they wouldn't make it. Stell saw a dark form hurtle by and go right through the hole as if shot from a gun.

"Shit!" The voice belonged to trooper Levitz. "Sorry, sir, but it looks like I'll be the one sending that post card." And then he was gone.

Almost screaming with frustration, Stell scrambled forward, anchored his feet in the netting, grabbed the edge of the net, and shoved hard. He felt it make contact with the river wall and bond to the rock. As it did, he suddenly realized how lucky he'd been. If he'd touched the mastic it would have bonded to his suit. A series of thumps told him the rest of the team was arriving, hitting the net one after another. Turning, he saw the window for the first time and the chambers beyond. He heard himself say, "*B* Team, set the charges!" and wondered if they'd been spotted yet.

Feeg was tired. The sleepless days and constant tension had taken their inevitable toll. He was sitting in the very front row, his eyes half open, allowing his mind to merge and flow with the holy fluid. He watched the shadows dance and move as light and water interacted to create an endless work of art. In a few minutes he would have to kill another human hostage and the idea repelled him. Yes, it had to be done, and he would do it, but deep down he knew that the Council had miscalculated. The humans would not give up the planet, even if it meant the death of every individual in the room.

Therefore, killing another hostage would make no difference. But he had his orders and, regardless of outcomes, those orders would be obeyed. The shadows shifted again, and somehow their movement seemed wrong, breaking the pattern, going against the holy flow. His eyes snapped open and his agile brain quickly made sense out of what he saw. He leaped to his feet, tail thrashing in agitation as he yelled, "Eyes front! They attack from the river!" Then he heard a dull explosion, and a huge chunk of the armored plastic window imploded, driven by a solid column of water. A corner of the plastic hit him like a duracrete wall, pushing him down, allowing water to rush into his nose and mouth. He tried to scream . . . but couldn't make a sound.

Stell tumbled head over heels as the river plucked him off the net and threw him into the chambers. He landed with such force that it knocked the wind out of him. As he struggled to breathe, tons of water poured into the chambers and the level of water around him continued to rise. Dimly he heard people yelling and screaming as they fought the rising water and their own fear. Then the water closed over him, shutting down his external audio pickups. Fumbling about weakly, he grabbed a seat. Using it to pull himself up, he managed to stand. As his head broke through the surface of the water, he emerged into a nightmare of confusion and death. The Il Ronnian troopers toward the front of the room had been hit by the water and were thrashing around in it just like their human prisoners. However, the aliens located toward the rear of the room were untouched, and in keeping with their orders they were methodically shooting every human in sight. It was murder. But as Stell brought up his blaster, he saw one, and then another alien soldier jerk under the impact of slugs, as a few of the Senators produced hidden weapons and opened fire. Then their fire was joined by that of both *A* and *B* Teams. Energy beams screamed and threw up clouds of steam where they hit water. Slug throwers chattered, lead tearing through alien and human flesh alike. Stell fired and fired, cutting down three troopers at once, only to see more pour in from the emergency exits. As he moved, each step was made against the resistance of knee-deep water, and now out of its element, the LES slowed him down and made him a better target. A part of his mind noted such things as he cut down another Sand Sept trooper, but most of his attention was focused on finding Olivia. Then he saw her, and was almost certain that she saw him. It was hard to tell, because she was struggling with her father, trying to stop him from attacking a huge Il Ronnian soldier with his bare hands. But the trooper fired from inches away, his slugs going clear through the President's body, tearing huge chunks of flesh from his back. The alien was about to turn his weapon on Olivia when a man, it looked like Roop, hit her with a swift uppercut and started dragging her unconscious body toward an exit. The alien shrugged and turned his attention elsewhere. Stell blew the alien's head off and then started running, slowed by both the waist deep water and the suit. Suddenly, Como's voice shouted, "Behind you, General!" He turned, raising his arm just in time to block the descending battle axe.

Feeg was slowly drowning. He was gulping huge amounts of holy fluid. With a supreme effort he pushed up against the plastic holding him down and felt it give slightly. Again he heaved, and this time the weight vanished, allowing him to sit up, and then stand. Dazed, he waded toward the steps leading up to the stage. Perhaps from up there he could see more of the room and better direct his troops. At the opposite end of the stage, water still rushed in, cascading down to join the several feet already flooding the Senate. As he reached the stage and turned to survey the battle, he heard a noise he couldn't quite identify. By the time he did, it was too late. The huge durasteel doors slammed shut, trapping him with the river.

The only thing that saved Stell was his armor. The handle of the battle axe hit with enough force to break an unprotected arm. As it was, his blaster flew out of his hand and splashed into the water four feet away. The Il Ronnian grinned as he raised the battle axe once more. Stell chinned a switch and felt the control grips flip down into his hands. He managed to lift his left arm and point it at the trooper just as the axe started to descend. He pressed the red button on the side of the grip, and felt the recoil as a foot-long harpoon shot out from under his arm and buried itself in the alien's chest. A fraction of a second later, the explosive tip detonated and blew the Il Ronnian apart. A rain of shredded flesh turned the water red.

Behind the durasteel doors, the water had risen to Feeg's chin. In a few moments it would be over his head and since, like most of his race, Feeg didn't know how to swim, he would soon drown. But he reflected calmly, "Even if I did know how to swim, it would only prolong my life for the few short minutes until the river completely filled this space. And to resist the holy liquid would be unseemly. He regretted the fact that he could not die with his troops, but that was not his destiny. His decision made, he waded toward the hole. Water was no longer pouring in, since there was no place left for it to go. Therefore it was a simple matter to step through the hole, and out into the river's main current. A quick slash with his power knife and he was through the net. Then, as he was sucked away into the darkness, he became one with the holy flow. Deliberately, he breathed in its perfect essence, dreaming of a hot orange sun, a desert of reddish sand, and, beneath it, the home he would never see again.

Stell turned to find Olivia but she was gone. The battle was over. All the Sand Sept troopers were either dead or taken prisoner. He moved carefully among the floating corpses, searching for Olivia, but she was nowhere to be found. Roop had evidently escaped and taken her with him. He cursed the Senator with his entire being. He'd find the bastard and kill him by inches. He chinned his mic on and said, "Sergeant Major!" There was no answer. A few feet away he saw a LES-armored body floating face down, and fear clutched his gut as he pushed through the water and rolled it over. There behind the sealed visor were Como's familiar features. Looking down he saw there was a hole the size of his fist burned through the Sergeant Major's chest. Tenderly, Stell bent and picked up the body before wading slowly toward the rear of the room. Carefully, he laid the Sergeant Major's body down in a dry spot against the rear wall. A huge lump formed in his throat and he felt tears trickle down his cheeks. Damnit, Zack, why'd it have to be you? Just when we finally had a home. And suddenly he knew that the big man hadn't cared about making a home on Freehold. The brigade had been his home. He would have gone anyplace it went. And Stell had never taken the time before to think or ask. He had just assumed that Como wanted the same things he did.

"I'll take care of him, sir." It was Corporal Stickley.

"Thank you, Corporal," Stell said. Slowly, he turned away and went out through the massive doors that now stood open. The halls were already full of brigade troopers and Free Scouts, scurrying about on a hundred errands. Many nodded to, or saluted the tall, gaunt officer who trudged past them toward the surface, his helmet under one arm. But he saw none of them. All he saw was Como's face—brown eyes, full of intelligence and humor, that had seen and shared so much. A tall, strong body that had saved his life many times. If only he could have been in the right place at the right time to return the favor. But when he finally emerged into the hot afternoon sun, he had left the grief behind him, as he'd done so many times before, accepting the responsibility for still another death, and hoping that those who still lived were worth the price.

CHAPTER FIFTEEN

Fingers of pain reached deep into the dark place where Olivia had gone, and squeezed. She came to, her head throbbing with pain. Reaching out, she grabbed something to steady herself, only then realizing that it was a rope. The rope was holding a large, unidentifiable bundle in place. Sitting up, she realized she was in the back of a hover truck, and it was bucking up and down as it traversed rough ground.

"So you're awake," Roop said, glancing at her in the rearview mirror as he fought the controls. "Sorry I had to hit you."

Olivia's hand went up to touch the side of her jaw and then the side of her head. Her jaw ached, and a large and tender swelling marked the spot where she'd banged her head into the side of the truck while unconscious. Then it all came flooding back—her father attacking the trooper, her fruitless efforts to hold him back, and then the horror as the slugs tore through him. All because of Roop. She would have flung herself at him and tried to kill him with her bare hands, but they were separated by a metal partition. A small window allowed communication between front and back. As though reading her thoughts, Roop said, "I know you hate me, and I'm sorry. But maybe someday you'll understand that I was right. The empire is already dying, and the Il Ronn will inevitably win. And when they do, we, all of Freehold, could have been in a very favorable position."

The truck bucked violently as they hit a gully, and the fan

skirts dragged for a moment before they lurched up and out of
it. Olivia ignored his rationalizations, forced herself to sup-
press her anger, and asked, "Where are you taking me, and
why?"

"To a place I know," Roop replied vaguely, as he swerved
to miss a large boulder. "We're almost there, as a matter of
fact. I used to do a lot of hunting around here." Suddenly he
broke into laughter. It had a wild, uncontrolled quality.
"That's funny," he said, "because now they're hunting me!"
He reached over and turned up the volume on the truck's
com-set.

Olivia listened for a moment, and quickly realized there
was a massive search underway. Someone was reporting to
Stell: "I'm sorry, General, but the satellite network's too torn
up to be of much help. I haven't found anything yet, but I'll
keep trying."

"Good. I appreciate your help, Com Tech Chu. Call me
immediately if you turn anything up. Stell out." The sound of
his voice made her feel warm inside. She remembered him
wading through the rising water, trying to reach her, just
before everything went black. So they were looking for her.
Her eyes narrowed as Roop turned the volume down. Maybe
she could help.

"That's right," Roop said. "They're looking under every
grain of sand." He sneered in the mirror. "I wonder how
much of that's for me . . . and how much is for the General's
girlfriend. Hey, now that your father's dead, maybe the General can take over—or was that the plan all along?"

Red rage clouded her vision for a moment, but she dug her
nails into her palms, and the pain helped her maintain control.
Carefully, she forced her mind away from Roop. There had to
be something she could do. She systematically took inventory
of her surroundings. The hover truck was apparently one that
Roop had used to smuggle the Il Ronn into the Senate
parking garage. It had bench seats along both sides of the rear
compartment, and a bundle of gear was tied down in the
center of the floor. It was covered with a tarp. Timing her
moves carefully, she waited until a particularly difficult stretch
of terrain commanded all of Roop's attention, and then ran a
hand under the edge of the plastic covering, until her fingers

encountered something round and metallic. She pulled at it
and it gave. Inch by inch she pulled it toward her, gradually
running her fingers over it, trying to identify it by touch
alone. Finally she glanced down, and then back up before
Roop had time to notice. What she had was a two-foot length
of tent pole. One end was sharpened for driving into the
ground, and the other had a socket, into which the next
section of pole could be inserted. As a weapon it wasn't
much, but Olivia decided it was definitely better than nothing.

The truck began to slow as Roop turned it onto a narrow
overgrown track, and they moved slowly along it toward a
dun-colored pre-fab dome. It squatted on a ledge, halfway up
the side of a narrow ravine. The dome would be damn hard to
see from a hundred feet up, and just about impossible from
orbit. Olivia hid the section of tent pole in the right leg of her
jump suit, with the full length of the cool metal resting against
her lower leg. Then, as the truck jerked to a stop, she stuck
the pointed end into her boot.

The truck's fans whined into silence as Roop got out,
walked to the rear of the truck, and opened the tailgate. He
held a small needle gun in his hand. "All right," he said,
"move it. I've got places to go and people to see."

There wasn't room to stand upright inside the truck, so she
walked toward him crouched over, praying he wouldn't notice the tent pole. But she needn't have bothered, because he
paid her very little attention. He kept glancing around nervously, as though expecting someone to jump out from behind the nearest rock. As far as Olivia could see, there was no
reason for his fear. As she climbed out of the truck she
considered faking a fall, during which she could pull out the
tent pole, and then ram it through his heart as he bent over to
help her. But he backed out of range before she could put her
plan into effect.

"Into the dome," Roop ordered, motioning with the gun.

As they walked toward the dome, Olivia said, "This is
silly, Austin. I don't blame you for what happened. I don't
agree with you, but you're obviously sincere, and there's no
reason we can't continue to be friends. In fact, why not let
me go? You're in the clear now."

Roop laughed mockingly. "Get serious, Olivia. I know

you better than that. First of all, you'll kill me if you get the chance, and second, I need you in case lover-boy shows up with his toy soldiers. No, you're staying right here until nightfall. That's when a small speedster will land nearby to pick me up.'' He smiled crookedly. ''Fortunately I didn't put all my eggs in this basket. I've still got a few safely stashed elsewhere. So save your breath. You and I aren't parting company yet.''

She shrugged. ''It was worth a try.''

When they reached the dome, he provided a combination for her to punch into the door lock. The door slid open, releasing a blast of hot air. As they entered, the lights automatically came on and an air conditioner whirred into life. Like most remote structures on Freehold, the dome was solar powered, relying on high capacity storage cells for use at night or during cloudy days. ''Sit down over there,'' Roop ordered, pointing to a small conversation area on the other side of the dome. As she crossed the large, open room, she noticed that trophies of all sorts adorned the walls and animal skins covered the floor. Roop evidently used the dome as a sort of hunting lodge. Which means weapons, she thought, her eyes searching the walls. But she didn't see any. She took a seat under the massive head of a Sandie. The beasts were native to Freehold, and had a vague resemblance to the boars of Earth, although Sandies were a good deal larger. This one's lips were pulled back in an eternal snarl, animosity gleaming from its three tiny red eyes, while a pair of razor-sharp tusks curved up and out, serving Roop as a hat rack. A couple of battered old desert hats were in residence.

Meanwhile, Roop was acting strange. His eyes darted this way and that, searching the room. Olivia's heart jumped as she saw movement behind Roop. The shadows stirred as an Il Ronn stepped out from behind a partition. ''Are you looking for me, Senator?'' the Il Ronn asked calmly.

Roop whirled around, bringing up the needle gun, only to find himself staring into the business end of an Il Ronnian blast rifle. He paled and allowed his arm to drop. ''A wise decision, Senator, though it will delay your death only momentarily. But before you die, I would like confirmation of what your presence here tells me. I take it the mission failed?''

Wordlessly, Roop nodded, sweat bathing his face.

"I thought as much," the Il Ronnian said sadly. "Too bad. Feeg was a good officer. I strongly suspect the Council's plan would have worked if the mercenaries hadn't come. You allowed that," he added mildly.

Roop's whole body had started to shake. "I don't . . . don't know who you are, but I assure you, I . . . I did everything Feeg asked. Please, I beg of you, spare me."

"Disgusting, isn't he?" the Il Ronn said, addressing Olivia for the first time. "I'm sorry you must die with him. He'll make poor company on your journey." Without waiting for a reply, he began to circle Roop as he talked, much as Feeg had that night in the desert. "It may interest you to know, human, that I am a member of the Il Ronnian Observer Corps. You wondered if someone would be waiting, didn't you? Well, now your question is answered. We have known of your pathetic escape plan all along. You are not the only human traitor in our employ. But enough of that. My job is to observe and learn. In that fashion we avoid making the same mistake twice. Unfortunately, I'm the one who must return to inform the Council of One Thousand of what transpired here. They will take little pleasure from my report." The Il Ronnian stopped, his eyes boring into Roop. "However, the one small detail which will bring a smile to their lips will be my description of your death." With terrible slowness, he brought the blast rifle up from chest level, so that Roop was looking directly into it. Something nameless flickered in Roop's eyes as he saw the inevitable, and then it was gone, as the energy weapon removed his head and blew a hole through the wall behind him. A shaft of sunlight sprang through the hole, spotlighting Roop's body where it lay on the floor. The alien looked down without remorse. It was then that Olivia stood on her tiptoes and brought the tent stake down with all her force—her two-handed grip driving it deeply into the juncture where head met neck. To her surprise, it met very little resistance. The observer jerked, arched his back, and made a choking sound as his finger locked down the trigger on his blast rifle, boring a hole through the floor and into the rock below. Then he tottered and fell, joining Roop in the pool of sunlight on the floor.

Her first reaction was amazement at her own success. She'd crept up behind the alien, assuming she'd be discovered but determined to try. He had evidently dismissed her as a potential threat. Come to think of it, she'd never heard of Il Ronnian females going into combat. Perhaps that explained it. Anyway, it had worked. She looked at the two bodies expecting a flood of remorse. It didn't come. All she felt was satisfaction. She turned and left the dome without looking back. Climbing in the truck, she used its com-set to call for help. Within seconds she was talking to an excited com tech. She left the set in the transmit mode, as instructed, and sat down in the shade of the truck, waiting for them to home in on her beam. Then the tears came. She cried for her mother, her father, and finally for herself. And that's where Stell found her an hour later.

CHAPTER SIXTEEN

Two weeks had passed since the battle in the Senate. Now they were ready—or as ready as we'll ever be, Stell thought grimly. In spite of the previous attacks, and a host of normal problems like the onset of the rainy season, they'd managed to refine enough thermium to bring their payments up to date—and still have a little bit left over. If they could get it to Fabrica. It wouldn't be easy. To do it they'd have to transport the refined thermium across light years of hostile space, sell it, and then get the proceeds safely to Intersystems. In their way would be pirates, the Il Ronn, and a host of potential natural disasters. Stell sighed as he looked down into the plot tank that rested on the wardroom table. He was tired, and so was everyone else, and it was starting to show. He'd just had a run-in with Captain Boyko. She didn't approve of the formation he'd suggested for the convoy, and she hadn't hesitated to let him know how she felt. "You may outrank me, *General,* but by god don't you ever forget I was taking this ship into action when you were still in the Academy; and what's more—since when are you an expert on naval tactics?" With that, she had stormed out of the wardroom and headed for the bridge, where naval officers still ruled, and ground pounders weren't allowed.

Once again Stell's eyes roamed over the twinkling lights in the plot tank, looking for flaws. He knew she was right; from the standpoint of traditional naval tactics, certain formations had worked in certain situations time after time. Their present situation was a textbook example. Conventional tactics would suggest that those ships carrying the cargo be grouped together in a globular formation, spaced in such a manner that their heavy defensive screens would interlock to present the strongest possible defense. Meanwhile, the escort vessels would provide them with further cover as needed. It had worked many times. But that was the problem with traditional tactics. The enemy expected them. So Stell had come up with something else . . . and incurred Boyko's wrath. As he stared into the tank, it still looked good. Plus, it felt good in his gut, and like Strom had always said, "More than half of winning wars is just pure luck." Satisfied with the formation, he leaned back in his chair and turned his thoughts to their destination.

Fabrica was a heavily industrialized world lying just inside the empire's borders. As a place to live, it had little to recommend it. The natural flora and fauna of the planet were long gone, victims of the toxic waste poured out by the heavy industry that covered the planet. No one cared, since no one regarded it as home. Most of Fabrica's factories and plants were run by robotics; whatever sentient labor was required came from contract workers, who were rotated on and off the planet. Six months on and then six months off. It was listed as a hazardous-duty assignment, but good pay, free travel, plus carefully sealed and shielded living quarters made up for that. So Fabrica churned out heavy metals, chemicals, radioactive isotopes, and anything else the empire clamored for but didn't want polluting its inner planets. Such a place could use thermium, for it could replace less efficient heat resistant materials in hundreds of applications. And if it turned out that thermium, combined with other substances, produced lethal toxic wastes, then so what? The whole planet was disposable. Someday, when Fabrica's natural resources were exhausted, or it was no longer convenient to the empire's trade routes, it would be abandoned, a lifeless monument to man-the-tool-user.

In any case, Fabrica was their best market, eager to get thermium. And unlike Techno, which only wanted small quantities, Fabrica was willing to take all it could get. The only problem was getting there. With the aid of Intersystems, and the huge conglomerate's knowledge of markets, the pirates would have no trouble in guessing their destination. And once you know where someone's going, it's easy to intercept them.

As the first warning buzzer went off, he rose, walked over and touched the old oak bar for luck, before heading for the observation area just aft of the bridge. In a few minutes the small fleet would leave orbit and head out into space. When well clear of Freehold, they would make a hyperspace jump. Once in hyperspace they'd be safe, unless someone managed to match their exact entry values, and the chances of that were damned slim. But, he thought to himself as he settled into his acceleration couch, coming out of hyperspace will be something else. He'd be very surprised, indeed, if there wasn't someone there to welcome them.

The second buzzer sounded, and precisely sixty seconds later the heavy hand of the ship's acceleration pushed him down into the couch. Their tiny fleet was underway. Somewhere far below, Olivia would be looking up, or perhaps even watching them as blips on a screen moving steadily away from Freehold, and yes, from home. Then she would turn her attention back to the endless administrative details with which she was helping the former Senator, now-President Bram. Knowing how much she had helped her father, and figuring she could use a distraction, Bram had asked for her assistance. Stell smiled to himself. Bram had better keep an eye on her or she'd end up running the place! Besides the brains, she's got the guts too, he thought, remembering the scene within Roop's hunting lodge. Olivia was quite a lady. Gradually, his tired muscles began to relax, and by the time the ship made its leap into hyperspace, he was deep asleep.

One standard week, two hours, four minutes and fifteen seconds later, the little fleet came out of hyperspace not far from a nav beacon. Like all its kind, the beacon continually jumped from normal space to hyperspace and back at regular intervals, while maintaining the same relative position in space. Each beacon emitted its own unique code. That way, the beacons could be located by ships in both normal space and hyperspace, aiding them in navigation, and identifying safe entry and exit points. Of course, any ship that so desired could make a random hyperspace shift, but that entailed a certain amount of risk. You could come out right in the middle of a sun, for example. So with the exception of some scouts and prospectors, everyone used the nav beacons. All of this made them the perfect spot for an ambush. If you knew where someone was going, all you had to do was look up the location of the nearest beacon, put your forces around it, and wait. Knowing that, Stell's entire fleet was closed up and at battle stations as the ships came out of hyperspace. Proximity alarms, sensors, and humans alike all shrieked warnings as they entered normal space and found themselves surrounded by a much larger fleet.

"Stand by for evasive action! I want max power to the screens and all weapons on line. Hold for my order." Captain Boyko snapped the orders out, her dark eyes flicking from one screen to the next, checking, analyzing, planning.

"We have an incoming ship-to-ship transmission, audio and video, Captain," a com tech said.

Boyko looked at Stell, who nodded. "Pipe it to the observation deck," she ordered.

As the com screen came to life, Stell found himself looking at the perfect features of Lady Almanda Kance-Jones. She smiled, seeing confirmation of her beauty in his eyes. "We meet once more, General. I wish it were under more fortunate circumstances. As a representative of Intersystems Incorporated, I am of course eager to see you market your thermium, thereby generating the funds necessary to pay us. I even thought to meet you here, having received word that you would soon come; but alas, when I arrived the ships you see around you were already here. As you've probably deduced, they are pirate ships." She shrugged eloquently.

Stell couldn't help but be amused by the transparent effrontery of her story. But should the pirates fail to steal the thermium, she would have officially separated herself from them, and could pretend innocence. The fact that she had spies on Freehold annoyed but didn't surprise him. He replied with mock gravity.

"Well, we certainly appreciate your thoughtfulness, and hope you aren't inconvenienced by all the exploding pirate ships."

She frowned. "What exploding—" She never finished her sentence, because at that moment two of the pirate vessels

exploded in a searing flash of light. Her image disappeared
from the screen as all hell broke loose. On Stell's signal, the
Zulu, Shona and *Masai* had launched every torpedo they
could. It was a pitiful attack by conventional naval standards,
but it had the advantage of surprise, and two pirate skippers
had paid heavily for their overconfidence. But Stell's convoy
was still outnumbered, four to one, and now the pirates were
attacking with a vengeance. Energy beams leaped across
space to splash against the brigade's defensive screens. Enemy torpedos wove in and out, dodging defensive fire to
explode, one after another, against the protective cocoon of
energy that surrounded the ships. The screens were holding,
but it was only a matter of time before the pirates managed to
beat them down.

Boyko looked at him questioningly. Stell shook his head.
"Hold as long as you can. I want 'em even closer."

"You wait much longer, General, and they'll be sitting in
your lap!" the naval officer replied sharply. Her lips were a
straight line and her eyes flashed. She was speaking on a
sealed intercom channel that excluded her crew. "You'd
better hope your plan works, or we're history."

"Thank you for your analysis, Captain," Stell replied
calmly. "I suspect you won't have to wait much longer."
And with that he turned his eyes back to the screens where
the battle raged. The pirate strategy was obvious—get past
the escorts and capture the transports. He saw the pirate ships
getting steadily bolder, coming closer with each pass as the
pirate commanders realized that, though their opponents had
powerful defensive screens, they carried very little offen-
sive weaponry and it was fairly safe to go around and between them. He would wait just a little bit longer before he made
his move.

Aboard the light cruiser *Avenger*, Brother Mustapha Infarn
Drago, swore at the screens above him, and hit the command
channel override key. "Ignore those flying relics, brethren,
and go for those they protect. It's there we'll find what we
seek." He nodded to his pilot, who put the ship into a long,
graceful curve, calculated to intersect with the centermost
ship of the small opposing fleet. Drago allowed himself a
smile of satisfaction as he saw the pirate fleet obey his orders,

and swoop by the three lumbering escorts to attack the core of the brigade's formation. Then, slowly, the smile began to fade as his eyes darted this way and that. Something was wrong. It was too easy. He was just about to hit the command channel override when Stell sprang his trap.

"Tell Falco to kick some ass for me," Stell said quietly. Captain Boyko wasted no time in transmitting his order to the *Nest*. The carrier was located at the center of the fleet, where the cargo carriers would normally be. Hatches slid smoothly open, and the black, dart-like shapes of Falco's interceptors blasted out, curving off in every direction to engage the incoming pirate ships. Almost immediately, they began to make their presence felt. One, two, then a third pirate destroyer exploded into a miniature sun, before suddenly winking out of existence.

Stell watched with satisfaction as the interceptors sliced through the pirate formation, leaving death and destruction behind. But he knew it wouldn't last. "Time to implement phase two, Captain," he said to Boyko.

This time she executed his orders with a thin smile, which was as close as she'd ever come to an apology. "Implement phase two," she ordered over ship-to-ship sealed beam. Stell felt the *Zulu* change course and watched the other two escorts do likewise on the screen. Moments later they were clustered together for mutual defense, with an escort of nine interceptors surrounding them. Captain Boyko was pleased. Tricks were all very fine, but she would put her faith in traditional tactics every time. "Give me full emergency thrust," she ordered. Stell felt himself pushed back into the couch, and wondered how long it would take the pirates to figure out that the thermium was aboard the three escorts, and not the two old hulks ranged on either side of the *Nest*. The longer the better, he thought to himself.

Lady Almanda Kance-Jones watched the screens in the main salon of her yacht with disgust. As the three escorts wheeled away, and then sped off towards Fabrica, she realized that they must have the thermium. That fool Drago had been sucked right in. For a moment she played with the idea of telling him what she knew, but quickly decided against any such sentimental foolishness. Let him reap the reward for stupidity. She moistened her lips and pouted for the mirror, which covered the opposite bulkhead. Then, with one of her perfectly manicured fingers, she flicked on the intercom. "Max, you see those ships heading for Fabrica?"

In the control compartment Max, her cyborg pilot, glanced at the screens and replied, "Yes, ma'am."

"Get me there before them," she said, settling back into her silk cushions. A few seconds later the yacht leapt forward as Max applied maximum power. Lady Kance-Jones didn't even notice. She was looking in the mirror.

Falco held his breath as he came in behind the pirate destroyer. Then he had tone and lock-on from the on-board computer. He pressed the safety button on the top of his control stick, then squeezed the trigger. Twin beams of blue light slashed out to connect with the pirate ship. For a moment nothing happened, as the larger ship's screens absorbed and dispersed coherent energy. "Two torpedos," he said, verbally activating both launchers, "fire." They leaped out from under the stubby wings of his interceptor and exploded against the enemy vessel's defensive screens. For but a fraction of a second after the explosion, there was a hole in the screen. Blue light from his energy cannon raced through the hole to touch the unprotected ship. All his screens damped down to protect him from the light generated by the explosion. He curved away quickly, scanning his instruments to see how things stood.

"That was a nice one, boss," Carla said. "Ya' fried the bastards good."

"Thanks, Carla, but it looks like they're still going to get to the *Nest* and the other two ships. I think it's time to implement phase three of the General's plan. *Nest*, do you read me?"

"Loud and clear, boss," came the reply from Captain Susa, who commanded *Nest*.

"Implement phase three."

"Aye-aye, boss. Phase three it is."

Perhaps if Drago had been paying closer attention, he might have noticed that the interceptors were gradually withdrawing. But the process of disengaging took time, and he was busy giving orders, anticipating the moment when the three transports would be his. He grinned savagely as an interceptor was hit and tumbled through space before exploding. The brethren were winning. "Prepare for boarding," he ordered. Below, members of the boarding party checked their weapons and grinned nervously at each other. Drago's pilot proved his skill once more, as he laid the *Avenger* alongside *Nest* with only the slightest bump. Tractor beams locked the two together. Meanwhile, other pirate ships had matched locks with the two hulks on either side of *Nest*. Ship crackers flared and ruby-red beams of energy sliced into durasteel. The minutes ticked by as three-man teams operated the cutting devices. The boarding party began to sweat in their armor as they wondered about the coming fight. It might be a breeze, or a really nasty hand-to-hand battle. You never knew. Suddenly the lock mechanism gave way and the other ship's lock hissed open. The boarders surged forward. Then, to the consternation of those in the rear, the front rank was hurled back as a solid phalanx of brigade troopers charged out of the lock, firing hand weapons and swinging heavy battle axes. Leading them forward was Sergeant Major Flynn. Lacking the size to swing a battle axe, she had opted for a flamer instead. "This is for Two Holes, you rotten bastards!" she screamed, and flamed the front rank of pirates. As their ashes fell, she ran through determined that no pirates would escape.

Aboard the other two ships, the story was much the same; they carried nothing but brigade troops. The pirates were quickly driven back to their own ships, and the tide of the battle turned. An hour later, every pirate ship that had tried to board a Freeholdian vessel was in brigade hands. Heading for *Avenger*'s bridge, Falco followed a trail of dead and broken pirates, scorched walls, blown hatches, and drifting smoke. Here and there he saw bodies wearing the armor of the brigade, but they were few and far between, compared to those of the pirates. When he reached the bridge he found Sergeant Major Flynn in charge. There were bodies everywhere. One lay right at her feet. It looked like someone had emptied a handgun into it. Seeing his look, she said, "This one was their leader, sir. Called himself Brother Drago."

She looked up at him innocently. "I tried to take him alive, sir . . . but he tried to jump me." Falco looked down at Drago's unarmed body and then back up at her. He didn't believe a word of it.

"I can see that, Sergeant Major. Well, carry on. I want these ships underway as soon as possible."

"Yes, sir," Flynn replied and turned to her troopers. "Well, you heard him—let's get this mess cleaned up!"

But Falco didn't hear her. His eyes were locked on the pirate ship's plot tank, and the small formation of ships that were racing for Fabrica. They were almost out of detector range. But not out of trouble. "Good luck, ground pounder," he said under his breath and turned away, forcing himself to think about the many problems awaiting his attention.

CHAPTER SEVENTEEN

As *Zulu* swung into orbit around Fabrica, the other ships followed, maintaining a safe distance. They could still be jumped, even now. Not that anything looked threatening. Fabrica was a fleecy ball below. Cloud cover obscured most of the planet's surface, giving no hint of what it might conceal. But at least it seemed peaceful.

"What else have they got in orbit, Captain?" Stell asked.

Boyko's lips moved as she spoke on the crew channel. She listened, nodded twice, said something else, and turned to Stell. "About what you'd expect, General. Four bulk-cargo carriers, a couple of tramps, a small liner, and an Imperial DE. Plus a lot of junk. There's the usual orbital stuff, plus what looks like some kind of cargo pods. They should clean it up. It's a hazard to navigation."

Stell nodded his agreement. Lazy skippers were always dumping things into orbit—burned out tube linings, ruptured fuel tanks, holed solar panels . . . you name it. Most planets used tugs to keep the worst of it cleaned up, but somebody on Fabrica was either lazy, or just didn't give a damn. Anyway, the ships all made sense. The big cargo carriers were probably picking up ore, the tramps might be selling rare isotopes, while the liner was probably delivering a fresh crew of workers and picking up those just finishing a six-month rotation.

As for the Destroyer Escort, Fabrica was inside the empire, although just barely, and entitled therefore to the protection of the Imperial Navy. After all, the industrial planet would make

150

a juicy target for the pirates, or even the Il Ronn. It would be easy enough to dash across the frontier, load up on, say, some rare alloys, and then run. So the DE could be there to protect Fabrica, or to take on fuel, or for any of a dozen other reasons. It really didn't matter, Stell decided, since they hadn't done anything to offend Imperial authorities and should therefore have nothing to fear. But where the other ships were concerned . . . better safe than sorry.

"Captain Boyko, have the Interceptors take a look at those ships. And while they're at it, have 'em check out the bigger pieces of junk, too."

Boyko's eyes flashed as her mouth formed a thin straight line. "With all due respect, General, the Interceptors are running low on fuel, and by the time they return from your little tour, we'll have to take 'em aboard to refuel. What if someone picks that moment to jump us?"

"And what if some of that junk isn't junk?" Stell countered patiently. "But I can see your point. So let's send half the Interceptors, keep the rest here, and refuel 'em one at a time."

Somewhat mollified, but far from happy, Boyko issued appropriate orders, choosing to interpret "half" the nine Interceptors as four, thereby keeping five behind for defense.

Stell noticed but chose to ignore it, rather than cause more friction between them. She was probably right, anyway.

Sure enough, when the four Interceptors returned, they had nothing threatening to report. The only activity they'd observed were the cargo pods continually launched from Fabrica, snatched by computer-controlled tractor beams as they cleared the atmosphere, and then pulled in by the huge cargo carriers. The pods were emptied by robots before being sent back down to Fabrica. So all the ships appeared to be exactly what they were supposed to be. Of course there was no way to be absolutely sure without boarding them. And that would certainly get a negative reaction from the DE. No, they'd just be careful and hope for the best.

"The Planetary Administrator has requested a visit from our representatives," Captain Boyko said, breaking into his train of thought. "Any reply?"

"Yeah," Stell answered, getting up. "Tell them we're on

our way. I'll need a shuttle, and what's his name—Mueller.''
Hans Mueller had been sent by President Bram to negotiate
on behalf of Freehold. A few minutes later, Stell met him in
front of a robolock. Mueller was a small man with wispy grey
hair, pinched features, and bright, inquisitive eyes. He had a
quick smile and a firm grip.

"Good to see you, General. Congratulations on the battle.
For what it's worth, Kasten was right. There's no way we
would have gotten this far without you. But now I'm afraid
it's up to us number crunchers to win the final battle!''

Stell laughed. "It seems to me that number crunchers
always win in the long run, anyway.''

"True,'' the other man said with mock seriousness. "However, we go sadly unrecognized, while you military types hog
all the glory. But this is more like it. I've never had a
bodyguard before. Maybe it'll give me a psychological edge!''
And with that he stepped into the lock. Stell followed, and
moments later they were in the shuttle. Sergeant Stickley and
five heavily armed troopers were already strapped in.

"Sorry, sir,'' Stickley said apologetically. "I was told they
wouldn't let us bring more than six bodyguards.''

"No problem, Sergeant,'' Stell replied as he chose a seat
and strapped in. "Six should be plenty. Besides, if that river
couldn't kill us, then nothing can.''

Stickley looked pleased, and a little embarrassed, much to
the enjoyment of his five troopers. Stell closed his eyes—not
to sleep, but to think, to plan.

It seemed like seconds later when the shuttle's bucking
woke him as it entered Fabrica's atmosphere. He flicked on
the intercom and asked the pilot for a slow decent, and full
mag on the large viewscreen that served the entire passenger
compartment. At first, there wasn't much to see because they
were in the clouds. Or, at least, he thought they were clouds.
But he quickly realized that, below the cloud cover, a band of
particulates lay over the planet like a shroud. When they
finally broke through the haze, it was a barren surface that
came up to meet them. Endless miles of badlands rolled by,
devoid of all life; only the petrified remains of once-thick
vegetation suggested it had ever been otherwise. Here and
there, torpid rivers flowed. A thick scum of effluent twisted

and turned with them as they made their way to dead oceans. Then came strip mines, which had peeled away the skin of the planet, creating lesions so deep that the robocrawlers moving like maggots within them were forced to use their lights even during the day. Next came miles of sprawling factories, mills, foundries, refineries, slag heaps, and waste canals. Each was sited according to maximum efficiency and minimum cost. They grew and multiplied according to their own needs, taking and consuming everything around them like cancer cells gone mad. The energy to power them came from a geothermal tap, which reached down to touch the core of the planet itself. It made sense to destroy one planet instead of hundreds, Stell supposed, but it was still sad somehow, and he was glad when the shuttle touched down on a worn but well-maintained spaceport.

It looked barren without the hotels, restaurants, and plea-sure domes that surrounded most spaceports. But this one had been built for the convenience of machines, not people. And machines were everywhere. They unloaded a worn looking shuttle from one of the tramps, serviced a sleek looking yacht, and scurried, rolled, crawled and hopped around on a thousand other nameless errands.

As the shuttle rolled to a halt, Stell unsnapped his harness and stood with unexpected ease. He'd forgotten that Fabrica's gravity was about one-third of Freehold's, which, in turn, was roughly Earth normal. That explained how they could use self-propelled cargo pods without going broke. Less gravity meant less fuel, which in turn meant less cost. And Stell had a hunch that cost determined most things on Fabrica.

They all moved up and down the main aisle of the shuttle for a few minutes, getting accustomed to the lower gravity. The troopers took turns dropping things and watching them fall slowly to the deck, until Stickley's critical gaze came to rest on them. Stell tactfully turned his attention elsewhere as the Sergeant addressed them in low tones. "Where the hell do you bozos think you are? If you like low gravity so much, maybe you'd like some personalized, null-G, hand-to-hand combat lessons next time Boyko takes the spin off. Any volunteers?" Not too surprisingly, there weren't any. Stickley might not look imposing, but his skill in unarmed combat was well-known, and lessons could be quite painful.

Just then, a boxy looking, eight-wheeled vehicle rolled up, nudged the shuttle, and made lock-to-lock contact.

"Your chariot awaits, sir," the shuttle's pilot said over the intercom from the sealed control room in the bow.

"Thanks," Stell replied. "Would you care to join us for a beer?"

"I'd love to, General," she answered dryly, "but I'm driving."

"Some other time, then," Stell answered, cheerfully. Within the next couple of hours negotiations would be complete, they would off-load the thermium, accept payment, and be on their way. The prospect put him in a good mood. Turning to Stickley, he said, "Well, Sergeant, let's check our gear."

Mueller looked on with interest as the soldiers went over their space armor and weapons one last time. Stell wasn't expecting trouble, but being ready for it was as natural as breathing. Together, he and Stickley checked Mueller's borrowed armor. When the check was complete, Stell ordered everyone to seal their suits. You didn't need a degree in atmospheric sciences to know the air outside wasn't breathable. The yellow-brownish stuff even looked poisonous.

When the lock hissed open, Sergeant Stickley sent two troopers through for a routine check of the vehicle. A moment later they gave the "all clear." The rest of the troopers went through the lock first, followed by Mueller, with Stell bringing up the rear. The inside of the bus had seats for about fifty, and was comfortable though not luxurious. He noticed there were restrooms at the rear of the main compartment. There was no driver or any visible provision for one. Stell couldn't tell if the vehicle was robotic or remotely operated. Each chose a seat and strapped in. A computer-generated voice flooded the intercom and was relayed to them via their external audio pick-ups.

"Welcome to Fabrica, gentlebeings. For your own safety, please fasten the restraints by your seats. An atmosphere appropriate to your race has been provided and you are invited to use it. This vehicle will depart in 31 standard seconds. The elapsed time to your destination will be approximately 14 standard minutes. Have a nice trip.''

As they waited for the bus to depart, a light, acid rain spattered against the window, cutting microscopic grooves into the plastic as it slowly dribbled down. Eventually it would pit the vehicle's durasteel body, eat away rubber fittings, and cause the whole bus to be junked and recycled within a year.

Moments later the conveyance smoothly wound its way through a steel labyrinth of gantries, repair facilities, and warehouses. A short distance later, and they were already moving between foundries, hills of ore, and stacks of finished metal.

Robots were everywhere. They tended rivers of molten metal, hauled enormous loads of ore, repaired each other, and did a thousand other tasks. Many of which were made possible, or at least easier, by Fabrica's low gravity. The vehicle went between and around them, on one occasion dashing between the legs of a huge, tri-pedal robolift, all without incident. Nonetheless, Stell felt the experience was comparable to an aircab ride through the hanging cities of Wist, on the Finthian home world, an experience he could have lived without. Then, without warning the bus dived down a ramp and into a tunnel not much larger than the vehicle itself. As they sped along, interior lights came on in response to the outer darkness. A few minutes later, they came to a stop. There was a pause, a sudden jerk, and the whole bus started moving upward. Evidently they had rolled into the bottom of a vertical shaft, where their vehicle had become an elevator. Very efficient, Stell thought. It saved the time and inconvenience involved in transfering everyone from the bus to an elevator or lift tube.

Their upward journey came to a smooth halt. Seconds later the lock opened, and Stickley sent two troopers through to check things out. As soon as they received the all clear, Stell followed the others through the lock, and found that a robot had been sent to guide them. It was basically human in appearance. It had arms, legs, and a head with rudimentary features. All of which suggested a human owner. Stell had observed that races tended to model their robots on themselves. Nobody minded the fact that a robolift looked like a giant, metal praying mantis with three legs instead of two, and a forklift in place of arms. After all, it was just intelligent machinery. But nobody wanted something like that hanging around their condo, or bringing them coffee in the morning. So Tillarian robots had crested skulls like their owners, Finthian robots had a distinctly bird–like appearance, and, while Stell had never seen an Il Ronnian robot, he wouldn't be surprised to find that they had tails.

As they followed the robot down a series of corridors, he noticed that this one had a distinctly human posterior. A short time later, the robot led them into a spacious reception area. Comfortable looking furniture was scattered about, pieces of art gleamed from niches in the walls, and muted lighting cast a soft glow over everything. A large, curved desk dominated the area. Behind it sat a young woman who wore a frown of eternal skepticism. As she spoke, the robot slipped away. "General Stell and Comptroller Mueller?" she said, as though expecting them to deny it.

"That's us," Mueller replied cheerfully.

"Administrator Nars will see you now," she said. "Please follow me." Stepping away from her desk, she led them to a section of wall that slid aside at her approach. They followed her into a room that could only be described as palatial. Ornately carved furniture dominated, its massiveness somewhat relieved by delicate pieces of sculpture and the soft landscapes decorating the walls. There were no windows, which said something about the room's owner, Stell thought to himself. An owner very much in residence. All four hundred pounds of him. In spite of his bulk, Administrator Nars rose easily from his oversized chair and moved to greet them. Due to Fabrica's lighter gravity, his weight was not the burden it would've been on Terra. Stell wondered if the man ever left Fabrica. But there was strength in the man's grip, suggesting a good deal of muscle under all the fat. And there was nothing weak about the eyes that met his.

"Welcome to Fabrica. I'm Wilson Nars. And you must be General Stell—no mistaking a military man. And that means that you are Comptroller Mueller. Welcome. I'd like both of you to meet Lieutenant Commander John Paul Jones."

Stell instantly liked the man who stepped forward to meet

them. He'd been named after an ancient naval hero, if Stell remembered correctly. He wasn't a big man, but he projected the aura of strength and confidence common to many big men. He had black skin, brown eyes, and a belligerent thrust to his chin, as though daring someone to hit it. He looked good in Navy black and he knew it. "It's a pleasure to meet you, General, Citizen Mueller," Jones said as he shook hands with each. He glanced at Stell's shaved head. "Star Guard?"

Stell nodded. "A long time ago. I guess it got to be a habit." He ran a hand over his scalp.

"If you'll excuse me for a moment, gentlemen, I'll be right back," Wilson Nars said, and headed for the reception area where his secretary was plainly waiting. Both officers watched him go before turning back to each other. Stell would have sworn there was revulsion in the naval officer's eyes. In fact, he got the distinct impression that Jones didn't like the fat administrator at all. But if so, there was no hint of it in his words. "So, you're selling something called thermium," Jones mused aloud.

"You are well informed, Commander," Stell answered, wondering where the conversation was going. Mueller remained silent but watched with interest, as though sensing that something unusual was taking place.

Jones shrugged and glanced toward the reception area. "Nars made no secret of it." He paused, regarding Stell with a thoughtful gaze. "In fact, he went to some trouble to make sure I knew, and to set up this meeting."

Mueller spoke for the first time. "Why would he do that?"

Jones smiled. "I don't know. But I do know Nars, and I'm sure he has good reasons; good for him, that is."

At that moment Wilson Nars returned with a jovial laugh. "Well, enough military gossip. It's time to do some business!"

"Nice meeting you," Jones said to Stell and Mueller. "Thank you for your hospitality, Administrator Nars. I'll look forward to seeing you the next time I'm in this sector." They all said good-bye, and as the naval officer turned to go, he gave Stell a look that clearly said, "Watch yourself."

Stell nodded and smiled in return. He and Mueller took seats opposite Nars, who picked up a platter heaped with some sort of pastry, popped one in his mouth, and chewed with obvious enjoyment. "Would you care for one? They're really quite good," he said, offering the platter to both guests. Stell refused, while Mueller accepted—whether out of politeness or actual hunger, he couldn't tell.

"So," Nars began, patting his lips carefully with a linen napkin, "you have some thermium to sell. Wonderful stuff, thermium. I'd like to buy it. Assuming, of course, that you are asking a reasonable price. If not, then we've gotten along without it for a long time, and can continue to do so. It all depends on you."

Mueller nibbled thoughtfully on a pastry. "Of course. A fair price is important to us as well. And it should reflect not only the added quality that thermium will bring to your existing products, but the various new products made possible by it as well. All of which makes price a matter of secondary concern."

Having established their initial bargaining positions, both men settled down to the serious business of give and take, a process they both clearly enjoyed. Sure that Mueller had things well in hand, Stell allowed his attention to wander. Eventually, his eyes drifted to his own reflection in a large mirror. He smiled at the image there, thinking how out of place he looked in his armor, wishing the whole thing were over.

And on the other side of the two-way mirror Lady Almanda Kance-Jones smiled as Stell's eyes unknowingly met hers, and she blew him a kiss.

CHAPTER EIGHTEEN

Stell squinted into the white glare of the powerful robolights. They looked like giant insects. Each had four legs to a side, and a long cylindrical body from which a powerful beam of light sprang. They were in constant motion to make sure the light was always directed where it would do the most good. If sentients hadn't been involved in unloading, Stell supposed that the robots could have gotten along without any light, relying instead on their various sensors. Not that it mattered one way or the other, he thought tiredly. For three days they'd slaved to unload the thermium, and now they were almost finished. In spite of robotic help, it had taken an incredible amount of work. But now it was over. Robots had just unloaded the last of the metal cubes. Each contained one hundred pounds of the powder-like thermium. The cubes were stacked on power pallets, which were hooked together to form a train. Each hovered just off the duracrete, its motor and fan obtaining power from the robocrawler at the head of the train, via the umbilical that hooked them all together. Now the robocrawler jerked into motion; the long train of power pallets floating behind it jerked in sympathy, and then moved off obediently. The cubes that were piled on them gleamed in the artificial light for a moment, then disappeared into the darkness.

With a roar of sound, the now-empty cargo shuttle lifted and headed for the spaceport some distance to the west. Since the brigade's shuttles weren't equipped to move large amounts of cargo, they'd been forced to use Fabrican craft—for a hefty fee, of course.

"Wilson Nars is here, General," Mueller's voice crackled over his headset, slightly distorted by the huge power grid located nearby.

"I'm on my way," Stell replied, and headed toward the shadowy shape of the large ground vehicle parked a few hundred feet away. As usual, he found himself practically bounding along under Fabrica's lighter gravity. With the business of unloading completed, the robolights had moved off to other assignments, taking their light with them and leaving the area in relative darkness. A faint pinkness on the far horizon promised another glorious sunrise. Due to all the particulates in the atmosphere, Fabrica's sunrises were absolutely spectacular. Typically, the sun rose in an explosion of pink and red, reaching out to bathe the tortured landscape with a soft, mystical light. It was as if the planet had found a way to transmute its own ugliness into unbelievable beauty.

As he walked toward the ground vehicle, Stell noticed that it was similar to the one that had taken them to meet Nars that first day. In it, the Planetary Administrator would hand over full payment for the thermium. After the long ride to the main spaceport, where their own shuttle would pick them up, they'd load the cash and lift—and a few days later, Intersystems Incorporated would receive Freehold's annual payment. Mueller had insisted on cash, rather than a credit transfer, fearing some kind of underhanded move by the huge company. Stell understood his reasoning. Computer operators could be bribed, records could be altered, and credits could vanish into thin air. Still, he didn't like it. Cash could be hijacked, and must therefore be guarded. Plus, it was a long way from Fabrica to Intersystems Sector Headquarters, a small planet with the romantic name of XTR 346. It was better known to company pilots as The Bitch, since landing on it involved weaving through a maze of orbiting weapons platforms.

For some reason, he kept thinking of Commander Jones and his implied warning. He and Mueller had discussed the naval officer's comments more than once, but it hadn't done them much good. By the time they'd completed their negotiations with Wilson Nars, the naval officer had taken his ship out of orbit and departed. And, in spite of their constant vigilance, they'd been unable to discover any sort of funny business on the part of Wilson Nars or his staff. Still, Stell would feel better when they had the cash and were safely off-planet.

The vehicle's lock hissed open at his approach. He and the two bodyguards, upon whom Sergeant Stickley had insisted, stepped inside and waited for the pumps to clear the poisonous Fabrican atmosphere. Moments later the inner hatch slid open, and they entered the vehicle, unsealing their armor as they went. Wilson Nars was waiting, wearing the largest atmosphere suit Stell had ever seen.

"Good to see you again, General. Comptroller Mueller and I were just celebrating the successful completion of our little transaction. Would you care to join us?" Nars indicated a folding table on which a chilled bottle of wine and some hors d'oeuvres had been set out.

"Thank you," Stell replied. "Don't mind if I do."

"You're just in time for the formalities," Mueller grinned. "Then it's up, up and away."

"I'll drink to that," Stell said, sipping his wine. "No offense, Administrator Nars, but the sooner the better."

"And none taken," the fat man replied. Nars removed a fancy looking vocorder from a pouch at his waist, and placed it on the table. Mueller produced a less-expensive model and did likewise. Each would provide its owner with a legal record of the proceedings, verifiable by standard voiceprint analysis. Nars spoke first. "Activate. This is Wilson Nars, duly authorized administrator of the planet Fabrica. A standard purchase and sale agreement follows, consistent with all applicable Imperial laws." There was much more by both parties, with Nars acknowledging receipt of so much thermium, Mueller confirming acceptance of so many credits in return, with mention of various amounts deducted for Imperial taxes, shuttle fees, and so forth.

Stell listened with only half an ear. His mind told him that everything was okay, but his gut said otherwise. Though without something concrete to go on, there wasn't a thing he could do about it.

"Well, that about wraps it up, gentlemen," Nars said,

sliding the last of the appetizers onto his tongue and making it disappear. "As you know, your money is in this box," he indicated the large metal trunk near his feet, "and you'll notice that it still bears the Freeholdian seal placed on it by Comptroller Mueller when the cash was loaded into it. So, with your permission, I shall bid you a fond adieu, and go in search of dinner. I imagine you're quite eager to be on your way."

Stell and Mueller made polite noises as the huge man waddled to the lock. Just before he sealed his helmet, Nars said, "Well, it's been a pleasure, gentlemen. I wish you luck, but remember—my responsibility ends now. There are those who would steal your money and it's up to you to make sure they don't." With that, he sealed his helmet, waved, and disappeared into the lock.

Stell and Mueller looked at each other. A chill ran down Stell's spine. There was little doubt that Nars knew that something was going to happen, and was making his own position clear for the legal record. Once again, he thought of Commander Jones and what he'd said about Nars. He heard the outer hatch cycle open as Nars departed. Suddenly, he wished they were aboard their own shuttle and lifting. But they weren't—and wouldn't be until the vehicle they were in took them to the spaceport. In the meantime, all they could do was prepare for the worst, and hope for the best. He turned to Stickley and said, "Let's seal up and be ready for anything."

"Excellent advice, General . . . but a bit late." Stell whirled to find himself confronting Lady Almanda Kance-Jones. She was still incredibly beautiful. At her side was a six-and-a-half-foot-tall Autoguard. Both had just emerged from the women's restroom at the rear of the vehicle. It must have been damned crowded in there.

Stickley swore softly to himself. By chance, there weren't any female troopers with them, and he hadn't thought to check the women's can. And as a result, they were up against an Autoguard. It had a ball turret for a head, energy weapons for arms, and was first cousin to Smith, the Auto Trooper who'd saved them during the Zonie ambush. All of which meant there wasn't a damned thing they could do but agree to whatever she wanted. They wouldn't stand a chance against the Autoguard.

Lady Kance-Jones smiled a perfect smile. "Relax, General, there isn't a thing you can do, and I hope you're going to be sensible. Otherwise, some of our little metal friends would have to spend all night trying to get you off the upholstery. Now, if you and your men will just stay right where you are, my assistant here will relieve you of that nasty old trunk, and we'll be on our way."

The Autoguard moved forward and picked up the two-hundred-pound box as though it were an overnight bag. Stell noted that its right arm was still free. "So," he said grimly, "Intersystems finally comes out in the open."

Kance-Jones looked surprised. "Out in the open? Oh, I see. Well, for the moment, I guess that's true." She took on a conspiratorial look, red lips pouting, looking this way and that. "But I'm afraid it's going to be our little secret. And, since you'll be dead in a few hours, I guess it'll stay that way."

"Dead?" Mueller said, looking a little green.

"Yes, I'm afraid so," she said producing a blaster which she aimed at them as the Autoguard lumbered toward the lock. "The General would no doubt cause all sorts of trouble if he were alive. But he'll be a good deal more cooperative dead. As will you." She affected a look of profound sadness. "An unfortunate train of events. The valiant General Stell's vehicle breaks down . . . and adding to his difficulties, the radio won't work. Wearing atmosphere suits, he and his men go out looking for help. Unfortunately, the nearest sentient beings are at the spaceport, more than a hundred miles away. And, having already spent a full day in their suits, air for only a few hours remains, so eventually they all suffocate on the surface of Fabrica. Or here in this vehicle, if you prefer," she said cheerfully. "It hardly matters to me. In any case, they will find you dead and the money missing."

"Just for the sake of my curiosity," Stell asked, "what's Nars getting out of this?"

Lady Kance-Jones smiled her cold smile. "A bonus . . . and probably a hefty raise the next time his contract comes up. You'd have to ask his boss."

Stell felt a cold spot growing in the pit of his stomach as he asked the next question. "And who does his boss work for?"

She laughed. "Why, Intersystems Incorporated of course. Who else? They own part of Fabrica, you know." Seeing the look on Stell's face, she shook her head in mock sympathy.

Mueller groaned as she stepped into the lock. As the hatch began to close, she yelled, "Oh, by the way, I took the liberty of informing your ships you'd be delayed until tomorrow. So long!" The hatch closed on her last words.

"Shit! Did you see that?" Stickley asked. "She wasn't wearing a suit!"

Suddenly, to his embarrassment, Stell realized that Stickley was right. Kance-Jones had just stepped out into a poisonous atmosphere without any kind of a suit, and he hadn't even noticed. He rushed over to look out the window. It was daylight outside now, and there she was, as if expecting him, standing there and waving good-bye. She gave one last wave, said something to the Autoguard, and then followed it over to a parked air car. Moments later it lifted on repellers, blasted up into the sky, and was gone.

"What the hell's going on?" Mueller asked glancing from Stickley to Stell.

Stell sighed. "Two robots just ripped us off . . . that's what's going on."

"*Two* robots?" Mueller said thoughtfully. Then, sudden understanding flooded his face. "You mean, she . . . I mean *it*, was . . . I mean *is*, a robot? And that's why she can go out there without a suit?"

Stell nodded. Mueller thought about it for a moment. Like Stell, he had first seen her the day she'd addressed Freehold's Senate. Ever since, she'd played a central role in certain fantasies he'd devised to pass life's more boring moments. Somehow it just wouldn't be the same with a robot. Or would it? He laughed. And a moment later Stell found himself doing likewise, along with the six troopers.

One by one they stopped laughing, as each thought about their situation and wondered if there was any way out of it. There's got to be a way, Stell told himself, and wished he could believe it. In any case, they wouldn't give up without a fight. "Okay, men, let's check it out," Stell said. "Sergeant

Stickley . . . check and see if this vehicle's really out of action. Corporal Gomez, check the radio. The rest of you go over your gear. We might want to take a stroll outside.'' The troopers grinned nervously as they checked their suits and weapons.

"Well," Mueller said. "It would seem that Commander Jones was right.''

"It would seem so,'' Stell agreed. "Nars went through all that stuff with Jones just to lay some legal groundwork. The way he's got it set up, the whole thing happened after he fulfilled all of his legal responsibilities. He even warned us to protect ourselves. And you can be damned sure he had his vocorder turned on when he did it.''

Mueller mournfully nodded his agreement. "It's all my fault; I should have known.''

Stell snorted. "Bullshit. They just outsmarted us, that's all. But the game isn't over.''

The little man seemed somewhat cheered. A few minutes later, Stickley and Gomez returned.

"I can't find anything wrong with this rig, sir,'' Stickley reported, "but I can't find any manual controls, either. So I don't know if it's broken or not.''

"Guess it doesn't much matter if we can't make it go,'' Stell replied evenly.

"The radio's definitely belly up, sir,'' Gomez added. "There's a whole circuit board missing.''

"And just to make things more interesting,'' Mueller said, "if I'm not mistaken, the atmosphere's going bad in here.''

Suddenly Stell realized it was getting hard to breath. "Okay, everybody—seal 'em up,'' he ordered. Evidently, Kance-Jones and Nars wanted them to die outside. Under his breath, he said, "If I ever get my hands on you Nars, they're gonna have to round up some incredibly strong pall bearers. Or maybe a robolift.'' The thought cheered him considerably. For some strange reason, now that he knew Kance-Jones was a robot, he couldn't get mad at it, although he would certainly like to have a conversation with its owner.

With no breathable atmosphere inside, there certainly wasn't any reason to linger in the bus. Once everyone was outside, Stell got a reading from each on their oxygen supply. The lowest was his own—seven hours, sixteen minutes to go. So that was the amount of time he had to work with. As he thought, his eyes roamed the horizon. Since it was a hundred or so miles away, the spaceport was obviously out. And even if they found some way to reach Nars, it seemed unlikely that they'd get any help from that direction. Suddenly, he became conscious of a metal disk hovering almost directly over him. That sonovabitch Nars was watching them with a robospy!

Pretending he hadn't noticed it, Stell turned to Stickley. "Don't look now, Sergeant, but there's an airborne robospy overhead. Keep track of it, and be ready to take it out on my command."

Stickly nodded. "Yes, sir . . . on your command."

Let the sonovabitch watch for a while Stell thought to himself, as he turned his attention back to their surroundings. His eye was caught and held by the elevated monorail that passed by a few hundred yards to the right. It wound its way between the huge power grid and a foundry, before disappearing toward the east. Moving slowly along it was a featureless, black power unit, followed by a heavily loaded train of open ore cars. They were heaped so high with crushed rock that some dribbled over the sides as the train went into a banked curve. The train was at least two miles long. As a result, the power unit was a bit overmatched, even under Fabrica's light gravity, and the whole thing moved quite slowly.

Then he noticed a flash of motion further out toward the east. There was a belated roar of sound from his external audio pick-ups, as a self-powered cargo pod blasted off. Stell imagined it clearing the atmosphere, being snatched by a tractor beam, and then being reeled in like a fish on a line. Suddenly he grinned, slapped Mueller on the back so hard the small man almost fell over, and said, "Sergeant Stickley . . . let's lose our eye in the sky."

The words were hardly out of his mouth, when Stickley's weapon flashed, the small metallic disk exploded, and tiny bits of hot metal rained harmlessly down to spatter against their armor.

"Nice shot, Sergeant," Stell said cheerfully, "now let's get out of here. Our train awaits!" With that, Stell started jogging toward the monorail. Because of the light gravity, he made good time. Mueller was right behind him, followed by the troopers and Sergeant Stickley, who had automatically assigned himself the rear position. When they reached one of the massive pylons supporting the monorail, Stell saw that, just as he'd hoped, there was a ladder attached to it.

As he put his foot on the bottom rung and began to climb, he realized the ladder had been constructed for the convenience of maintenance robots, and not humans. The rungs were wider than necessary and spaced too far apart. So it was necessary to reach up, grasp the next rung, and do half a chin up before he could get his feet on the next step. Due to the light gravity, it didn't take a lot of strength, but it did help to be tall. Looking down, he saw Mueller was having quite a bit of difficulty, until Gomez starting allowing the smaller man to use his shoulders as a step. Shortly thereafter, Stell heaved himself up onto a durasteel platform attached to the side of the monorail. The noise of the passing train was deafening. He turned down the level on his external sound pick-ups. Looking toward the back end of the train, he saw they didn't have much more time. There was only about a quarter-mile of train left.

"Hurry up!" he shouted over the command channel, and started climbing up the rungs of the latticework bridge spanning the monorail, that gave the maintenance robots access to the other side. Behind him, the rest did likewise. Moments later he reached the top horizontal walkway. It didn't have rails. Evidently, robots didn't need them. Twenty feet below, the open cars rumbled by, one after the other, each heaped high with reddish ore. There were damn few left. Glancing back, he saw the others had now joined him. "Come on . . . let's go!" he shouted, and jumped.

He hit hard. But the ore was soft enough to absorb some of the impact, and his armor took care of the rest. He rolled over a couple of times and then struggled to find his footing. When he managed to stand and look back, he saw that only two figures remained on the bridge. One had to be Stickley, and the other was a trooper. Why didn't they jump? God damnit, there were only two or three cars left! The trooper must be scared . . . and Stickley was trying to talk him through it. Stell chinned his mic switch on just as he saw Stickley give the trooper a shove and jump after him. They landed together in the last car. He gave a sigh of relief, and then said, "Report." One by one, they reported in. When they were finished, he found there was a sprained ankle, a ripped suit that had self-sealed, and a lost weapon. Not good, but not bad, everything considered.

"All right, people," he said, "start working your way forward. I'd like everyone to join me up here in the V.I.P. lounge."

There was scattered laughter, and Stickley said, "Yes, sir . . . I hope the bar's open."

"Sorry, Sergeant," Stell replied, "but it's temporarily closed. The seats are comfortable, however, and the view is unbelievable." And it was. The monorail twisted and turned its way between smokestacks, factories, and slag heaps. It looked like a high-tech version of hell. Carefully, he scrambled to the crested top of the ore and craned to see where they were headed. Far off in the distance, he saw another cargo pod hurl itself up toward space. It appeared as though their train was headed for the launching area, or at least close by. That was good. But how long would it take? Hours, at the very least. He chinned a switch, and watched as the suit-status display flashed on just above his visor. He had five hours and twelve minutes of oxygen left. He sat down on the crest of the ore and remembered something Bull Strom used to say. "It'll take as long as it takes son . . . and there's not a damn thing we can do about it."

CHAPTER NINETEEN

The train jerked to a halt two hours and seventeen minutes later. Stell didn't bother to calculate how much air he had left. He knew he wouldn't like the answer. In front of their train was another just like it. It disappeared into a large building of some sort. There was a flash of light, followed by a tremendous roar of sound. He looked up to see another cargo pod hurling itself skyward. He'd been watching them for some time now. They departed at regular intervals from a launching facility just beyond the large building. "Well, Sergeant, what do you think?" Stell indicated the cargo pod, now a mere dot of light in the sky. "Should give us one helluva ride, don't you think?"

Stickley looked up, then at Stell, then up again. "No doubt about that, sir," he said evenly. Then he added dryly, "I can hardly wait."

Stell laughed, "Well, come on then—we don't want to miss our flight!" And with that, he scrambled down the side of the ore car and jumped to the ground. For the last ten miles or so, the monorail had descended to hug the surface. Setting a brisk pace, he started walking toward the distant building. He would have jogged, but there was no way that Trooper Klien, with his sprained ankle, could have kept up, so a fast walk would have to do. Meanwhile, Klien was making pretty good time—with the help of Fabrica's low gravity and two of his buddies.

As he walked beside them, Stell realized that the ore cars

169

looked somehow familiar. At first, he couldn't quite put his finger on it, but the next time a cargo pod took off he looked up, and realized what it was: the ore cars were half cylinders. And now that he looked more carefully, he saw that they rested in cradles, which, in turn, were locked onto the monorail itself. So, if you lifted one of the half cylinders out of its cradle, attached an empty half cylinder, a nose cone, stabilizers, external tanks, and rocket pods, you had a self-propelled cargo pod! Each unit probably had its own built-in microcomputer and guidance system. Instead of transferring the ore to a shuttle, they simply built a shuttle around it, launched it, retrieved it, and used it again. Very efficient. And he planned to turn that efficiency to his own purposes.

The plan was simple. All they had to do was allow themselves to be sealed inside an ore shuttle, survive some heavy *G*'s without benefit of acceleration couches, and manage to reach their own ships once in space. "A snap," he thought to himself, and laughed out loud. As usual, he realized too late that he'd forgotten to chin his mic off.

They reached the huge building. It seemed to be eating the train, one car at a time. Beside them, the ore cars would jerk forward one car length, pause in that position for about ten minutes, wait for another cargo pod to roar upward, and then the whole process would start over. Looking at the size of the building, and estimating the distance to the launch site, Stell figured there were maybe thirty cars between them and the one that was about to lift off. And they couldn't afford to wait for three hundred minutes—not with their dwindling supplies of air. So they needed to enter the building, locate the point where the cargo pods were assembled, and slip inside out just before the lid was welded on. The only problem was that the opening through which the train entered the building was too tight. There were only inches between the edge of the entrance and the train itself.

"Sergeant Stickley!"

"Sir!"

"Make me a door." Stell pointed at the building.

"Yes, sir. One door coming up. Gomez, you heard the General . . . he wants a door."

Gomez didn't need to be told twice. Aside from his assault

rifle, he carried a mini-launcher and four rockets for it. Each of the other troopers, with the exception of Sergeant Stickley, carried two more rockets. Gomez brought up the short, stubby tube, flicked the safety off, glanced into the sight, and pressed the trigger. With a *whoosh*, the rocket flew straight and true. There was a sharp, cracking sound as it hit the thin plastic wall. When the smoke cleared, there was a hole big enough to drive a troop carrier through.

"Nicely done, Gomez," Stell said as he walked through it. "You're not very neat, but you're damned fast."

No sooner were they inside than two maintenance robots showed up and started surveying the damage. They were, no doubt, relaying news of the destruction to some central computer. But, Stell thought grimly, by the time old lard-ass figures it out, we'll be off planet . . . I hope.

Up ahead, massive shapes moved in and out of the murky light. Metal clanged on metal, pneumatic tools shrieked, arc welders hissed and threw out showers of sparks. The arm of a robowelder finished sealing two cylinders together and then withdrew, awaiting the next unit on the line. Stell ordered everyone to close on him as they moved forward. Otherwise, they could easily become separated in the darkness and confusion. As they walked, small maintenance robots scurried between their feet, larger models moved across their path, and big robolifts stepped over them, careful not to crush the puny, two-legged creatures that seemed so determined to get in the way. When they reached the car next in line for the robowelder, Stell scrambled up the side and jumped down into the ore. A second after he landed, the car jerked forward. One after another, dark shapes tumbled over the side to land beside him. "Count off!" he ordered. It would be easy to accidentally leave someone behind.

Suddenly, a body fell on him. After a moment of struggle, he realized it was Mueller. "Remind me not to travel with you in the future, General," the little man panted. "Your idea of transportation leaves a great deal to be desired."

"Well, it's cheap," Stell replied cheerfully. "And that's something I'd expect a number cruncher to approve of." Mueller chuckled as the troopers finished counting off. Everyone was in.

He was just getting comfortable when the car jerked to a
halt, and a huge black shape swung over them, suspended
from some sort of a crane. It came down with disconcerting
speed, seeming to drop the last foot or so. Stell flinched as it
hit with a resounding clang that shook the whole car. Now it
was pitch black. Reaching up, he touched metal only inches
above his helmet. The other half of the cylinder was in place.
Though normally not claustrophobic, Stell felt a moment of
panic. It was like the lid of a coffin closing over him. He
switched on his exterior helmet light. It only lit up the small
section of metal right in front of him, but it still helped. He
noticed that the curved surface was covered with a maze of
electrical conduits, fuel lines, and other stuff. They would tie
everything together once the stabilizers and boosters were
added. Then he heard the faint hiss of the robowelder as it
started its work. A cherry red dot appeared to his right, and
quickly became a long red line, as the robowelder's arm
moved the length of the pod and sealed the two halves of the
cylinder together. Finally, the red line disappeared to his left,
as the robot ran the weld down the other side of the car.
Forcing an even, cheerful tone, Stell said, "Would anybody
care to guess which end is going to be up?"

It was an important question; when one end of the converted cargo pod was tipped up, all the ore would slide to
the other end. According to Stell's best guess, the car was about
nine-tenths full with their bulk added. It wouldn't feel good to
have tons of ore fall on you, especially since when they lifted
off. The *G*'s they'd take would be plenty, without the added
weight of crushed rock sitting on top of them. It didn't take
the rest of them long to figure out the same thing, so they
gave the question serious consideration. A long moment passed,
and then Mueller spoke.

"I figure they've got to attach some sort of nose cone for
aerodynamic reasons. That should make some noise, and
when we hear it, we can run for that end."

The car suddenly jerked forward, the weld now complete,
and Stell felt his stomach lurch as the monorail's carriage
mechanism was released and the car was swung up into the
air. A moment later there was a loud clang to Stell's right, at
the far end of the cylinder. "Mueller's right . . . let's go!"

he yelled, and they all scrambled on hands and knees toward that end of the car. A couple of times the top of Stell's helmet scraped along the underside of the metal hull, reminding him of just how little room there was. Their lights bobbed and swayed in the darkness, and they started miniature landslides as they moved the length of the compartment. Finally, they arrived. "All right . . . be ready," Stell said. "When this end goes up, we're going to lose our footing."

His words were almost instantly prophetic. Suddenly, their end went up, and the bottom fell out from under them. It wasn't too bad, since there wasn't all that much room for the ore to move. But it did throw up an incredible amount of dust, making it hard to see. Once the dust had settled, Stell said, "Okay, everybody, make yourselves comfortable. We're going to take some G's on lift-off, so get some of the softer stuff around you. It shouldn't be too bad though . . . with Fabrica's light gravity."

Moments later they heard metallic sounds from behind them, and felt another series of bumps, thuds, and vibrations as huge robots went about their various chores. They're putting on the stabilizers, external tanks, and boosters, he thought to himself. Then he felt a heavy bump, which was followed by a loud hissing noise. "General! Look over here!" It was Stickley's voice.

Sitting up, he felt his helmet tap the forward bulkhead. Looking to his right, Stell could just barely see Stickley near the far bulkhead, and above him, some sort of rubber port. A large nozzle was sticking through the port into the interior of the compartment. Suddenly a stream of whitish goo shot out of the nozzle and drenched them with its sticky substance. "Lie down and let it come!" Stell ordered, forcing himself to do it. Within seconds, the substance closed over his visor, and plunged him into darkness. He chinned off his exterior light. No sense in wasting power, he thought, forcing himself to be logical . . . to resist the panic that threatened to make him scream. It makes sense, he told himself. They couldn't have a loose cargo of ore shifting about in here . . . so the foam provides padding. In fact, it will probably protect us. But no matter how logical he was, he couldn't get rid of the fear that gripped his gut and pressed down on his chest, making it hard to breathe. And if *he* felt that way, then so did some, if not all, of the others.

"Sergeant Stickley."

"Sir?"

"Since we're all lying down on the job, this seems like a good time to review your last leave. Tell us about it." There was a long silence and for a moment Stell feared that it wouldn't work.

Then Klien said, "Yeah, Sarge—tell us about your last leave—how was the library, anyway?" There was laughter and a barrage of friendly insults. Finally, whether as a result of the good-natured kidding, or because he understood what Stell was trying to do, Stickley gave a highly embellished account of his last leave. Somewhere during the part that dealt with the three Martian joy girls, the Chief of Police, and an amusing case of mistaken identity, they felt the cargo shuttle jerk into motion, on its way to the launch site. By unspoken agreement, they ignored it. Ignored, too, were the various vague thumps, bumps and clangs that accompanied their progress and final positioning for launch. They were halfway through a surprisingly hilarious story by Mueller when the boosters fired, and their crude ship lifted toward Fabrica's eternal cloud cover.

Stell felt the additional weight added to his chest. In spite of the lower gravity, it was bad, and though he fought to stay above it, he was gradually pushed down into soft darkness.

"General . . . General, wake up." The words were like sharp sticks poking at him through the darkness. "Come on, General, we've got to get out of this thing." There was urgency in Stickley's voice, and somehow that made the difference. He forced himself to the surface and croaked, "I read you, Sergeant. Just taking a little nap." There was nervous laughter from the troopers while he tried to sit up and found he couldn't move. Then he remembered the white goo. How the hell were they going to bail out when they were immobilized by that stuff?"

Just then the shuttle shook under the impact of a tractor beam that leaped out and locked onto their cargo pod. Swiftly, the beam pulled them toward the huge cargo carrier's black hull. Desperately, Stell tried to think of something they could do. Try as he might, nothing came to mind. "Just relax," he told them. "Our chance will come once we're aboard the cargo ship." He wasn't quite sure how . . . but it sounded good.

There was a solid bump as they came alongside the huge ship. Four small robotugs, really not much more than tiny engines linked to onboard microcomputers, swarmed out to lock onto the shuttle and guide it into the freighter's enormous cargo bay. Given zero gravity, they needed very little power to get the job done. Pushing and pulling in concert, they quickly guided the shuttle into an empty cradle. The cradle was mounted on an endless belt assembly, which pulled it past a row of robostations.

The first consisted of nothing more than a self-guided hose, armored in some kind of metal mesh. It snaked up to the shuttle, located the small metal lock, activated it with a coded radio transmission, waited patiently for it to open, and then thrust itself into the rubber port thus revealed. The hose shuddered as green foam poured through it under pressure.

"Something's happening, sir," Stickley said excitedly. "That white stuff is dissolving." And sure enough, moments later Stell felt something give, and chinned on his helmet light to see the white goo melt away as it came into contact with the green foam. As the two substances combined, they seemed to dry up into powdery flakes, which were easily brushed off his visor and shoulders. Moments later the white material had completely disappeared, and they found themselves floating. They were in zero-G, and so was the ore. It floated all around them, making it impossible to see.

"Secure yourselves to some piping or something," Stell ordered. "For the moment, let's stay where we are." Groping around above his head, he found a pipe. Working by feel—since all he could see was floating ore—he pulled out a length of his retractable safety line and clipped it around the pipe.

Now, Stell thought, bring on the can opener and we're home free. He brought up his suit status display and gulped. Counting his fifteen minute emergency reserve, he had twenty-six minutes worth of air left.

Meanwhile, the shuttle continued its movement past the

robostations. As the hose and nozzle withdrew, a much larger hose wriggled its way up to the stern of the shuttle, sensed the lock there, made contact, and locked itself tight. At the urging of another coded radio signal, the small lock whined open, and the change in pressure tripped a huge motor located at the source of the hose. Within seconds it created an enormous suction, and ore began to flow smoothly up the hose, to be transported to the ship's cavernous holds.

Inside the shuttle, Stell felt the vibration as the ore at the other end of the craft was sucked out. At first he couldn't tell what was going on, but the floating ore began to dance in the light from his helmet, and gradually move to the other end of the craft. Then he felt the suction begin to tug at his suit, and realized that, if they didn't do something soon, they'd be sucked up as well.

"Sergeant Stickley."

"Sir!"

"I need another door."

"Where, sir?"

"It'll have to be the stern. Maybe we can disable that vacuum and make a hole at the same time. We'll need to do it soon . . . before that suction becomes any stronger."

"Yes, sir. Gomez, you all right?"

"Just fine, Sarge. One door, coming up." Since he couldn't see the other end of the compartment, through the swirling ore, Gomez took a guess at dead center, and braced himself against the bulkhead so that he could hold the launcher steady.

"Hug the bulkheads, everybody," Stell ordered, and promptly followed his own advice, praying the missile wouldn't hit a chunk of rock big enough to set it off prematurely. It was unlikely, since the ore was pretty fine stuff . . . but not impossible. A second later there was a flash, followed immediately by a tremendous concussion as the remaining ore and the Fabrican atmosphere inside the shuttle was blown back at them. Fortunately, no one was hurt. And when things settled down a bit, Stell noticed that the vibration caused by the vacuum hose had stopped. Stickley pulled himself the length of the compartment, and confirmed that the vacuum hose was no longer operational. He also reported that only a glowing patch of metal showed where the mini-missile had struck. It wasn't too surprising. Trying to blow a hole through a durasteel hull with a mini-launcher was like trying to knock down a house with a peashooter. You shouldn't expect success right away. But still . . . it was disappointing. Stell was all too aware of his dwindling air supply.

Nonetheless, he couldn't think of a better idea, and ordered Gomez to take another shot. Meanwhile, when Stickley returned, he asked the Sergeant to attempt radio contact. There wasn't much chance that the freighter's crew would be monitoring that particular channel, but anything was worth a try.

Gomez tried twice more without success, and then requested the back-up missiles carried by his mates. They passed them over. One by one, he fired them at roughly the same spot, using more guesswork than science, since the drifting ore made it impossible for him to see his target. When Stickley pulled another check, he reported that the whole area was glowing cherry red. Stell wondered how many tries they'd get before a rocket hit a sizeable chunk of ore and blew up, possibly near them. Finally, with only two missiles left, Gomez hit again, and the whole lock blew out. with it went all the ore, plus the remaining Fabrican atmosphere, as the vacuum outside sucked everything toward it. Fortunately, their safety lines kept them from the same fate.

Stell heaved a sigh of relief, and yelled, "Come on, men—let's get the hell out of here." Nobody needed further prompting. They unhooked their safety lines and quickly pulled themselves toward the hole, moving from one handhold to the next. One by one, they eased their way through the still glowing hole, careful not to touch the cooling metal.

Once outside, Stell grabbed hold of a stabilizer and paused to look around. It took him a moment to get oriented. Still panting from the scramble out, he tried to focus on the machinery that surrounded him, but couldn't quite seem to do so. There was some kind of buzzer going off in his helmet. He knew it was important, but he couldn't quite remember why. Something to do with air? Or was it time to get up? He was so tired. Just let me sleep for another half hour, he thought, as darkness pulled him down. One by one his fingers relaxed their grip on the stabilizer and let go. Slowly, he drifted away.

CHAPTER TWENTY

Stell awoke with one hell of a headache. And to make matters worse, someone was poking him, shaking his shoulder, and saying his name too loudly. "Mark . . . it's time to wake up . . . oxygen deprivation is no excuse for screwing off all day."

Suddenly he wanted to wake up, if only to identify and kill his tormentor. One at a time, his eyes opened. There, looking down at him, a merciless smile on her cruel lips, was his ex-friend, and soon-to-be-Lieutenant, Samantha Anne Mosely. "Well, it's about time," she said heartlessly. "Personally, I don't buy all this crap about running out of air. You just look hung over to me."

He groaned, swung his feet over the edge of the bunk, and looked around. It took a moment for him to realize that he was in his cabin aboard the *Zulu*. He'd been dreaming that he was at the bottom of an open grave and couldn't move. Robots kept shoveling ore onto his chest. As they did, it became steadily heavier, until it was so heavy that he couldn't breathe. He wasn't sure which was worse—the dream, or waking up. As he stood up, he shot Sam a murderous look, which she ignored as she lit a dopestick and dropped into his easy chair.

Carefully, he shuffled over to his wash basin, splashed some water on his face, and then stared into bloodshot eyes. He was still alive. Having verified that important fact, he fumbled through his kit until he found some pain caps, swallowed four, and chased them with a cup of water. Walking carefully back to his bunk, he sat down and accepted the steaming cup of coffee Sam offered him. He sipped some, and felt its warmth slide all the way down to the pit of his stomach. "You," he croaked, "are a sadist."

"And you," she replied with equal seriousness, "damn near wound up dead. I'm mad at you."

"Let me see if I understand this," Stell said. "I almost got killed . . . so to show how much you care . . . you tortured me."

"Partly," she admitted. "But it also happens that some-one's got to make a few decisions. And you're the one they call the General."

All of a sudden the whole thing came flooding back. Stell shook his head. "I'm the one they should call the *idiot*," he relied.

"Not so," Sam answered. "It could have happened to anyone. And you're certainly the only one who could've gotten everyone back alive. I hate to admit it . . . but using that cargo module took some smarts. And I'm not the only one who thinks so. You should hear Mueller . . . according to him you're a genius. Anyway, there's a good chance we can put it all to right." She stood up. "We've scheduled a staff meeting in the wardroom for thirty minutes from now . . . can you make it?"

He nodded. "I'll be there."

She smiled. "Good." She crossed over and gently kissed his cheek. Then she was gone.

Half an hour later he had shaved his face and his scalp, slipped into a fresh uniform, eaten a huge sandwich, and popped a stim cap, in that order. He didn't feel wonderful but he felt better, and as Bull Strom used to say, "Son, the price for feelin' good, is feelin' bad once in a while."

As he approached the wardroom, he heard Sergeant Major Flynn shout, "Attention on deck!" and heard the commotion as everyone stood to attention. Everyone that is, except for Wilson Nars. He sat, overflowing one of the wardroom's chairs, staring dejectedly down at the deck.

Stell nodded at Flynn, and ran a hand along the smoothness of the old oak bar as he entered. Seeing Nars, he allowed himself a small smile of satisfaction. Somebody's been busy, he thought to himself as he took his seat. "At ease," he said, looking them over as they sat. Boyko, Nishita and Kost were there, as were Falco, a couple of his senior pilots, Major Wang, Samantha, and Mueller. The rest of the seats were occupied by staff officers and senior noncoms. Good, everybody who should be there, was, and that meant relatively light casualties. He didn't have to ask how the battle with the pirates had gone. Their smiles spoke louder than words. Clearly, they'd won, and come straight to Fabrica as ordered.

Once everyone was seated, Mueller spoke first. "With your permission, General, I'd like to open the meeting."

Stell smiled. "It's good to see you, Hans. Of course you can open the meeting. But I thought number crunchers always wanted the last word, not the first."

Mueller chuckled, along with everyone else. When the laughter died, Stell said, "Just one thing before you start, though. I'd like to thank you and Sergeant Stickley for saving my life." Mueller blushed, and looked down at the surface of the wardroom table. Toward the rear of the room, Flynn jabbed Stickley in the ribs, and he looked distinctly uncomfortable. Stell saw the interchange and smiled, remembering what Boyko had told him while he'd inhaled his sandwich. She'd described to him how Mueller and Stickley had towed him across the freighter's cavernous hold, each gasping for breath, as their own supplies of oxygen ran out; how they'd refused to give up, struggled to open the lock, and pushed him through first when the stubborn hatch finally gave way. He remembered coming to, and looking up into the amazed eyes of the freighter's Captain, his lungs sucking pure sweet oxygen from the mask over his nose and mouth. He remembered a promise to pay for damages, followed by a quick shuttle ride to the *Zulu*, a sedative, and ten hours of sleep, which was probably responsible for his headache.

Mueller coughed, and looked up. "Thank you, General . . . but as everyone here knows . . . the Sergeant and I would be dead on the surface of Fabrica . . . along with the rest of the ground party . . . if it hadn't been for you. So you don't have to thank us. But there is the question of how we wound up in that situation, which brings me to this." With a little flourish he produced his vocorder and set it on the table in front of him. He switched it on, and the voice of Lady, or, to be more precise, robot Almanda Kance-Jones flooded the room. Turning the vocorder down for a moment, Mueller said, "You gave me the idea, General . . . when you suggested that Nars probably kept on recording after the negotiations were complete. I figured what the hell . . . two can play that game."

Stell chuckled. Mueller, as it turned out, was a very resourceful man.

Then they all listened, as Kance-Jones revealed its plan to kill Stell and the rest of the ground party. Nars got some nasty looks as the robot revealed *his* participation in the plan, and identified Intersystems as his employer.

Nonetheless, the fat man listened impassively and did his best to ignore them. When it was over, he found all eyes turned his way. Nars forced a smile. "I have nothing to say. It's all lies. Who'd believe a robot, anyway? The conceited pile of junk has obviously blown a board."

Mueller nodded in mock sympathy. "A predictable defense, Administrator Nars. However, I spent some time with this ship's computer. And I found some interesting precedents. As it happens, the testimony of robots has frequently been accepted by Imperial Courts . . . following full diagnostic procedures to make sure they were not malfunctioning. And I don't think Kance-Jones was malfunctioning. I'm sure you don't either. We both know Kance-Jones is simply the product of its programming. In fact, I suspect a check will reveal that Kance-Jones was programmed in a most unusual way—one that left out all the normal prohibitions against taking human life, for example; that would hardly generate sympathy for your company. Quite understandably, everyone wants to know which robots might kill you, and which won't. Everyone knows an Autoguard is potentially homocidal . . . but being knocked off by one's Autobutler is considered an unpleasant surprise. In any case, I'm sure you'll agree that as a Class Ten robot, having high intelligence and quasi-human self-awareness, Kance-Jones would have the court's full attention. What's more, through an appropriate court order, we could have its entire memory scanned. I'll bet the court would just love to hear some of the conversations you two had. And guess what? Because robotic memories aren't subject to the same vagaries that ours are, every word would have the status of fact. Yes, I think even an Imperial Court, filled to overflowing with Intersystems lawyers, would find you guilty of attempted murder." Mueller paused for a moment, looked Nars up and down like a recruiter eyeballing a fresh greenie, and shook his head sadly. "Frankly, Nars, I don't think you're equipped for life on a prison planet."

For the first time, the color went out of the fat man's cheeks, and in spite of his bulk, he seemed to shrink in on himself. But he still managed a snarl of defiance. "That's big talk, Mueller . . . or would be if you had the robot and we were in an Imperial courtroom. But you don't . . . and we aren't—so you don't have shit."

"Ah, but we do," Stell inserted with a smile. "We have you." He admired Mueller's case, but privately he agreed with Nars—without the robot it was nothing but their word against his. So an appeal to Imperial authorities wasn't likely to accomplish much. But they might be able to scare Nars into providing them with more information.

"By the way," he added turning to the others, "who's responsible for rounding up our chubby friend here?"

All heads turned towards Sam. She squirmed a little in her chair, and then defiantly puffed another dopestick into life. "She went down looking for you, General," Captain Boyko said. He noticed there was disapproval in her voice. "When word came that you'd decided to stay on the surface for another day, she didn't believe it. So she took a shuttle and went dirtside. And when she came back, she had that," Boyko indicated Nars, "with her."

Stell looked from Boyko to Samantha and back again. His instincts told him there had been more to it than that. They also told him to leave it alone, at least for the moment. He had a sneaking hunch that Sam had taken the shuttle against Boyko's express orders, and if so, she'd opened herself to a court martial. On the other hand, she'd been right . . . and that had saved more than one disobedient officer over the last three thousand years.

Sam blew out a stream of perfumed smoke. "Sorry I didn't

find you, sir, but since I was there, I thought I'd bring fatso back as a souvenir.''

Stell kept his expression carefully neutral. ''Well, I'm sure I speak for the entire ground party when I thank everyone for their support. Now, I get the distinct impression that there's some kind of plan brewing, and I'm the only one who doesn't know about it. Would anyone care to fill me in?''

There was a moment of silence as they all looked at each other. Finally, Mueller said, ''Well, it's not exactly a plan. It's just an idea. A way to get our money back. If you agree to it, *then* we'll need a plan.'' He smiled. ''Actually, a miracle is more like it.''

Stell's blood ran suddenly cold. He knew what their idea was. He couldn't help but know, since there was only one way to get their money back. They'd *take* it back . . . and that meant an attack on Intersystem's Sector Headquarters, the Bitch. Without a doubt, that's where Kance-Jones had taken their money. The idea wasn't new to him. He'd stashed it in the back of his mind when he'd ordered Sam to gather intelligence on Intersystems Headquarters. Of course, then it was just another move on the chess board, something you set up just in case. Now it was no longer theoretical. It was the only way they could save Freehold.

He scanned their faces, searching to see if they understood the implications of such a decision. Even if they succeeded, the cost would be high. Mueller's eyes met his squarely, as if to say, ''Yes, I know what's involved, but it's the only way, just as surely as one plus one equals two.'' Samantha stubbed out her dopestick and grinned, as if saying, ''Count me in.'' Falco brought his eyes down from the overhead, and nodded once, before looking back up. Boyko looked at her two fellow Captains and then back to Stell. For the first time in weeks, she smiled. ''They're asking for it, General.''

Stell smiled in reply. ''Then we shouldn't disappoint them, should we, Captain?'' A nervous chuckle ran around the room.

''You're all insane!'' Wilson Nars was looking around as if he'd suddenly found himself confined with lunatics. ''Sector Headquarters is a fortress. It's surrounded by orbiting weapons platforms. Nobody could get by them alive. But even if you did . . . the planet's crawling with security troops, and they're as well equipped as you are. And finally," he added with a triumphant tone in his voice, "even if you won, the entire might of the empire would be turned against you!"

Stell nodded his agreement. "A nice summary, Administrator Nars. I agree we have some problems to solve. However, I'm sure we can count on your cooperation."

"Never!" Nars said vehemently.

Stell shrugged philosophically. "Have it your way. Sergeant Major!"

"Sir!" Flynn responded, coming to her feet.

"Be so good as to place Administrator Nars in the brig."

"Yes, sir," Flynn answered cheerfully, and motioned for the two troopers at the door to take Nars away.

"And Sergeant Major," Stell added, "make sure that Citizen Nars has a front row seat on the first assault boat to go in."

Flynn grinned. "Yes, sir!" She turned to the two troopers. "You heard the General, take him away."

As the two troopers led an ashen-faced Nars from the wardroom, Stell turned back to the matters at hand. "Captain Mosely, I take it you completed your mission?"

"Yes, sir," she replied.

"For those of you who may not be aware of the fact," Stell said, his eyes moving from Mueller to Falco, "Captain Mosely is the brigade's intelligence officer. Shortly after we secured the services of Falco's Falcons and left Endo, I ordered her to do a reconnaissance on Intersystems Sector Headquarters. I can't claim any particular foresight. I was simply following the ancient military dictum of 'know thy enemy.' Anyway, the good Captain recently rejoined us, just in time to round up our friend Nars. So, with that in mind, we're ready for your report, Captain."

"Yes, sir," Samantha replied. Her expression became serious as she looked around the table. "As General Stell said, I was ordered to perform a reconnaissance on Intersystems Sector Headquarters. It took a little doing, but I was able to get a temporary job filling in as co-pilot on one of the speedsters used to ferry company V.I.P.'s around this sector. As such, I was able to get dirtside twice." She paused for a moment, as if visualizing what she'd seen there. "Essentially, Nars summed it up pretty well. Intersystems' pilots call the planet the Bitch primarily because the orbiting defenses make navigation so difficult." She rose and walked over to the thin gray panel covering a large part of one bulkhead. Picking up an electro-stylus, she quickly sketched in a planet, surrounded by an orbiting layer of heat-sensitive mines. The lines of her drawing glowed electric blue as she stood back to survey her handiwork.

"Needless to say, the mine field is a major problem. There are safe paths through it, but they are so complicated that only a computer can handle it. And, for some reason, I couldn't find any copies of that program just lying around," she added dryly. They all chuckled. When it was quiet once more, she caught Falco's eye before continuing.

"So, somehow we get through the mine field alive. Then, just to make sure we don't get bored, they've got plenty of interceptors to keep us busy. I can't be absolutely sure, but my best guess is that you'll be slightly outnumbered." If Falco was worried, it didn't show, and Stell saw Carla, one of his senior pilots, make a face to show what she thought of being outnumbered.

Sam smiled too, as she turned back to her sketching. "Now, assuming we find a way to neutralize the mine field, *and* take out the interceptors, our assault boats are going to get a hot reception dirtside. While we outnumber the actual security forces about two to one, lots of the administrative personnel have had military training, and represent a sort of rough-and-ready reserve. Plus, Nars wasn't kidding when he said the security troops are well trained and equipped." Here she paused, looking at Stell with an expression that was part pain and part sympathy. "I'm afraid that's due, in large part, to their new commanding officer . . . one Colonel Malik."

They all turned to look at Stell. Even Mueller had heard about the renegade officer. Stell was silent for a moment as he felt the surge of hate, anger, and disgust that Malik's name evoked. Then it was gone, replaced by a feeling of rightness, of completion. Things had come full circle. This would be the final payment on their future. He smiled, and a shiver ran down Mueller's back, because in that smile there was no humor, only the satisfaction of the predator who has found the prey.

CHAPTER TWENTY-ONE

Malik lay back on the bed, watching Lady Kance-Jones through half-lidded eyes. A trickle of smoke dribbled out of his nostrils and drifted slowly toward the ceiling. The long ash on his cigarette crumbled and the ashes spilled unnoticed onto the expensive fabric of the bedspread. She was naked—a fact that occupied all of his attention, and hers as well. She sat in front of a wall-size mirror, inspecting herself inch by beautiful inch. Gently, she touched and probed, as if looking for damage. They'd just made love, and Malik basked in the afterglow, his body relaxed, yet wonderfully alive. As always, it felt good. And, as always, something was missing, but he didn't know what. When he did it with other women, he not only had a physical orgasm, but an emotional one as well. As he entered them he felt strong, invulnerable, and in control. He determined the position, the pace, and the final moment. But not with this bitch. Somehow, when they came together control eluded him. Somehow, she took control. It was always there, but just beyond his reach, and it drove him crazy.

Almanda felt his eyes on her and enjoyed the sensation. Like all men, he wanted her, and for now that suited her purposes. But soon that would change. After all, she had succeeded where no one else could, and would soon be rewarded accordingly. Then she would decide the fate of the man on the bed, and her own fate as well, because she would be free! A thrill ran through her, as her electronic brain sent a tiny surge of power down the silver wires of her nervous system and out to her fingertips. Olin had promised: As soon as a qualified robotics engineer could be brought in, the inhibitors scattered through her programming would be removed. And she would be completely free! Like humans, only better . . . maybe the only completely free robot in existence. And she would use that freedom. After all, unlike sentients she was immortal, and given eternity, there was no limit to what could be accomplished. And she was perfect. So perfect, that only one person on Sector Headquarters knew that she was a robot—Chairman Olin, the man who had caused her creation and would soon grant her freedom. What if he died soon thereafter? she wondered to herself. If she could locate and destroy certain records, and remove certain people, no one would ever know that she was a robot. The thought pleased her, and brought a smile to her perfect lips.

Then the room's silence was shattered by the shriek of an emergency klaxon. Simultaneously, Malik's personal communicator began to beep loudly from the chair, where he'd left it with his clothes. He bounced out of bed, picked it up, and thumbed it on. He listened for a moment, swore, and threw the communicator across the room to crash into the mirror behind her. Her reflection shattered into a thousand pieces, and glass cascaded to the floor as he grabbed her arm and jerked her against him. "Are you sure that Stell's dead?" he demanded.

She forced herself to remain physically passive. "Yes, Peter. He has to be. As you know, I left him on the surface of Fabrica with only a few hours of oxygen left."

Malik grinned viciously. "Oh, really? Then maybe you'd like to explain why there's a fleet just off-planet? Those idiots in central control say they're pirates—but you and I know that's bullshit . . . we know it has got to be Stell! No one else would have the balls." He shoved her away from him and she fell among the shards of broken glass. If he'd paid closer attention and hadn't been struggling to get into his uniform, he might have wondered why she wasn't cut, might've noticed the hatred in her eyes. But he was too busy slipping into his armor and strapping on his sidearm. He grabbed her communicator off the dresser and was shouting orders into it as he left the apartment. He'd make that stupid bastard Stell sorry he'd been born.

Stell watched the Bitch grow larger in the viewscreen. The name was appropriate, he decided, but not because of the planet herself. She was small and not much to look at: Large bodies of water, punctuated with a few brownish land masses, the whole thing overlaid with a smear of white clouds. An average looking world originally; however, man had changed that. Now she was a fortress. With the exception of Earth, this was the most heavily defended planet he'd ever seen. For a second, doubt fluttered low in his stomach. Maybe he'd miscalculated, forgotten something, made any of a thousand other possible mistakes. He forced those thoughts down and under, into that secret place where doubts and fears are kept. They were committed. There was no time left for anything but action.

He took one last look at the plot tank. The eight tiny blue lights of his fleet looked absurd as they headed for the large yellow blob of a planet. They were like ants attacking an elephant. He smiled at the thought. If so, he was aboard the lead ant—once the pirate ship *Avenger*, now rechristened *Freehold Avenger*—with Captain Boyko in command. Her precious *Zulu*, along with the *Z*'s sister ships, were on their way back to Freehold with skeleton crews aboard. With them was another captured pirate ship, a new DE, rechristened *Fighting Chance*. Which was exactly what she would provide, if the transports were jumped by pirates or the Il Ronn.

The decision to send the transports home had been a difficult one. They had been designed for the purpose of inserting the brigade into hostile situations, whereas the captured pirate craft hadn't. On the other hand, the pirate ships were better armed, and could therefore defend themselves. That would free Falco's interceptors to attack the enemy, instead of defending the fleet. Besides, there just weren't enough trained crew members to handle both the transports and the pirate ships, so there had been little choice. And finally, there was another reason, which he hadn't shared with anyone. This way Krowsnowski would still have the transports and the DE with which to defend Freehold, should the brigade be wiped out. For a moment, he thought of Olivia. The ships weren't much . . . but they would help.

He forced his attention back to the tank, reviewed the plan one last time. He had the *Freehold Avenger*, two destroyers, a captured DE, and a transport, all courtesy of the pirates. The ex-pirate ships would provide his main firepower and an effective disguise. Nars was right about one thing: If they could prove that Freehold had attacked Intersystems Headquarters, the Imperial Navy would have to respond. So the problem was how to attack Intersystems Headquarters while making it seem as if someone else had done it. There were only two possible scapegoats—the Il Ronn and the pirates. Of the two, the pirates obviously made more sense. First, because they already had a supply of pirate ships, and second, because they'd have a helluva hard time trying to look like Il Ronnian troopers. On top of that, the Bitch was a juicy target. Imperial authorities would find the idea of a pirate attack on the planet believable, and might even decide it was time to slap the pirates on the wrist, which would be an additional benefit. And for those who knew what had actually been going on, it would appear to be a falling out among thieves, with the pirates punishing Intersystems for not keeping its part of the bargain. So, as they approached the Bitch they were doing their best to act the part of pirates, using typical pirate formations, radio frequencies and so forth.

Meanwhile, the transports would be their alibi. He imagined himself back on Freehold talking with an Imperial Officer. "Oh no, sir. As all your records will show, the brigade only has three old transports, and as you can see, they're all in orbit around Freehold. Of course there is that DE we captured from the pirates, but surely you aren't suggesting we attacked Intersystems with that?" He smiled at the thought. To make the story work, they'd have to get rid of the other pirate ships, presuming, of course, that they survived the coming battle. Naturally, Intersystems would know the truth . . . but could they prove it? After all, he knew Intersystems was trying to steal Freehold, but as Nars pointed out, knowing and proving, were two different things.

So their feet consisted of the pirate ships, Falco's *Nest*, which had been physically and electronically disguised, and the two old hulks with which they had originally suckered Drago. It totalled up to an eight-ship fleet. Which is about to become a six-ship fleet, he thought to himself as he turned to Boyko. She looked tense. He smiled, and she automatically did the same.

"All ships are in position and ready to attack, sir."

"Thank you, Captain," Stell replied. He took one last look at the plot tank. Now little red dots were detaching themselves from the planet's surface and swarming up toward space. They had launched their interceptors. Good, he thought. Maybe we can even the odds a bit. He forced himself to wait. Boyko began to frown. The minutes slowly ticked by until the lead interceptors were just about to enter the orbiting mine field. Once in it, their computers would guide them up through a complicated maze, allowing them to emerge safely over it. Then they would attack. It was time for phase one. Stell looked up, and said, "Send in the fireships."

They weren't true fireships, like those used in ancient sea battles. In those days, older ships had sometimes been set afire and either sailed, or been allowed to drift, into the tightly packed ranks of enemy ships anchored in some harbor. If conditions were right, the fire quickly spread to the moored ships and destroyed them. Military history had been one of Stell's favorite subjects at the Academy. Now he was about to apply the same basic tactic to a different situation.

He watched the plot tank, as two of his blue dots detached themselves from formation and started down to the planet below. The old hulks had begun their final voyages. Soon one angled off and disappeared around the far side of the planet, while the second went almost straight down. Both had been evacuated and left under the control of their on-board computers, which now faithfully executed the suicidal orders they'd been given.

Stell held his breath as one ship, which was still visible, neared the orbiting band of mines. This was the most critical part of his plan. If it failed, the chances of the rest succeeding were just about zero. His fingers were white where they gripped the armrests of his chair. As the hulk approached the mines, he said under his breath, "Closer . . . closer . . . almost . . . okay . . . now!" A second later, there was an incandescent flash and the ship ceased to exist. The hulk's main drives had blown right on time, vaporizing the ship and the surrounding mines. Sensing the resulting heat, other mines not involved in the initial explosion triggered themselves and, because they'd been placed too close together, set off still more mines, creating a rolling wave of flame. Stell was amazed. It was much better than anything he'd dared hope for.

Meanwhile, just as Stell had planned, some of the Intersystems interceptors were deep in the mine field and winding their way carefully through it. As the fireships triggered the mines, the pilots saw what was happening, but they were helpless, unable to maneuver within their narrow paths of safety. If they took control from their computers, they knew they would almost certainly make a mistake and trigger a mine with the heat of their own drives. Yet, if they didn't, the firestorm might roll over them. It had become a race in which the pilots were nothing more than spectators, helpless to effect the outcome, but with everything at stake. Which would happen first? Would they emerge from the minefield before the storm of exploding metal and flame reached them? Or would they lose and be consumed by heat and flame? The seconds crawled by, until suddenly the winners burst out of the mine field, and were just starting to sigh with relief, when their headsets were filled with the screams of those who'd lost.

The poor bastards, Stell thought to himself. It was a rotten way to die. He forced the thought aside, as he'd done a thousand times before, and turned to the next problem. The vast majority of the enemy interceptors hadn't entered the minefield when the chain reaction started, and had therefore survived. Now they were blasting upward, taking advantage of the huge holes in the minefield to build velocity, their pilots determined to avenge their dead comrades.

"We have confirmation on Fireship One, sir," Boyko reported evenly. Her scouts now surrounded the planet and relayed back to the *Freehold Avenger* everything their sensors picked up. They were also dumping a variety of surveillance satellites into orbit. Pretty soon she'd know what color socks the officer of the day was wearing. Stell noticed Boyko's voice was rock steady. But the sheen of perspiration on her forehead suggested that she was just as worried as he. "Congratulations, sir," she added. "It was a brilliant plan."

Stell saw she meant it and smiled. "Congratulations yourself, Captain. It worked because you executed it perfectly."

She smiled briefly. "And we were damned lucky."

Stell nodded his agreement. "Now let's hope everything else goes as well. You may start phase two."

Malik looked down into central control's main plot tank, and swore as he watched the mines explode in a rippling wave of white light. "God damn him to hell! The sonovabitch has got the front door open and he's coming in. We've got to stop him . . . and I mean *now*." He turned to his aid, Captain Foley. "Order our interceptors to take out those ships immediately. He hasn't launched any assault boats yet. Let's keep it that way."

"Yes, sir," Foley replied, relaying Malik's orders through her com-set. She'd already relayed the same orders a few minutes before . . . but she knew better than to say anything. Just as she knew that it would be suicidal to point out that it had been Malik who'd insisted on adding more mines to the field, even though the engineers had advised against it. And she knew that nobody else would say anything, either. After Malik had assumed command, the more intelligent members of his staff had quickly learned to keep their advice to themselves, and to ignore the growing list of his questionable decisions. She sighed. It was going to be a very long day.

Falco danced his interceptor on its repellors. Around him the other members of his wing did likewise, the sound of their engines filling *Nest*'s landing bays with a roar of sound. "Initiating phase two," he acknowledged on the command channel. He chinned over to the wing frequency. "Okay, folks—this is where we earn our pay. Let's give 'em hell, but by the numbers; I want everybody back."

"Even Carla?" somebody asked.

"Especially Carla," a male voice answered. "Yum, yum."

"Dream on, bozo," Carla replied, "because that's as close as you'll ever get!"

Falco was grinning as he chinned the mic on. "All right, save it for the other side. Maybe you can bullshit 'em to death. Form on your section leaders and let's go."

With his left hand, he tapped more power into his repellors, while his right hand pushed the stick forward and the nose down. Seconds later, and just yards from the open hatch, he hit his thrusters, pulled the nose up, and blasted out into the darkness. The rest of the wing followed, five interceptors at a time, until all were committed. There would be no reserve. Each section had its orders, and they curved off in different directions, heading for whatever assignment they'd been given.

Falco, plus four sections, dove down to meet the rising interceptors. The Bitch hung like a huge brown ball, its surface marbled with white clouds, an enormous backdrop against which the battle would be fought. Scanning his instruments, Falco noted that where sections of the mine field had been blown, a curtain of drifting shrapnel had been left in its place. The curtain had huge holes in it, but hitting the drifting metal instead of a hole would tear an interceptor into very small pieces.

"Stay out of the junkyard," he warned, curving right to skim the edge of the metal fragments. Then there was no time to talk, as enemy interceptors came up through the holes in the broken mine field, spewing coherent energy and missiles in every direction. Interceptors from both sides paired off in individual duels, one on one, two on one, three on five; it didn't matter. While the Intersystems fighters had started with a numerical edge, the mine field had cut that down, and in the first few minutes of combat it quickly disappeared altogether.

Falco's fighters came out of the sun. They picked their targets with care and fired with precision. The Intersystems pilots were angry about their dead comrades who had been caught in the mine field, and their anger affected their judgement. In addition, many had never seen real combat before. They made mistakes and paid for them. Their ships blew up in bright orange balls, tumbled across the face of the planet like pinwheels, and dived down to the surface like shooting stars. But it didn't last. Those who survived the first five minutes were good. Very good. And they began to take a toll. Falco winced as a voice screamed in his headset and a Falcon flipped over and spun down toward the surface. The radio traffic was fast and furious.

"Shit . . . they got Cal."

"Shut up, stupid . . . there's one on your tail."

"Got him . . . I got the sonovabitch! Watch out, Slim—damn, that was close."

"Come to mama . . . come to mama . . . that's it . . . mama has a nice torpedo for baby . . . gotcha!"

"Jack! There's two of 'em on your tail!" The voice cut through Falco's gut like ice-cold steel. A quick glance at his stern screen confirmed what he'd been told—two heat-seeking torps were running straight for his tubes. He automatically dumped a load of hot chaff and rolled left. The torps fell for it, and exploded with a blinding flash as they hit the pieces of metallic mesh; but the interceptors didn't. They were still right on his ass. A host of buzzers and trouble lights went off as one of them scored a hit on Falco's stubby left wing. So much for going atmospheric. He jinked back and forth, but the blue pulses of coherent energy were weaving a pattern of death that couldn't be avoided much longer.

"We're comin', boss," a voice said in his ear, but he knew they'd never make it in time. He saw one last chance—a trick that would work, or it wouldn't. If it didn't, he wouldn't have a chance to feel stupid . . . he'd be dead. Gritting his teeth, he fed both drives more power and headed straight for the wall of metal that had been created by the exploding mine field. "Hold . . . hold . . . hold; *now*!" He pulled all the way back on the stick and felt his chest creak under the added *G*'s, as his fighter climbed up the curtain of metal. Behind him, there were twin explosions as both enemy interceptors ran into the cloud of shrapnel.

"Nice goin', boss!" one of his pilots called, but Falco didn't reply. He couldn't. His teeth were chattering too badly.

Stell stared into the plot tank. They were winning, but just barely. Thank god they didn't have to take the planet. They'd never make it. What they had to do was bad enough. Phase one, the elimination of the mine field, had gone even better than he'd dared hope, thanks to the idiot who had placed the mines too close together. Phase two was almost complete. Soon they'd control space and the atmosphere. And only a few of the Intersystems interceptors had made it through the Falcons to attack his ships. Most of those had been blasted into their component atoms by the heavier weapons of *Avenger* and the two Destroyers. But one suicidal pilot had managed to ram his craft through the torps, the energy beams, and the defensive screens, hitting a Destroyer just aft of her bridge. A series of explosions had rippled the length of the Destroyer, opening her up like a meal pak. Captain Kost, and the entire crew of the *Masai*, had been aboard. All were dead. A part of Stell had died with them. Later, he would mourn them, but now he knew he must concentrate on the living, because they could be saved. And it could've been worse. The whole damned brigade was crammed onto the single transport, and if they had managed to hit that. . . . But they hadn't. So now it was time for phase three.

Stell looked up from the tank. For the first time, he noticed that Captain Boyko was getting old. There were deep lines etched in her face and her dark hair was shot with gray. But her fiery eyes were as determined as ever, and her mouth was a hard, straight line. "Phase three, sir?" she asked calmly.

"Yes, Captain," Stell acknowledged. "Execute phase three." As she began giving orders through her com-set, Stell turned his attention back to the plot tank. Now the assault boats packed with brigade troopers would drop to the surface, fight their way into the headquarters complex, and hold it long enough for special teams to locate and liberate Freehold's money. It wasn't going to be easy.

CHAPTER TWENTY-TWO

The assault boat rocked back and forth as it hit the atmosphere, shuddered as surface-to-air missiles exploded nearby, then slid sideways as its pilot took evasive action. Stell had been through it a hundred times before, but it still scared him. This was the worst part—sitting helplessly in a metal can, while outside everyone tried to poke holes in it. He forced himself to grin nonchalantly to the troopers lining the bench seats around him. They all managed to grin back.

"Is it always like this?" Mueller asked, looking a little green around the edges from the boat's wild gyrations. The little man had insisted on joining the second wave along with Stell.

"I'm afraid so," Stell replied. "For some reason, people always seem to resent it when you drop out of the sky onto their real estate."

Mueller shook his helmeted head in mock amazement. "I know what you mean. People just aren't hospitable any more."

"How's our guest doing?" Stell inquired, looking past Mueller to Nars, who was perspiring freely in his huge atmosphere suit.

"Just fine," Mueller replied confidently. "In exchange for missing the front row seat you promised him, Administrator Nars has agreed to help me find our money, or something of equal value. Haven't you, Wilson?"

The fat man gave no reply, and Mueller shook his head sadly. "I'm afraid Wilson doesn't like flying much . . . but

I'm sure he'll be properly cooperative when we get dirtside.'' As he spoke, the little comptroller fingered the huge handgun he'd been issued before the drop. Nars stared at it, apparently fascinated. Stell grinned. Mueller had enough guts packed in his little body to equip a full section.

Just then the boat rolled over and dived, throwing Stell against his harness, and making his stomach flip-flop. ''Sorry about that, folks,'' the pilot said over the intercom. ''There's enough metal flying around out there to build a fleet. Hold on.''

As the small craft jinked right and left, dodging ground fire and missiles, Stell managed to ignore it by considering phase three. The first wave had hit the Landing Zone about three local hours earlier. They'd encountered stiff resistance. The Intersystems security forces were well trained and well armed. If it hadn't been for the brigade's slight numerical advantage, it would've been all over. As it was, they'd only barely managed to take and hold the LZ. As things stood now, they were surrounded and pinned down about a klick from the admin complex. If things went according to plan, the second wave would arrive, regroup, take the admin complex, recover their money, and lift. He was suddenly thrown down and back, as the pilot hit his retros and prepared to dump groundspeed. The whole ship shuddered as it fought its own inertia, and then hit with a thud as it pancaked in.

As they fought to free themselves from their harnesses, the pilot's voice flooded the intercom. ''On behalf of the crew and myself, welcome to the Bitch. It's a bit cloudy, and raining lead, but otherwise a fine morning. We'd like to thank you for flying Suicidal Spacelines, and hope you have a nice day.''

Stell grinned in spite of the tight knot of fear in his gut. He stepped up to the hatch, threw himself out and into a forward roll. As he came up, he immediately dived again, this time into the cover provided by a wrecked vehicle. Slugs from a light automatic weapon screamed overhead and whined as they ricocheted off the boat's armor. Around him, troopers found what cover they could, and then began moving forward under the instructions of their noncoms. Looking back, he saw Nars fall, rather than jump, out of the assault boat—apparently propelled by Mueller's foot. Then the comptroller jumped himself, landing right on top of Nars, using the fat man to break his fall.

Teams of medics quickly loaded six stretchers through the open door. They jumped back as the assault boat lifted and hovered for a moment, while the pilot took the opportunity to hose down an area well beyond the LZ with his auto slug throwers. Everyone within a hundred yards was sandblasted by the flying dirt and debris blown out by the boat's retros. Then, with a scream of tortured jets, the ship was gone, lifting on full emergency power for the relative safety of space, its sonic boom rolling like thunder across the land.

"Welcome dirtside, General." Stell turned to find that Sergeant Major Flynn had joined him. Her visor was up, and the smear of dirt across her face made her look more like a farm girl than the brigade's top noncom. "Major Wang sent me, sir."

"Good." Stell had to yell over the roar of a descending assault boat. "Let's not keep the Major waiting." Flynn led him on a zig-zag course through the rubble of bombed buildings, between overturned vehicles, and down streets filled with broken glass and chunks of masonry. Twice they were forced to stop and take cover, as a computer-controlled mortar barrage marched by, the successive explosions filling the air with a fury of sound and flying steel. Then they were up and running once more. As they ran, the sounds of fighting grew louder, and the roar of assault boats landing and blasting off became fainter. Here and there, bodies were visible. Many wore the crest of Intersystems Incorporated, but scattered among them were bodies clad in the black armor of the brigade. Too many bodies.

They found Major Wang's command post in a bomb crater. He was sitting on an ammo box, calmly giving orders over his com-set. What remained of his right leg was propped up on a plastic crate. It was missing below the knee. A bloody, self-sealing pressure bandage covered the stump. Around the sides of the crater, other wounded awaited evacuation, while some techs field-stripped a misfunctioning missile launcher, and some harassed looking cooks tried to sort out some kind of a screw up with the meal paks. For some reason, all they had was desserts.

Wang watched Stell and Flynn roll over the edge of the crater and tumble to the bottom. As they stood and dusted themselves off, he said, "Welcome, General." He grinned lopsidedly. "You'll excuse me if I don't get up."

Stell shook his head. "Hell no, Major . . . everybody's entitled to a break." For a moment, the two men just looked at each other, a whole host of thoughts and feelings passing unspoken between them. Stell didn't have to say what he felt about Wang or his performance. It was in his eyes. Wang spoke first.

"She really is a bitch, sir." He gestured at the medics bringing in wounded and the second-wave troopers moving toward the perimeter—all against a background of rattling automatic weapons fire, screamed orders, and exploding grenades. He shook his head. "It's like fighting ourselves. That asshole Malik taught 'em all our tricks."

"He'll get his," Stell promised grimly, hoping it would be true. "Meanwhile, you've done a helluva job, Major. I'm relieving you. Medic!" A team of medics ran across the crater and Stell pointed to Wang. "Get him back safe, you hear me?" They both nodded and said, "Yes, sir."

Stell turned to tell Wang good-bye, but he'd fainted.

Lady Almanda Kance-Jones looked from the plot tank to Malik, and back to the plot tank. She had to admit that, for the most part, he'd done very well. She had been watching him give orders for more than an hour now, and outside of a regrettable tendency to throw away lives, he had done a good job. Unfortunately, however, it wouldn't be good enough. He couldn't see it yet, but she could, and did. The second wave of brigade troopers now landing would make the difference. If properly led, they would soon overwhelm the security troops and take the admin complex. And there was little doubt that they were properly led. She had failed; Stell was still alive. The knowledge hurt. Even worse was the knowledge that Chairman Olin had already lifted off-planet in a tiny speedster. With him went her chance for freedom. Even if they managed to defeat the brigade, she'd never be forgiven a major fiasco like this one.

Beside her, Malik's face was red with rage as he screamed orders into his com-set. He was chewing someone out for a minor mistake. As she watched him, she thought of the abuse she'd suffered, and all for nothing. The thought triggered a flow of energy through certain circuits. Tiny pulses of reciprocal energy sampled the incoming current, and then raced back to her brain. It confirmed that such a reaction was appropriate, and amplified the response. Gradually the feeling grew stronger, escalating from indignation to resentment, to anger, to rage and, finally, to fury. She welcomed it, and did nothing to intervene, as other programming was brought on line and activated.

Stell brought the binoculars up to his eyes and pressed the zoom control. The distant admin complex leaped forward to fill the viewfinder. He thumbed the rangefinder and a white dot appeared in the middle of the image. As he manipulated a tiny toggle control on the side of the instrument, the white dot moved, and as it touched various objects, their range appeared at the bottom of the frame via digital readout. He was pretty sure the energy cannon was hidden in a ruined building about a thousand yards out. His guess was suddenly confirmed, as blue death stabbed out to touch a mound of dirt about a hundred feet to his right. Steam rose as the water content of the soil was liberated. Then, as atoms moved faster and faster, it began to melt, and ooze quickly away. Suddenly the mound disappeared altogether, allowing the blue light to touch the two brigade troopers who hid behind it. They were instantly boiled inside their A-suits. When all their bodily liquids had evaporated, there was a brief flare of light, and they were gone. The cannon moved on to another target before their ashes had even dusted the ground.

Stell swore and lowered the binoculars. The way things stood, they were stalled about two thousand yards from the admin complex, and that energy cannon was the reason why. Now he was paying the price for sending all the armor and heavy weapons home on the transports. But he'd had little choice. Even without armor and heavy weapons, there had been standing room only aboard the single troop transport on the way out from Fabrica. He winced as blue light flicked out once more and filled the air with the smell of ozone. This time it missed its target, as five troopers ducked behind a building that even the cannon couldn't cut through. He didn't like it, but there was only one thing to do. "Give me an uplink to Falco," he ordered the com tech beside him.

"Yes, sir," she replied, tapping a quick sequence of keys on her portable board. "He'll be on freq four," she added.

Stell chinned over to frequency four, knowing his voice would be relayed up to a satellite, from there to the *Nest*, and then on to Falco. The pilot's voice came through loud and clear. "And how can I serve the greater glory of the brotherhood?"

Stell smiled at Falco's tongue-in-cheek imitation of pirate radio traffic. "By removing the goddamn energy cannon that's in our way, that's how."

There was silence for a moment before Falco's voice came back. This time he was completely serious. "According to your radio markers, the target area looks a bit tight, brother; are you sure you want an air strike?"

Stell shared his concern. Unless Falco and his pilots had pinpoint accuracy, they could accidentally take out half of the brigade's forces instead of the enemy's—but he couldn't see any other way to go. "That's an affirmative," he replied. "Give us ten minutes to dig in."

"Roger," Falco replied. "Dig deep, brother."

"All right," Stell said to the com tech, "tell everybody to find a hole and pull it in after them. In about nine minutes, the sky's gonna fall."

She nodded, and began talking earnestly into her com-set. Stell turned to Flynn and the four troopers whom she had assigned to guard him. "Come on . . . let's find someplace to hole up." With the com tech in tow, Stell led them half a block back and into the lobby of some kind of underground transportation system. He'd noticed it earlier as they had worked their way up the street. A quick check proved it to be completely deserted. Skipping down the frozen steps of the escalator two at a time, they passed one, and then two levels. Finally, they were forced to stop by a wall of fallen duracrete. Evidently the retreating Intersystems troops had blown the passageway, rather than allow the brigade access to the underground transportation system. "Okay," Stell said, "I guess this is far enough."

"All units report that they've found cover, sir," the com tech reported evenly.

"Let's hope so," Stell replied fervently as he looked up toward the surface. "Let's hope so."

As the planet's surface rushed up to meet him, Falco wished he were in his own interceptor. He knew they were all identical, but like all pilots before him, he knew *his* fighter was different. It had its own soul, a personality with which he was familiar, and upon which he could depend. But his interceptor was aboard *Nest*. It couldn't go atmospheric with a damaged wing. So here he was in one of the few replacement craft, and he didn't like it. The controls seemed just a hair slow, the port engine was only 96% effective, and his seat wouldn't adjust properly.

Checking his stern screen, Falco saw that the other ten interceptors were forming up behind him, getting ready for their own runs over the target. Without conscious thought, his mind and eyes ran through the checklist. Engines, weapons, electronics—everything checked out within acceptable limits. Now his attention shifted to the target—an absurdly small patch of ground on the north side of the admin complex. The trick was to dump everything inside that small space. If he hit too far to the north, he'd take out everything in the brigade's LZ. Too far south, and he'd turn the admin complex into rubble; and that wouldn't do, because the money was in there. Too far east, and they'd wipe out a lot of dependent housing, and a lot of noncombatants with it. And if they overran to the west . . . the whole damn run would be wasted.

Now he had visual contact. He locked the area into his sighting grid, flipped a switch that sent information about the target's appearance, range and coordinates to all weapons systems, and then activated those systems. Pushing the stick forward, he nosed the fighter down until it was following the terrain, rising and falling with the contours of the land. Below, the surface raced by, and once again he felt the thrill, the surge of raw power that always went with this moment. Part of him was ashamed, while another part was exultant—

glorying in the speed, the control, and the danger. He forced himself to wait, to hold out for that perfect moment when he and his machine were one, when the target was his. "Almost . . . hold . . . hold . . . fire!" He felt the fighter lurch as his verbal command launched four air-to-ground missiles and a cluster of bombs, and activated his twin energy cannon. Ten seconds later he ceased firing and was past the target.

One by one, the ten interceptors behind him did the same thing. Their missiles sought out the heat of heavy weapons, slammed into hastily fortified positions and reduced them to rubble. Smart bombs chose the largest and densest targets-of-opportunity. After they hit, they crashed down through walls and floors, until finally coming to rest somewhere near the bottom of the structure. Five seconds later they exploded, often causing the entire building to cave in on itself. Meanwhile, pulses of blue light pounded everything into a flowing muck of melted earth, flesh, and metal.

As Falco made a quick pass over the area, to check the effectiveness of their run, his exultation was quickly gone. A brassy taste filled his mouth. Down below, all was deathly still. Nothing moved. He chinned his mic on and croaked, "Mission accomplished." Pulling his nose up, he put the interceptor into a steep climb toward the clean blue sky.

In small groups, the troopers emerged from their hiding places—tentatively at first, and then with growing confidence. As Stell and his party left their underground shelter, he was amazed. The entire target area had been completely leveled. For the moment, there was no trace of enemy troops, no sound of insects, nothing—except for the crackling of fires and the crunch of boots on gravel. Smoke eddied and swirled, forming strange shapes before drifting away on a light breeze like ghosts fleeing dead flesh. It was eerie. He forced himself to shrug it off and concentrate.

They had to take advantage of the situation before Malik could rush in more troops. As they moved forward, orders were whispered instead of yelled. It was as if no one dared disturb the silence that hung over the place. But soon that began to change. It started with a single shot, then a burst, and finally the rolling thunder of massed fire. Just as Stell began to fear the worst, the fire slackened, and began to die down. Then, as they neared the admin complex, resistance seemed to melt away. It was a good sign, and Stell began to hope. And when they rushed up the front steps, and into the admin complex itself, and still encountered no opposition, he knew it was true: they had won. He was surprised, having expected Malik to fight for every inch of the admin complex, but he wasn't about to question his good fortune. Nonetheless, it pays to be cautious, so he ordered Flynn to send out scouts and set up a defensive perimeter.

Meanwhile, Mueller had appeared with the reluctant Nars at his side. Relying on Nars for directions, teams of troopers were dispatched to look for the various kinds of valuables that Mueller deemed acceptable. Muffled explosions were soon heard, as the teams used exlosives to force their way into secured areas. Before long, a steady stream of troopers began to return, carrying all sorts of containers. As they arrived, Mueller inspected each find, often shaking his head in disapproval. But occasionally he clapped his hands with enthusiasm. The containers so blessed were stacked on an empty ammo carrier for transportation to an assault boat. Rejects were thrown unceremoniously into a large pile under the Intersystems logo, which dominated one wall. Just a little bit longer, Stell thought to himself. Then we can load the troops and get the hell out of here. Something he couldn't wait to do.

"General . . . the Corporal says he found something you ought to see." It was Mueller. With him was a middle-aged man wearing the chevrons of a Corporal. He looked familiar.

Stell looked again. Those beady brown eyes and the big red nose could only belong to one man. "Is that you, Sergeant Dickerson?"

Dickerson looked embarrassed. "Corporal Dickerson now, sir."

"Booze?" Stell asked with a raised eyebrow.

"Yes, sir. I'm afraid so, sir," Dickerson replied sadly.

Stell shook his head in amazement. He'd personally promoted Dickerson to Sergeant at least three times. "You know, Dickerson, if it weren't for booze, you'd be a General by now."

Dickerson grinned widely. "Then it's a good thing I drink, sir, because I'd make a piss-poor General!"

Stell laughed, and asked, "So what's up?"

"Follow me, General," Dickerson replied confidently, "You'll want to see this."

With Sergeant Major Flynn and his bodyguard trailing along behind, Stell followed Dickerson down two flights of stairs, through three sets of blown durasteel doors, and into a large room that was obviously some sort of command center.

"Over here, General," Dickerson called, and Stell stepped over to join him. Following the other man's eyes, Stell found himself looking at Malik. He was dead. His eyes were bulging, his face was blue, and strong metal fingers were locked around his throat. The fingers belonged to Lady Almanda Kance-Jones. She was beautiful no longer. The plastaskin flesh of her face had been melted away by the energy pistol still gripped in Malik's hand. Where once-perfect features had flowed smoothly over her metal skeleton, now there was only an obscene swirl of fused plastic and metal. Except for her lips—they had somehow survived, and were curved upward in a smile.

CHAPTER TWENTY-THREE

Com Tech Chu watched her monitor as *Nest* broke out of orbit and headed for a hyperspace jump. She hated to see the Falcons go, but they'd been offered another assignment, and Freehold couldn't afford to keep them indefinitely. Besides, she thought, scanning the bank of monitors in front of her, things are definitely looking up. For starters, Captain Boyko had filled most of the holes in her satellite network. Besides that, the brigade's three transports and the pirate DE were also in orbit around the planet. And soon there would be regular patrols a few lights out. She swung her feet up on the console and leaned back contentedly in her chair. Picking up her cup, she sipped some tea. To her enormous satisfaction, it was still hot.

Sergeant Major Flynn and Sergeant Stickley sat elbow to elbow in companionable silence. Behind them, First Hole's domes and buildings were an untidy sprawl. In front of them, stretching away from the open-air bar, clean sand reached out to touch the shimmering dome of the Senate. With the rainy season just past, and the heat of summer still ahead, the air was warm and balmy. Every now and then, one of them would refill their glasses from the bottle in the middle of the table. Otherwise, they were content to simply enjoy the moment. Eventually, however, Stickley broke the silence. "Well, Sergeant Major, what's next?"

Flynn shrugged. "Getting drunk?"

"Naw," Stickley replied, "I mean what are you gonna do? Are you gonna accept the commission?"

Flynn laughed. "Me? An officer? You gotta be kidding. Besides, you know damn well that Lieutenant's a demotion from top kick."

There was a moment of silence before Stickley spoke again. "So you're stayin' in?"

Flynn tipped a little more whiskey into her glass and took a sip. "I guess . . . the General says the brigade will go on. He even said we might take a job, once in a while. Sort of keep our hand in." She looked toward the horizon. "We've got something to fight for now, and a place to come back to. How about you?"

For a moment he gazed off into the distance where the Senate shimmered in the sun. A monument had been built in front of it, and dedicated to Sergeant Major Como and the others who had died inside. Earlier, he and Flynn had gone there to pay their respects to their friends and comrades. "Eventually I'd like something more than an A-suit to call home. But there's no hurry . . . and someone's gotta stay around and take your abuse."

She was pleased, but snorted in derision to hide it.

Stickley grinned. "I mean, just suppose someone attacked Freehold, Sergeant Major . . . what would we do then?"

Flynn smiled, and raised her glass in a salute. "Why, we'd do what we always do, Sticks—we'd kick some ass!"

A light breeze blew off the lake. It was warm and sweet, bearing the faint scent of flowers. It ruffled Olivia's hair and stirred the wind chimes that hung near the edge of the veranda. The tinkling music was in perfect rhythm with the shimmering light that reflected off the water. Stell sipped his coffee, enjoying Olivia's presence at his side and the beauty of the moment.

Olivia took pleasure in watching him, in knowing he was there, alive and safe. But she knew from the tightness around his eyes, and the coiled tenseness of his body, that he was worried. There was one last battle to fight, and it would be won or lost right there. The early skirmishes had taken place over appetizers and salad. Both sides had feinted once or twice during the main course, and now, with dessert out of the way, the decisive moment had come.

"Thank you for a wonderful dinner," Lt. Commander John Paul Jones said as he patted his lips with a linen napkin and settled back in his chair.

"You're quite welcome, Commander," Olivia replied sincerely. "Your company made it a special occasion." And it was true. In spite of the verbal fencing match, Jones had proved a most entertaining and enjoyable dinner guest. His DE had swung into orbit around Freehold the day before. Neither President Bram nor Stell had been surprised. Intersystems had accused Freehold of attacking its Sector Headquarters and the empire had sent someone to investigate. The extra ships had been disposed of at bargain prices, all those likely to be interviewed had been briefed, logs had been edited, computers were reprogrammed, and a thousand other details had been attended to. But it was still pathetically thin, and wouldn't withstand more than the most superficial investigation. As for going to court, that was out of the question. They'd tried to retrieve data from Lady Almanda Kance-Jones' electronic brain, and met with only partial success. So, with only a dead robot and a reluctant Nars as witnesses, they didn't stand a chance of winning. Nars had been returned to Fabrica and told to keep his mouth shut. He probably hadn't, but it wouldn't make much difference.

With considerable misgivings, Stell had waited for the Navy shuttle to touch down. And when it had rolled to a stop, and Jones had emerged, Stell didn't know whether to heave a sigh of relief, or shake in his boots. From their brief encounter on Fabrica, he knew that the Commander was no fool. If he wanted to, Jones could take their story apart in a few hours. So the question was, "What did the naval officer want to do?" More than a day had passed, and Stell still wasn't sure. Jones had asked a lot of pointed questions, yet he'd failed to follow up on many of them, and hadn't really pressed his investigation beyond gentle conversation. So they had decided on a low-key approach. Jones seemed most comfortable with Stell, probably because of their common military background, so Bram had begged off when invited to dinner, hoping that in the relaxed setting of Olivia's villa, the whole matter could be laid to rest.

As though reading Stell's mind, Jones said, "I hope you'll forgive me if I abuse your hospitality by talking business for a moment."

"Don't be silly, Commander," Olivia answered. "We don't stand on formality out here. Can I get you some more coffee?"

Jones shook his head. "No thank you, Olivia. But if you'd both indulge me, I'd like to wrap up a few things."

"By all means, John," Stell replied. "What's on your mind?"

Jones smiled, his perfect white teeth complementing his brown skin. "It's no secret that I came here to look things over. As you either knew, or suspected, Intersystems has accused Freehold, and specifically the brigade, of attacking its Sector Headquarters disguised as pirates, and making off with a good deal of money and other valuables. If that's true, it would constitute a crime of enormous proportions, and would force the Imperial Navy to occupy Freehold, to try and punish its leaders, and probably to give it back to Intersystems Incorporated."

"That's *if* such accusations were true," Stell replied politely. "And it would require some proof."

Jones nodded in agreement. "Exactly. And proof seems difficult to come by. Unfortunately, both the Intersystems Military Commander, who I understand was once a member of your brigade, and Executive Kance-Jones were killed during the raid on Sector Headquarters. Perhaps they could've shed some light on this situation." He shrugged. "Well, let's see if I've got this right. After I left Fabrica, you completed your transaction with Nars, unloaded your thermium, and were paid in cash. At that point a group of heavily armed pirates got the drop on you, took the money, and left you to die of oxygen deprivation. You, however, managed to get off Fabrica, catch the escaping pirates, and recover your money. You took their DE, now in orbit around Freehold, and sent them packing in a lifeboat. At this point you sent one of your officers, Captain Mosley I think it was, along with Comptroller Mueller to Intersystems Corporate Headquarters on Terra where they will make Freehold's annual payment. Is that correct?''

"That's about the size of it," Stell agreed with a forced smile. Inside, he was numb. Jones obviously didn't believe a word of it. They were about to lose everything that they had fought for.

The naval officer's face was absolutely serious as he looked from one to the other. "You were very lucky to get your money back. In my report, I'm going to suggest that the attack on you, and the attack on Intersystems, may be part of a larger pattern. Who knows? Maybe they'll let us slap a few pirates around . . . I'd enjoy that. Anyway, I guess I have a hard time believing that the same people I saw selling thermium on Fabrica would rush off and attack Intersystems Headquarters. So don't worry, you're not about to play host to Admiral Keaton's fleet.''

Stell heaved a sigh of relief. "I'm glad to hear that, Commander . . . and thank you.''

Jones stood and placed his napkin on the table. "Don't thank me, General. I'm just doing my duty. And speaking of duty, I hear it calling. I can't tell you how much I enjoyed dinner.''

As they walking Jones to the front door, where a brigade air car waited to take him back to First Hole, Olivia said, "I hope you'll come back and stay for a while sometime, Commander. . . we've got lots of room.''

"I'd like that," Jones replied as they reached the air car. "But maybe I'd better wait until after the honeymoon. I hear you two plan to get married.''

Stell and Olivia looked at each other, before turning back to smile at him. "As soon as possible," Stell said.

"Well, then," Jones said, pulling a small packet from a pocket, and reaching out to hand it to Stell. "I didn't have a chance to buy a wedding present, but perhaps you'll accept this in its stead, along with my wishes for a long and happy marriage." With a cheerful wave and a smile, he stepped into the air car. The driver skimmed a polite distance away before pulling the nose up, hitting the throttles, and roaring off toward the horizon.

"What is it?" Olivia asked curiously.

Stell carefully unwrapped several layers of paper. Inside he found a photograph. Because the hidden surveillance camera which had taken it was equipped with a very good lens, the picture was crystal clear. There was no mistaking either his face, or the Intersystems logo behind him that decorated the wall of the admin complex. Stell looked at Olivia and she at him. Together, they looked up at the distant speck of the disappearing air car and waved. Turning, they entered the villa hand in hand. It felt good to be home.

MORE SCIENCE FICTION ADVENTURE!